SHERLOCK HOLMES AND THE CASE OF THE MISSING AMERICAN CULTURE

SHERLOCK HOLMES AND THE CASE OF THE MISSING AMERICAN CULTURE

A Novel

Kenneth Frawley

To order additional copies of this book, contact:
Xlibris Corporation
1-888-795-4274
www.Xlibris.com
Orders@Xlibris.com
19589

CONTENTS

Acknowledgements

Rolf Wicklund, artwork.
Veronica Lonsway, proofreading.

CHAPTER I

The Visitor

The day had started out like every other of the last eighty years, or thereabouts. I had risen at my usual hour of 8am, dressed and had gone down to the dining room to devour the breakfast that was always waiting for me by half past. And, as usual, it, and the morning paper, were meticulously laid out on the Victorian mahogany dining table I have had since the days of my first marriage. Mrs. Gale, my housekeeper for the last thirty years was not only the most efficient domestic I had ever employed, she was the most cordial and considerate. It seemed an impossible task to replace her. Yet that was exactly what had been occupying my mind for the preceding fortnight. She had elected to retire from professional life and settle in the Welsh seaside resort village of Tenby. Both she and her husband Bryn had long thought of returning to Wales, the land of their births, before they were too old to savor it and their retirement. One could not argue against that. After all, I had been enjoying my retirement immensely for the last eighty-five years. Nevertheless, it was with great sorrow and reluctance that I had accepted Mrs. Gale's resignation.

As I consumed the usual breakfast of grapefruit, nine-grain toast, tofu scramble, a pot of Russian Caravan tea and my pile of vitamin, mineral and herbal supplements, I searched through the classified ads in the Times. I knew the effort was an exercise in futility, but the act seemed to help me cope with the impending loss of my very good friend and housekeeper. Simultaneously, I found myself recalling an adventure from my very early days at

Holmes' side that I had yet to chronicle. Since Holmes and I had been out of the game for some ninety years now, he no longer minded if I penned detailed accounts of the cases he had believed were too delicate to speak of in any form, at the time. After all, the principal parties involved in them were long gone now.

BOOM, BOOM, BOOM, BOOM! Suddenly, my thoughts, and my morning read, were uncharacteristically interrupted by a strong, anxious pounding at the front door.

"Who could that be at this early hour? exclaimed Mrs. Gale as she sprang into the room. "How unbelievably inconsiderate. You haven't finished your breakfast, or done your yoga and stretching exercises yet," she added.

"I'm afraid it's my fault, Mrs. Gale," I answered. "Though I did not expect anyone at this early hour, I did agree to let the employment agency send someone round today."

"I'll send them off and tell them to return at a more civilized hour," she offered.

"No, no. You'd better show them in. Let's offer them a cup of tea while I finish this most outstanding breakfast of yours."

"Very well, Dr. Watson. Very well."

And with that she nodded her fine featured, gray head, took a deep sigh to help hold back the tongue-lashing she felt certain our early arriving visitor deserved and darted for the door.

While Mrs. Gale fetched our visitor, I put down my paper and concentrated on the food before me. However, I could only manage a single bite before Mrs. Gale returned with our unexpected guest.

"Excuse me, Dr. Watson. A Mr. Moore to see you, sir," she announced.

I looked up to see a tall, very well tailored, man of about forty-five-years of age standing before me. He was slender and appeared very fit. His dark, finely manicured hair revealed scarcely a gray hair and his clean-shaven face exposed a strong square jaw. Yet immediately I could see an anxiousness about him that clearly contrasted the image of the strong, confident man his physicality presented.

"Good morning, Mr. Moore. What can I do for you, sir? I

cooperatively asked. "I assume you have some people for me to consider?"

"Excuse me?" he responded with confusion and a refined, yet unmistakable, southern American accent. "I don't quite know what you mean, sir."

"Ah", I shot back. "Clearly you are not from the employment agency. Are you?"

"No, sir. I'm not. I'm from the U.S., sir."

"Yes. Well then, what brings you all this way, Mr. Moore?"

"I'm awfully sorry to interrupt your breakfast, Dr. Watson. Please, forgive me," he stated with a slight tremble and a genuine regret.

"Come, come, young man. It's quite all right. My ritualistic mornings can do with some variation now and then. What is it that inspires you to visit me this morning?"

"Well sir, to put it simply, I desperately need your help," he answered.

"What sort of assistance can I be to you, Mr. Moore?" I asked with a slight pitch in my voice that gave away my intense curiosity. "I have not practiced medicine in almost a century."

"No, sir. I have not come to seek your medical counsel. Although I am sure you are still quite—"

"You are very kind," I eagerly jumped in. "But I still would very much like to know the nature of your business."

"Yes, sir. Well—," he continued, trying to quickly swallow the nervous lump in his throat.

"Please, Mr. Moore, do have a seat. Mrs. Gale, would you mind pouring our guest of cup of this marvelous tea of yours?"

"Certainly, Doctor." she dutifully replied.

"Thank you, Dr. Watson," said Moore humbly.

"Now sir, again, how can I be of service to you?" I asked.

"Well, Dr. Watson, I am an American."

"Yes, I have observed that."

"And, well, sir, I have been sent here on a matter of the utmost importance and urgency."

"Really?" I said with a slightly feigned impression.

"Yes, sir. It's very, very serious, I'm afraid."

"That may be, but what use can I, an elderly retired physician, be to you in your time of need?"

"Sir, I am an employee of the United States government."

"Really?"

His face quickly lit up and he sat erect in his chair.

"Yes, really."

"What, may I ask, could the United States government want of me?" I asked.

"Sir, I am an attorney, specially appointed by the president himself to act in his behalf on the matter."

"I see. Well then, what is this urgent matter?"

"I cannot tell you, sir," he said coldly.

"Well then," I quickly countered, "how can I possibly assist you if I do not know what you require assistance with? I'm afraid you must enlighten me a bit more, young man."

Moore quickly retrieved a wallet and passport from the inside breast pocket of his jacket and tossed them onto the table before me.

"Excuse me, sir," he said with much humility in his tone. "I regret that I cannot."

He followed this with another item from his jacket pocket. It was a small identification card, complete with photograph, issued by the United States government.

"These, sir, should confirm I am who I say I am, sir."

"Very well, Mr. Moore. Let's assume you are who you say you are. I have no reason to doubt you. I only ask that you simply tell me what it is you wish of me."

"Yes, sir," he happily replied.

"Excuse me, but did you not, just a minute ago, say you were unable to explain to me the nature of the prob—"

"That is true, sir," he said quickly. "I cannot discuss the nature of the problem with you, Dr. Watson. However, I can share with you what it is we desire of you, sir."

"You perplex me, Mr. Moore. But, indeed, I am all ears."

"Thank you, sir."

His manner became slightly schoolboy-ishly giddy.

"Please, sir, let me start out by saying what a genuine pleasure it is to meet you. In fact, while on the plane over, I reread several of your accounts of the adventures you had experienced with Mr. Sherlock Holmes. Outstanding! Simply outstanding!"

I was growing fairly tired of this drawn out plea for help that I am certain I was less than polite when I lowered my brow and firmly stated, "I appreciate that, Mr. Moore. But I do have other business to tend to and—"

"Oh, yes, certainly. Do forgive me," he groveled.

"Now please, may we get on with the nature of your business with me?"

"Yes, Dr. Watson, of course."

He took another swallow.

"We, my government that is, has tried numerous times to consult with your good friend, the great master himself, Mr. Sherlock Holmes. But I am afraid we could not manage to get the time of day from him, sir."

"I should say not. Mr. Holmes has retired and is no longer interested in pursuing criminals or coming to the aid of governments, as he had done many a time during his great career. Surely you are aware of this by now?"

"Of course, sir, we are very much aware of that fact. But this is a matter of life and death."

His voice broke with such emotion I expected the man to begin sobbing.

"We, sir," he continued, "we, the United States of America, are a country very nearly on the brink of ruin. We sir, the world's sole remaining superpower, have reached the end of our rope. We, sir, have exhausted every measure available to us, and then some, and yet we can proclaim no success. Thus, the only recourse left to us, we very much hope, is to throw our fate into the hands of your good and wondrous friend, Mr. Sherlock Holmes."

I sat breathless, struck by the audacity of this man, and the government behind him. He looked squarely into my face as he sat waiting for my response to such an appeal. But I thought long and hard. He began to speak again, but I waved him off before he could utter a single syllable. I took a sip of my Russian Caravan, which, thanks to this very long-winded visitor, was now cold. That was the topper! My mind was made up. Holmes was my dearest friend. It is to him that I owe so much of what I am. It is he I place before all others, superpowers included.

"So if I hear you correctly," I began, "what you ask is for me to arrange an audience with Mr. Holmes?"

"Yes, sir," the nervy intruder answered with great enthusiasm. "Yes, that is exactly what we wish, Doctor."

Thinking for another second, I reached for my teacup. Feeling the coolness of it in my hand, I thought to myself, "He shall swing for this!"

And just as I was about to speak, Mrs. Gale, who had astutely observed the tea fiasco, quickly came to my aid with a fresh pot and another cup, the perfect antidote. Nothing like a hot cup of Russian Caravan coming to the rescue, his of course.

With myself now somewhat collected, I turned to the government servant beside me and calmly began to state my position on the matter.

"I am afraid that even I will not be able to persuade Mr. Holmes to meet with you. For as I have stated, Mr. Holmes has retired. Today he is a simple beekeeper, keeping quietly to his own. And he is vehemently opposed to any unwanted intrusion."

"But, sir, the matter is most grave!"

"I am truly sorry. However, my friendship with Mr. Holmes is far too valuable to risk on a matter I am certain he will have not the slightest interest in. Furthermore, I simply cannot allow you to invade his privacy in this manner."

Mr. Moore's face began to sag like a child's face that fails to persuade its parent to purchase for it that impulse candy at the supermarket checkout. It was rather pathetic for a man of his position and physicality.

"Dr. Watson," he said with an extreme seriousness, such as a man walking the plank might, "I implore you—No, I beg you sir, to reconsider. This is our only option."

He took another swallow.

"Mr. Holmes is our only hope."

"Surely you greatly dramatize the need for his assistance," I replied.

"Not by any measure, sir. Not by any measure. Why, if we cannot enlist Mr. Holmes' assistance, then, I'm afraid, we are done for and we must place the very existence of our great country entirely in the hands of God and pray for a miracle."

He spoke those words with such passion, such despair, I thought to myself, only the great *Olivier* himself could have given a more convincing, more moving delivery. And this man was no thespian. Clearly he must speak the truth. But was the United States really on the brink of disaster? Could such a thing really be? I read the newspapers. I found nothing alluding to any threat to the U.S. But, still his plea began to affect me. So much so, I was almost convinced.

"Mr. Moore," I started, "tell me something."

"Anything," he replied.

"How is it that you have concluded that Mr. Holmes, and only Mr. Holmes, can rescue your very powerful nation? It has every possible weapon, every conceivable arsenal at its disposal, manpower, technology, even forensics. What can a man of his age, a man long out of the game, do what such a powerful entity cannot?"

"That Dr. Watson, is a mystery to me," he replied. "I only know that he is the only human on the planet that is capable of seeing into, and right through, the very heart of evil. All one need do is read your accounts of his accomplishments to be certain of that. Surely, there is no other, only he."

"How can I assist you?" the words rocketing out of my mouth before I knew it. "Shall I ring him?"

"Heavens no, Doctor. He is certain to refuse us."

"Then what do you prefer I do?"

"I have a car outside. We could drop in on him together perhaps?"

I stepped away from the table, ignored the disapproving look on Mrs. Gale's face and started for the Georgian hat rack in the foyer to grab my hat and coat.

"He will be extremely angry with me when he discovers my treason."

"He will understand, I'm sure," offered Mr. Moore.

"I suggest we take my Range Rover. He'll recognize it immediately. Thus, effecting your audience with Holmes more easily," I said with great trepidation as I steered my very excited and relieved American visitor to the door.

"After you, Doctor."

CHAPTER II

Holmes

Spring was just beginning to reveal itself. Everywhere tiny wildflowers were awakening. Foxgloves and delphiniums were rocketing upward from the moist earth to drench themselves in the deliciously warm sunlight. Indeed, it was the perfect day for a drive through the English countryside, the kind of day that inspires the brightest of moods. But the thought of Holmes brought me back from my romance with spring. For if ever there was a potential dark cloud looming on the horizon, it was Holmes. Never have I been more fond of an individual, yet I knew all too well that my arrival with this desperately needy American passenger would set him off like a torrential winter downpour.

Holmes was a man of singular focus. Be it the toughest of mysteries, or his retirement, he would not stand for the slightest intrusion. Thus, I feared I had my work cut out for me. For decades Holmes has rested comfortably in the knowledge that I, of all persons, would not breech his trust in the slightest. Yet here I was defiling that trust in the worst possible way, actually delivering to him the very thing he was in seclusion to avoid, another life that was frantically claiming to be hanging by a thread. How on earth would I ever explain my part in this treachery? Oh, I was certain he would banish me to Elba the instant I presented my surprise visitor.

"My, this countryside is stunningly picturesque," said Mr. Moore, interrupting my internal panic. "This would be Sussex, then?"

"Yes," I replied, "it would be."

"How far do you suspect it is to Eastbourne?"

"Mr. Holmes' estate is five miles outside the city."

"Ah, I see. That would make sense," declared Moore.

"I am afraid you lost me, sir. I do not take your meaning," I said somewhat defensively.

"Well, you wouldn't want to raise bees in the middle of a city, now would you?"

"Ah, yes. But of course, you are right. How very keen a deduction on your part," I said with just a touch of sarcasm to subtly remind my passenger that I am first, and foremost, Holmes' friend and that my allegiance is entirely with him.

"I'm sure you're exceedingly tired of being questioned about your unsurpassed longevity, sir," he prefaced, which immediately put me on my guard, "but tell me, how is it that you and Mr. Holmes find yourselves in such spectacular condition for your ages? As I'm sure you are aware, it has been the topic of a great number of conversations for decades now."

"May I speak frankly, sir?" I asked.

"Of course, Doctor. By all means," Moore said with the excitement of a child who was anticipating learning the secret to a magician's most daring of illusions.

"Well then, let me put it to you as succinctly as I can. Let's see. How about, 'it is none of your business?'"

I watched Moore's mouth drop uncontrollably the instant I issued my standard reply. I knew exactly what thoughts were racing through his mind in that instant. Having witnessed such reactions to the reply Holmes had assured me was best in this situation I had come to enjoy watching people sulk when they were caught attempting to pry into my personal affairs. And like those before him who had dared to press me on the subject, Mr. Moore sank into a silent state of shock, which eventually transformed into a very a disgraceful display of pouting. It is amazing how the child never really leaves most people. As for me, I continued on with my duty as chauffeur in blissful silence as Mr. Moore gazed out the window like a disappointed adolescent.

Perhaps I should have apologized. But it was Holmes who had

learned the very secret of longevity and vitality. It was he who had acquired the formula for maximizing lifespan. It was he alone who sought out, examined and verified all aspects and components pertaining to one of Nature's most guarded of recipes. Specifics so astonishing, with ingredients so amazingly simple, that Holmes, quite correctly I believe, concluded the great mass not only unready, but unworthy of such a windfall. Like Columbus and Galileo had discovered before him, Holmes understood that be it the great governing powers or the herded mass, to these factions, wisdom and enlightenment might just as well be caster oil. Fortunately, I was a physician, in addition to his closest and dearest of friends. It was only natural that Holmes should share his precious findings solely with me.

Several minutes had passed and not a word had been uttered between Mr. Moore and myself and I was feeling a little like a cantankerous old coot. But we were fast approaching the Holmes manor and I knew the sight of it would certainly put Moore and I back on speaking terms. So, I began to drift into thought. Mr. Moore's question and his subsequent pouting triggered images Holmes had planted into my mind more than a century ago, images of him trekking the mighty Himalayas on his way to India from Tibet.

During the period of 1891 through 1894, Holmes traveled the globe in an effort to elude the late evil Professor Moriarty's many confederates. As circumstances would have it, only that bunch of psychopathic brutes and reptilian-minded roughs were privileged with the knowledge that Holmes had not fallen to his death, along with their leader, at the Reichenbach Falls in Switzerland. The rest of the world, most of all myself, mourned for years. And it was while Holmes was crossing that mountainous gateway to the heavens that he came upon the most fascinating of situations.

Now, as you may know, over the last five and a half score of years since Holmes' famed *disappearance*, there has been a great deal of speculation regarding that unaccounted for period of Holmes' life. Some of it has been rather inventive, I must admit. In fact, even as I chronicle this very adventure, it has come to my

attention that yet another account of that three-year gap in the
master sleuth's life has just surfaced. And while Holmes has found
them to be quite entertaining, I saw them as a respectful
compliment to a man whose obvious genius and substantial
contribution has single handedly made this unruly world a little
tamer. But now, for the first time, I will share with you the actual
facts of what transpired during that most curious of gaps in my
dear friend's famed life and career.

Doing his level best to give his evil pursuers the slip, Holmes
made his way to Tibet under the name of Sigerson. Once there, he
roamed the land for nearly a year, during which time he managed
to obtain an introduction to the thirteenth Dalai Lama, Thupten
Gyatso, where an immediate bond was forged between the two
men. They kept no secrets from one another. It was a relationship
that proved personally and intellectually beneficial to both men.
And it was through this connection that Holmes learned of a young
Indian solicitor, wise beyond his years, who had returned to his
native land after completing his legal studies in England. The Dalai
Lama himself had suggested Holmes travel to India to meet this
young man of peace. Thusly, it was on that journey that Holmes'
fantastic adventure began.

I have had no first hand experience with the terrain of that
rugged oriental landmass, but I assure you, from Holmes' account,
there may be none more treacherous on this earth. On his way to
Delhi, through Nepal and over the Himalayas, Holmes encountered
many a giant rock, protruding straight from the center of the earth
with ledges and ridges so narrow a sparrow could scarcely pass on
them. To look down at the distant earth below as you applied
yourself to the extremely delicate passing would have been the
gravest of mistakes. For those who could not bring themselves to
free their minds and 'become one with the peak', as the local
Lamas urged, were doomed. I needn't present you with the
number of men Holmes watched meet their end on that crossing.
Let us just say it was incomprehensible. And it was after
conquering one of the many treacherous peaks along the route
that the attack occurred.

Holmes, and his party of guides and other foreign adventurers, had just deprived the mountain of more victims by mastering one of the most difficult sections of the gigantic beast when they were ambushed by a band of, what appeared to be, renegade Nepalese. Though the bandits were not large in stature, their sinisterly snarling glares, gruff voices and great agility, not to mention their rifles, were extremely intimidating. They moved through the snow with the greatest of ease and were all too easily able to effect control of the situation. Two of Holmes' guides attempted to resist the villains, only to find themselves out-classed and flung off the mountain like discarded waste.

There were several other people in Holmes' party, yet it was Holmes the ruffians seemed to be interested in. They seemed to go to great lengths to make him as comfortable as possible, while the others were treated like enlisted men on the first day of basic training. It was a circumstance that Holmes found highly curious. Nevertheless, he, like the whole of the group, complied with every demand his captors made. The primary demand being that the group should follow them up, high onto the mountain. So follow the group did. Up, up, up. It seemed as though the strenuous vertical hike would last an eternity. Two members of the party, a New Zealand woman and an Argentine man, employed as anthropologists, fainted when their bodies became unable to cope with the low level of oxygen found at such an altitude.

This, however, was not a problem for the bushwhackers. For them, leaving the weak for dead was simply a matter of routine. Holmes, on the other hand, could not accept this and vehemently protested. The reaction of the brutes validated Holmes' earlier observation. For without the slightest hesitation, his abductors picked up the two unconscious hostages and proceeded to carry them along as they led on.

The relentless snow weighed heavier on the inexperienced body the higher it climbed. The air was like dry ice and the wind a stiletto, piercing its way through the strongest of garments. Holmes himself was finding it difficult to remain on his feet. He only managed to do so by employing a meditation technique taught to

him by the Dalai Lama. Suddenly, the procession came to an abrupt
halt. There in the midst of such nightmarish conditions, conditions
that would make Antarctica appear a paradise, a cave opening
presented itself to them. It appeared to be nothing more than a
dark, uninhabited grotto. Holmes and his party were immediately
ushered inside. It was dark. So dark they all assumed they were
looking at the end of a very short cave. Two American men in the
party started for a spot on the ground, thinking the cave merely a
resting point. But they were immediately reprimanded and ordered
to march forward, which they did with great haste.

On and on, into the black nothingness of the cave the group
pressed forward. Holmes described it to me as walking for miles,
as a blind man might do. You never knew if your head would
strike the ceiling or scrape a protruding rock. You just put your
faith in your other senses and hoped for the best. It was all one
could do. And then, in an instant, a tiny white dot suddenly
appeared in the middle of the blackness. About eye level it was,
resembling that white dot that temporarily remained on the screen
of an early tubular driven television set after it had been switched
off. But this one did not fade away. In fact, it began to increase in
size. Bigger and bigger the dot of light grew. Soon Holmes could
make out that the light was actually an opening. The cave had
actually been nothing more than a tunnel. But judging from the
size of the light source, the opening was still quite a distance away.

Sometime later, as the small brigade approached the final feet
of the tunnel, the intensity of the light from the opening became
almost unbearable. It was like looking directly at the sun. Then,
slowly, the eye adjusted. To the sheer surprise of everyone in
Holmes' party, the light had transformed into the most picture
perfect day imaginable. Out of the gloom of the mountain weather
and the pitch darkness of the tunnel, sprang springtime. Trees
wildly in bloom, birds singing, the breeze, sweetly aromatic and
gentle, all that one expects from a storybook spring was before
them. It was nothing short of miraculous.

Holmes stood mesmerized by the sight. Magically, his
abductors had transported him and his group out of hell and into

heaven with merely the snap of their fingers. Inexplicably, and despite their ruthlessly brutal methods, Holmes could feel nothing but grateful to them. Reason had not abandoned him, for he still despised the villains, but something existed in the air of the place itself which spoke immediately to Holmes of peace and of good will and of forgiveness. And as the party exited the tunnel completely, they found themselves on a wider, much friendlier ledge, whose vista overlooked the grandest of cities ever seen by Holmes, and Holmes was quite well traveled by then, as you are no doubt already aware. Holmes tried to persuade his captors to share with him the name of that picturesque land. But they had no interest in responding to any inquires and ordered the group to follow the ledge down to the magnificent city below. And so they did, with Holmes leading the way.

At the end of the trail, which the ledge had blended into, stood a tall middle-aged man. He was perfectly groomed, had a pompadour of thick white hair, a healthy hue in his cheeks and wore the most wonderfully ornate oriental-styled silk pajamas.

"Hello", his greeting began, "welcome to Shangri La. You must be Mr. Sigerson?" he said to Holmes. "We have been most eagerly awaiting your arrival sir", he cheerfully said with his rather cultivated colonial accent.

Now, as you have no doubt surmised at this point, this adventure sounds remarkably similar to one told by Mr. James Hilton in his novel, *Lost Horizon*. This, I assure you, is no coincidence. For it was long after Holmes and I had taken ourselves out of action, after the Great War, that I shared this story, not mentioning Holmes of course, with the talented young Mr. Hilton. We had run into one another in Picadilly and decided to take tea at the Café Napoleon. Over a glass of port, the then young writer and I discussed philosophy, my Holmes chronicles, the craft of writing and a few story ideas. The account of Holmes in the Orient had always pleased, as well as saddened me, for surely it merited a detailed account. Unfortunately, for my sake as well as Holmes', it was not one I could tell. And since Hilton found the tale so fascinating I urged him to put a pen to such a story as soon as he was able. Of course he argued that I should develop the idea into a novel myself. I assured him that I was far too busy organizing my case notes from the many adventures of Holmes' that I had not yet detailed. In truth, I knew that if my name had appeared on such a story, the world might have concluded that my protagonist was none other than Holmes himself. As fantastic and unbelievable the tale sounded, speculation into the complete adventure would have placed far more attention on Holmes and his life altering discoveries than was acceptable. Which is why, when sharing the tale with Mr. Hilton, I suggested the protagonist be a politician or diplomat. However, what I did not share with Hilton were the specifics of Holmes' meetings with the Lamas of Shangri La, including the High Lama himself, *Putung*, not Perrault, as Hilton had eventually named him.

Prior to departing Tibet for India, the Dalai Lama had authored a letter of introduction to Mr. Gandhi and had it sent on ahead by messenger. Though the messenger had successfully reached his destination and delivered the letter to Mr. Gandhi, he had been stopped along the way by Nepalese officials, who had found the letter during a routine search of his satchel. One of the officials also happened to be a representative and protector of the High Lama, as well as Shangri La. And it was he who passed on the news of Holmes' pending passage to the Lamas of Shangri La. Needless to say, the Lamas were very eager to meet the acquaintance of someone with such a remarkable reputation and thus set in motion plans to deliver the master sleuth to them.

Once at Shangri La, Holmes spent his time devouring the Buddhist, Hindu and Christian texts in the High Lama's extensive library. He also took many a meeting with each of the Lamas, gaining a wealth of knowledge from each and every one of them. In return, Holmes shared his own expertise in a variety of subjects. The Lamas were particularly interested in his immense knowledge of chemistry and appealed to Holmes for instruction in the area of chemical analysis so that they may be able to conduct a detailed study of some of their herbal elixirs and concoctions. Holmes was only too happy to oblige and, like his time with the Dalai Lama, what resulted was an intellectual and spiritual bond between Holmes and his hosts.

The Lamas had long known how to maintain exceptional health and vitality by paying attention to the relationship between body, mind and spirit. Their vast knowledge of human physiology, botany and nutrition had been developed primarily by trial, error and intuition over the centuries. Holmes brought them science. For this the Lamas would be forever indebted to him. From the Lamas, Holmes learned what to consume, what not to consume, how to eat, how to breathe and the practices of yoga and meditation. He was very keen on the herbal elixirs the Lamas had developed and incorporated them, along with the rest of his newfound knowledge of diet and exercise, into his daily regiment. He learned of the many benefits of tea, both green and black. He learned to drink only distilled water, avoid soft drinks, coffee, refined sugar and flour, fatty oils and, most of all, meat. He learned to eat moderately and to include the likes of apple cider vinegar, black strap molasses, kelp, brewers' yeast, wheat germ, fruits and vegetables, particularly tomatoes and broccoli, by the score and as raw as possible. Yogurt was the only dairy item allowed. The Lamas and the monks living at Shangri La quickly recognized that other milk products were more of a liability than an aid and began making replacement products from the soybeans they grew. Clearly, they were light years ahead of the world in the study and practical application of nutrition.

In the end, Holmes knew that even though the Lamas had expected him to remain at Shangri La, he could not. His was a life dedicated to serving the public at large, no matter how unworthy and unappreciative the great flock was. During his time at Shangri La, Holmes grew more protective of humanity, almost fatherly. He understood that humanity was just one big infant whose development was to be a painfully bumpy process. His contribution would be to patch up all the scraped knees and elbows he could. This, the Lamas, though regretfully, understood. For they saw the outside world as one single escalating argument that would eventually lead to the annihilation of the so-called *advanced* civilization and commended Holmes on his commitment and his bravery. And so Holmes departed, a better and wiser man, as they say.

"Forgive me, Dr. Watson," said Moore, bringing me back to the present. "You are correct. It was very rude of me to pry into your private life. I would very much like to apologize for that."

"Thank you," I replied. "I realise I was a bit rude myself, but you do not realise how often I have to contend with such questions. It is not mere speculation for the curious inquisitor. It is my way of life we speak of. I shall not, even indirectly, fuel the juvenile and petty gossip about myself, or Mr. Holmes."

"I understand, Doctor."

"Thank you. It is greatly appreciated. Ah, here we are."

I turned off the road and on to the long tree lined drive that led to Holmes' fairly modest estate, trembling all the way in anticipation of the blizzard I was certain would strike the instant Holmes set eyes on Mr. Moore.

CHAPTER III

The Problem

Reaching the circular gravel drive before the estate's ivy covered façade, Moore was stunned by the beauty and craftsmanship of Holmes' formal Italian-styled garden that surrounded that section of the grounds.

"This is amazing. Absolutely amazing!" he murmured, almost breathless.

"Yes, Holmes is quite a talented landscape architect," I proudly boasted.

"He never ceases to astonish, does he?"

"I believe 'astonish' is his middle name."

As I parked the Rover in front of the house I was praying that Holmes had not heard our arrival, despite the distant voice of experience, assuring me from the back of my mind, that that was not very probable. I put a finger to my lips, signaling to Mr. Moore to remain silent, then slid out of the car. Stepping onto the gravel beneath me, I felt my legs wobble. To counter this slight panic, I performed a quick little breathing exercise to compose myself as I escorted Mr. Moore to the large wooden door standing ominously before us. Once there, I took one last very deep and very nervous breath as I raised my index finger toward the small, lighted doorbell button fixed upon the main entrance's ornate framing. A second later, it was done. There was no going back.

Hollingsworth, a thin, smallish man in his early sixties, was Holmes' man. As always, he was impeccably dressed and very serious about his duties. Yet that never managed to get in the way of liking him. His stern, matter of fact manner might initially put a person off, as it did Mr. Moore when Hollingsworth greeted us at the door, but it never lasted.

"Good morning, Dr. Watson. We were not expecting you this day," he said firmly. "I'm afraid he does not like unscheduled visits." He took a look at Moore, then re-addressed me. "Or visitors."

"I am aware of that, Hollingsworth," I said strongly. "But this is a matter of the utmost importance. Please fetch some tea and bring it into the study," I said pushing my way into the house, "my friend and I will just slip in for a quick word."

"If you insist, Doctor," answered Hollingsworth, in a curt tone as he dutifully marched off.

I led Moore through the stately foyer and to the study door. Before opening it, I paused and turned to Mr. Moore.

"Brace yourself."

But as I reached for the doorknob, I heard that unmistakable voice travel through the door as if it were made of paper.

"Oh do come in, Watson. And bring in your American friend. I'm sure you are both tired and in need of refreshment after your long drive from London."

Though surprised by his initial pleasantry, I remained at the ready, poised for his first strike, as I opened the door. I waved Mr. Moore in and gestured him to stop and stand for a moment.

"Watson, my dear chap, how good it is of you to surprise me this morning," Holmes stated with a charity that I did not trust.

The large, stately room, was every bit the traditional wood paneled English library one finds photographed in books and magazines on proper English décor, the only exception being the large table set aside for Holmes' chemistry experiments and studies. Nevertheless, dark, cherry wood bookshelves, filled to the brim, covered all four walls in the room. Save for the windows and the fireplace, books were simply everywhere. Holmes sat with his back to us, occupied by the computer stationed upon the return adjacent to his grand mahogany desk.

"I'll be right with you," he said as he keyed frantically away on his computer keyboard. "Please, have a seat, gentlemen. I'm sure Hollingsworth will arrive with the tea you requested very shortly."

There were two large sofas facing one another on each side of an active fireplace. A large mahogany coffee table was stationed between them. With a wave of my hand, I silently gestured for Mr. Moore to take a seat, then took a seat across from him.

"Holmes," I said, "that's a new twenty-one inch flat monitor, is it not?"

"Yes, Watson. You know how susceptible I am to the latest in technology," he replied. "Please, one moment. Then I'm all yours."

What was he up to, I wondered? I looked at Moore who sat, nervously waiting and overwhelmed by the realization that he was in the same room as the legend himself. I didn't blame him. It was rather intimidating. But that was just what Holmes had intended. As if it were f2—f4 in a game of chess, intimidation was always his opening move. It was a relief to have Hollingsworth arrive with tea and several scones. It distracted us from the tension of the moment. And after pouring Moore and me each a cup, he carried another over to Holmes.

"Yes, thank you, Hollingsworth. Yes, quite right. This is a good place to break," said Holmes as he pulled away from the computer, took the cup from his manservant and turned to address Moore and I. "Well now, Mr. Moore, what is this tremendously nightmarish dilemma your government appears to have found itself in?" he said with a surprising calm and what appeared to be a genuine interest.

"Holmes," I protested, "how on earth do you know who this man is? I myself have only just met the man this morning. And I have yet to introduce him."

Holmes took a sip of tea then calmly sat the cup down on his large Edwardian desk. He then reached for his morning pipe and began to fill it with the herbal, spice and plant mixture, which he kept in a rather ornate oriental tin on the desk. He had developed the concoction to replace tobacco in the very early years of the twentieth century. For although he had greatly enjoyed tobacco by either cigarette or pipe, Holmes realised tobacco was not conducive to his good health and enlightened lifestyle. Yet he derived great pleasure from the vice and vowed to replace it with an acceptably healthy alternative. He succeeded, as usual.

"Come now, Watson," he began, "is it not obvious?"

My expression went blank.

"My dear friend, I fear you are slipping. Surely it is most elementary. I know your powers of observation and reasoning to be more than capable to piece together the facts which have allowed me to reach a correct assessment of what is before me?"

I was not in the mood for this challenge. I hadn't finished my breakfast, performed my morning yoga, or done my daily stretching exercises. The absence of these in my day was making me feel a little off the mark and the sight of Holmes, with his well groomed, distinguished head, his narrow face, with its slender lips puffing on his pipe, while clad in an elegant smoking jacket, really irked me. Sometimes that supreme confidence of his could be a real bore.

"No!" I grumped back. "This is beyond even your extraordinary powers of deduction. There simply is no possible clue to his identity by the mere sight of the man. He wears no monogram on his clothing. Neither is there one on his attaché. I grant you, you may recognize him as an American based on his style of suit, which is more conservative than fashionable, or his heavy Florsheim winged-tipped shoes, with the protruding sole, which are non-existent in England. But his name Holmes, no! Clearly you have had some advanced warning of our arrival."

"I have not," he replied. "However, I have expected you."

"How Holmes, how? And how do you know he is here representing his government? Really, Holmes! You must come clean. You have been informed of our visit in some way. Have you not?"

"You have me, Watson. I have been informed of such a possible visit."

"Ah ha! Who, pray tell, was it? Surely it was not Mrs. Gale?"

"No, it was not. It was Mr. Moore."

"What?" I said turning to Mr. Moore, whose face wore an expression of utter befuddlement.

"I have not even spoken—," Mr. Moore said with his veins swelling nervously in his neck.

"Quite inadvertently, of course. However, it was Mr. Moore who signaled me of his impending arrival," said Holmes in that very annoyingly calm, collected and certain manner of his. "You see, good Watson, a score of telephone calls were placed to this house from representatives of the United States in an effort to reach me, with several of them being made by a certain Mr. Moore. Hollingsworth has become quite skilled at screening my calls and correctly refused all such intrusions. In between calls, a few of Mr. Moore's colleagues paid an unannounced visit to my home, but, as you will no doubt conclude, they were also refused. So, the only logical choice for their next move was to enlist the aid of my oldest and dearest friend."

He stood up and began to professorially pace the room as he continued.

"Since only Mr. Moore's most heartfelt plea stayed with Hollingsworth, it became obvious the matter was now in his hands. And now, here you are."

"Why did you not warn me of this, Holmes? I would have—,"

"No, dear Watson. It is quite all right. After such a bombardment of pleas, I was quite intrigued. Consequently, I had no choice but to play it out."

"Holmes!" I barked.

"Yes, please forgive me Watson for putting you in a position I am certain must have caused you great stress. Truly, I do apologize, dear fellow."

He turned to Mr. Moore.

"Now, young sir, pray tell, what is this problem of yours?"

Holmes had that old sparkle in his eyes, the one he got when he suspected a good mystery was about to be placed in his hands. Moore sat up, swallowed another large lump in his throat and, trembling slightly, slowly began to speak.

"Well, Mr. Holmes," began Mr. Moore, as a child, caught with its hand in the cookie jar, might. "I am only at liberty to discuss the matter with you, sir."

"Then we shall discuss nothing!" Holmes shot back. "Hollingsworth," he shouted so as to be heard throughout the house.

With his back straight and his feet moving fast, the manservant reminded me of a traditional Irish dancer as he rushed into the room.

"Would you be so kind as to ring for a taxi to return Mr. Moore back to his hotel?" Holmes commanded.

"Right away, Mr. Holmes," answered Hollingsworth quickly, before rushing out to tend to the request.

"Wait!" began Mr. Moore. "Mr. Holmes, I desperately need to speak with you on a very, very serious matter, sir. Please—"

"You are wasting your time, sir," said Holmes curtly.

"Holmes," I said, "I don't mind. I'll just have a therapeutic stroll through your gardens."

"Nonsense!" he shouted. "Mr. Moore, have you no knowledge of my relationship with Dr. Watson? Do you not know that he is my right hand? If you cannot discuss the matter freely before myself and Dr. Watson, then I cannot, and will not, be of any assistance to you."

"But, Mr. Holmes, I am not authorized to—"

"Then I suggest you authorize yourself."

"But, sir."

"Why pester me with this infernal intrusion of yours in the first place? Surely you are aware that I am retired and have been so for quite some time. I am no longer the advisor I once was. I am a simple beekeeper. I tend to my studies, my garden and to my bees. That is all. Now, if you will excuse me, I have a schedule to keep."

Moore sat still for a second. His eyes moved about as his mind raced. As had always been the case, Holmes had him and he knew it. Moore could not come this far only to fail. But, like Hollingsworth, Moore had his orders to follow. He grabbed hold of his attaché and stood poised, ready to quit the room. He looked at Holmes, then to me.

"It goes beyond the violation of attorney/client confidentiality. I could be charged with treason, if I should share this with anyone other than Mr. Holmes, sir."

With a pained look of fear on his face, Moore nodded respectfully to me.

"I mean you no insult, Doctor."

"I understand," I replied.

"Well I do not!" Holmes interjected. "You know full well that Watson here has my complete confidence. Furthermore, I will simply have to relay all you share with me to him, for he is surely to assist me in this matter. That is, if the problem has merit and I am intrigued by it. So, young man, I assure you. Either you, or your story, shall be out within the next two minutes. Which shall it be?"

Moore stood frozen. Like all before him who had encountered the commanding presence of Holmes, he knew he was no match for the master. For things will be done as Holmes sees fit, or they will not be done at all. It may have seemed risky to Moore to yield, but reason told him it was even riskier not to take that risk.

"You are right, Mr. Holmes. Dr. Watson, I should be very pleased if you would join us." Moore humbly invited.

"Thank you," I replied.

"Very well, then," said Holmes, "Please sit down. Watson, perhaps you could pour our guest a little more of this most excellent tea?"

He looked directly into Moore's eyes.

"Now sir, how can I be of service to you?"

Moore began to tremble slightly as he spoke.

"Well sir, we, my country and I that is, are in the most desperate of states. We, the American people—"

"Good God, man!" raged Holmes. "Have all Americans been programmed to solely use the blasted term *American People*? You do not hear the English referring to themselves as the *English People*? No, sir, it does not impress, it infuriates."

Mr. Moore's posture became like that of Nagasaki, after the great blast.

"Holmes!" I refereed.

"Yes, yes. Forgive the outburst. Please continue Mr. Moore," offered an unapologetic Holmes.

"We," Moore cautiously resumed, "We *Americans* have been going along as normal, unaware for God knows how long, after all, we are quite an industrial people," he sucked in the deepest of breaths, "when all of a sudden it began to dawn on a few intellectuals and a tiny number of government officials that a theft had been committed."

"A theft you say?" remarked Holmes.

"Yes, sir, a theft. A theft, I believe, like no other in the history of human existence. A theft so bold and so clever that not a soul was ever aware of the crime."

"When did this theft occur?" asked Holmes.

"Quite some time ago, I'm afraid. Years, sir."

"Years!" shot Holmes. "Tell me, what exactly was stolen? Where was the item kept? And how is it no one should notice the missing commodity until just recently? Who was responsible for the item itself?"

"All of us, sir."

"What do you mean, all of you?" I burst in.

"Yes," demanded Holmes, "who exactly is *all* of you?"

"By *us*, sir, I mean we, we the American peo—, *Americans*."

Holmes and I looked at each other.

"Out with it, Mr. Moore," said Holmes firmly. "Just what is it that has been stolen?"

"It's hard to label it exactly—,"

"Out with it man! My powers are in deduction, not mind reading."

"Well sir, I guess I'd have to use the word *culture*. Yes, our culture, Mr. Holmes! They've taken our culture," answered Moore like a man who had just lost his deeply beloved.

Holmes burst out with a roaring laughter. And though I tried to contain him, it was impossible. Moore was offended, as was expected, and began to swell with anger.

"Holmes," I said, "this really is in very bad form."

Still, Holmes could not speak. In between guffaws, he was hunched over, tortured by his laughter. I pleaded with him to compose himself, but my efforts were in vain. It was not until Mr. Moore stormed for the door, that Holmes' laughter began to ebb. He quickly stretched out an arm to signal Moore to remain. Then, while wiping tears from his eyes with the handkerchief from his breast pocket, Holmes slowly began to regroup.

"Oh, that!" Holmes cheekily began. "Well, better late than never."

Holmes' comment and preceding outburst had infected me and the combination of the two caused me to accidentally let out a little chuckle of my own.

"Excuse me, Mr. Holmes, but I did not come here to amuse you and Dr. Watson," Moore scolded. "I came here for your help in retrieving my country's culture, not to be insulted, mocked and laughed at. It is quite unbecoming of a man with your reputation."

"You are correct, sir. My behavior is rather deplorable. Forgive this most juvenile and insensitive of reactions," replied Holmes. "However, you misunderstand me, sir. I do not mock you, or belittle your circumstance. I am merely surprised that someone in your country has actually noticed the absence of its culture."

"What do you mean, sir," Moore said sternly.

"What Holmes means," I interjected, "is that the rest of the world has been aware of this American condition, I dare say, for quite some many decades now."

"Is this true?" Moore asked of Holmes.

"I'm afraid it is."

Moore's face drooped and wrinkled like a pair of old and worn socks. He became quite agitated and silently paced the room. Holmes and I gave him his due. For such pills are extremely hard to swallow.

"You mean to tell me," said Moore, "the entire time we American's have been espousing the superiority of America and Americans, the rest of the world's population has been having a good chuckle at our expense?"

"I'm afraid so," Holmes answered rather bluntly.

"Behind our very backs?" cried Moore.

"Only in an effort to spare your feelings, I assure you," I quickly jumped in.

Moore was devastated and dropped back onto the sofa.

"Look here," demanded Holmes. "I, for one, had honestly come to believe, though reluctantly, that Americans simply preferred the quick, the simple, the easy and disposable when it came to the cultural aspects of their existence. Their hunger for it appeared insatiable. Therefore, you cannot blame the peoples of other nations for getting the wrong impression, if that is the case."

Moore turned a wounded eye to me.

"Do you agree with Mr. Holmes on this, Doctor?"

"Regretfully so," I answered.

"What, pray tell, finally brought the theft to your eye?" asked Holmes. "Travel I suppose?"

"Well Mr. Holmes, yes. The ease at which one can travel these days did have an affect. But it was much more than that, sir. We began to notice an influx of a great number of interior design and cooking books that were saluting the contributions of countries like France and Italy, in particular, in our bookshops."

"I see."

"We also began to see an increase in the number of sidewalk cafés popping up in American cities, as well as a real bombardment of foreign films filling the shelves in local video stores. And their popularity is growing by leaps and bounds. Add to this your own BBC, which has now infiltrated the U.S. cable television market with its BBC America channel. Why even our own Public Broadcasting System has increased its content of British television. I myself began to take notice that even I was watching more and more of it, preferring it, in many cases, to our own network programming. It is quite troubling, Mr. Holmes. Then there's the internet—"

"Did you begin an investigation into the theft yourselves?" Holmes interrupted.

"Why yes, of course we did. But sir, after months and months with no lead, no real direction in which to head in, our agencies are at a loss. And to put it frankly to you, most of our investigators are, shall we say, not up to the task. Why many were stunned to learn that Puccini was not a green vegetable—It doesn't look very promising, Mr. Holmes."

"No, I should say not," concurred Holmes. "So then, Mr. Moore, what is it would you ask of me?"

"Well, Mr. Holmes, I should think that was obvious. We want you to track down the thief and recover our culture."

Holmes broke out into a repeat performance of his earlier hysteria, then suddenly transformed back into the master pragmatist that was his nature.

"That is an insurmountable task," Holmes bombastically replied. "You forget, sir, I am no longer a detective, but a mere private citizen. I am retired and prefer to divide my days between my beekeeping, my gardening and my studies."

Moore straightened himself and, borrowing a dramatic gesture from Holmes, looked Holmes firmly in the eye.

"But sir, you must admit, this is no ordinary theft! This, Mr. Holmes, is a theft more dastardly, heinous in fact, than would be the theft of the Mona Lisa, the Portland Vase, or the British Crown Jewels," he passionately pleaded.

"This is true. Nevertheless, I cannot possibly get away at the moment. Even if I were a much younger man—,"

A sudden, deadly seriousness took hold of Holmes' expression and speech. He paced a bit, then cast that expression of great concern upon Moore.

"My good man," his tone now as serious as if they were speaking of the Crown Jewels, "you do not know what you are up against.

This is not an ordinary thief. This is a man of some cunning, of great intellect, great power and immense wealth."

"Are you saying you know who the thief is?" I quickly asked.

The psychology of Holmes' face hinted at the possibility.

"Is that correct, Mr. Holmes?" asked Moore with great surprise and a sense of hope in his tenor.

"Let us just say I have my suspicions," Holmes answered.

"Excellent! Let's get started then!" howled Moore.

Holmes abruptly broke away from the conversation to contemplate the matter. His shoulders began to droop as a thick, dark sense of gloom overtook him. This wasn't like him. Holmes had always been the proud warrior leading the charge. Yet his body language as he paced about, before stationing himself by the fireplace, unmistakably revealed apprehension, reluctance and, even more hair raising, great fear.

"Well, Mr. Holmes?" asked Moore with the enthusiasm of a vicar-like locker room coach before the big game.

But Holmes remained silent, lost in deep consideration of the problem put before him. Though not visible to Mr. Moore, I could see that Holmes was in desperate need of a few quite moments to collect his thoughts.

"More tea, Mr. Moore," I offered.

"Heck no!" he responded in that cocky manner Americans like to display when they're en route to march into some lawless land and save the day. "Let's get after the son of a bitch, who ever this thief is!"

"Silence!" Holmes sharply commanded. "Only fools rush in, as is the adage. You would be wise to remember that."

He stepped away from the fire and followed that dramatic bark of his with an extremely stern glare.

"Young man, you are correct in consulting me. But, there is much you do not know. This is the most serious of situations. It is none the likes of any Watson and I have ever, or ever will, encounter." He paused an instant. "You, my young friend, have opened Pandora's box."

"I don't understand, Holmes," I stated. "A moment ago you

were beside yourself with laughter. Now you behave as if we are talking about a plague."

"That is exactly what we are speaking of. A plague, my dear friend. A plague, indeed!" he announced with authority.

"Surely you exaggerate?" cried Mr. Moore.

I shook the very second the American unthinkingly blurted out such a challenge. For if ever there was the wrong thing to suggest of Holmes, it was that.

"I never exaggerate!" roared Holmes. "You are but a newborn babe playing with knives. You have no idea of what you are up against. No idea!"

"Holmes," I pleaded, "for the love of humanity, tell us what is the matter. How can your laughter and great ease with the subject suddenly turn into the realization of Armageddon?"

"Because, dearest Watson, it is a most grave situation. Most grave indeed. From the moment this man came to you we have all been in great danger. A danger so unparalleled, we will never encounter the likes of it again. Never!"

"I don't understand," belted out Mr. Moore. "We have not—"

"Not as of yet, Mr. Moore," Holmes cut in. "Not as of yet. But I assure you, not only are our lives now threatened, they are never to be the same again. And even if we are to catch this fiend, from this moment on we will not know a moment's peace. For this very second, I can say with utter certainty, our every move is being monitored."

"Holmes," I cried, "are you saying we are being watched?"

"That is correct, Watson."

Holmes strode over to the door.

"Hollingsworth!" he summoned.

In less than half a second his dutiful man appeared. The Olympic sprinter Michael Johnson could not have moved with such speed.

"More tea. Keemun I should think," ordered Holmes, before turning to me. "What do you think, Watson? Keemun all right with you?"

I hesitated slightly, surprised by Holmes' sudden hankering for tea in the midst of this panic.

"Yes, fine. Keemun sounds perfect. Thank you," I replied, knowing full well that Mr. Moore's eyes were on me as he tried, no doubt in vain, to make sense of what was going on.

"Good, then, Keemun it is," Holmes instructed the devoted domestic. "Also, prepare a hearty lunch for the three of us. We have a lot of work ahead of us and we will need sufficient nourishment."

"So you're on the case then, Mr. Holmes?" asked an astonished and beaming Mr. Moore.

"Could I refuse a starving child a meal? Could I not rush to the aid of a damsel in distress? In a word, *yes*. But, gentlemen, my decision is not, in all honesty, as benevolent as I imply. For in truth, I am afraid there is no other option, for any of us. For you, my good man," said Holmes, as he pointed a long, thin finger at Moore, "you have awakened the giant beast."

CHAPTER IV

The Slip

While Mr. Moore and I nibbled away for hours at an expansive lunch consisting of an arugula and slightly grilled portobello mushroom salad, accompanied by a dish of penne, showered in a mixture of olive oil, garlic and purple basil, grown in Holmes' own herb garden, Holmes spent the time pouring through his computerized notes and files. Periodically he would address us to ask a question or two of Mr. Moore, questions that neither Moore, nor I, could see as having any relationship to the theft. But like myself, Moore quickly came to learn that, when Holmes had the scent, our place was not to question. However, we were growing rather impatient waiting for Holmes to fill us in. No doubt he sensed the two pair of anxious, wondering eyes that were fixed upon his every move, for he suddenly sprang from his chair.

"Gentlemen, I implore you. You must do as I instruct. We must proceed swiftly, but cautiously. You will follow my instructions to the letter or, I'm afraid, we are done for," he announced, with an authoritative tone that reminded me of an old, domineering schoolmaster I once had. "Now, Mr. Moore, who was it that initially approached you on this matter?"

"The president himself, sir," replied Moore.

"Did he contact you directly, or did he do so by intermediary?"

"His personal secretary phoned me."

"That is unfortunate. Very unfortunate."

"Why so, sir?"

"Did you discuss the matter with her or the president alone?"

"Well, sir, President Clinton had Ms. Currie draft a memo on the matter to me prior to our meeting so that I may be prepared to discuss the matter when I arrived at the oval office."

"And where is that memo now?"

"In my file cabinet."

"At the White House?"

"Yes. Why do you ask?"

Holmes took a seat on the sofa across from us. As he formulated his thought, he looked long and hard into the fire, as if it were a crystal ball and he a soothsayer.

"Save for those that Watson and I share, there are no secrets in this world," he said to Mr. Moore.

The American froze in disbelief.

"None!" exclaimed Holmes. "I will wager ten to one that not a trace of that memo will be found in your office, the White House, or anywhere else for that matter. It, and the information contained in it, has been delivered to this master of thieves who must now silence you, and now us, in order to keep his tracks covered."

"But how, Holmes?" I asked. "And who, for God's sake?"

Holmes leaned forward.

"As I had suggested to you earlier, this is a man of immense wealth and power. Nothing in his realm goes unobserved. Nothing!"

He sank back into the sofa, as Moore and I sat stupefied and trying to calm our racing hearts.

"You two will leave here at dusk. Mr. Moore, you shall return to your hotel room and telephone Mr. Clinton directly. When his underlings answer, tell any and all of those that are aware of your visit to me that I have flatly refused you. I found our entire conversation to be ludicrous, utter and complete balderdash. When they ask why you were here so long here, if I had scoffed at your request, you shall say that after a period of pleading and groveling, the remainder of your time here was spent in hero worship, if I may be so bold."

He chuckled at the idea.

"That should put them off for a bit."

"But you haven't refused me, have you, Mr. Holmes?" asked Moore.

"Oh do come along, Mr. Moore'" Holmes rebuked. "*Time*, Mr. Moore. Time! We need to buy time!"

I could see the proverbial light switching on in Moore's head.

"Ah, I see," he said.

"Excellent!" cheered Holmes. "Now, you are to return to Washington tomorrow. Not on the first, but on the second available flight. Before that flight you will stop at Harrod's and pick up some gifts for whomever you can think of. We want these watchers, this school of ramora now clinging to us, to think you are not in line with your superior's thinking on this matter. We want them to think that this has been a mere errand, like any other, you have performed for Mr. Clinton. We must ease their concerns about you. Then, when their guard is relaxed, we shall slip in and strike. Do you follow me so far?"

"Yes, Mr. Holmes, I believe I do," Moore answered while managing to swallow yet another lump in his throat.

"Splendid! Now," continued Holmes, "when you return to the White House, you shall take a meeting with Mr. Clinton. But, this meeting shall be between you and the president alone! No one can know what you speak of. No one. I do not know how you shall manage this, but manage it you shall. Or we are sunk. Do you understand me?"

"Yes, Mr. Holmes."

"Excellent. At that meeting you shall inform the president that Watson and I are en route to Washington and that he is to meet us in the White House rose garden three days from now, on the eighteenth, at 2pm."

Moore suddenly became agitated.

"But, Mr. Holmes," he said, "the president is scheduled to meet Arafat at Camp David at that very time."

"Well, you will simply have to reschedule the man," Holmes callously replied.

"Holmes!" I shouted. "You cannot dismiss such world leaders to fit your schedule. Perhaps we could postpone—"

"Nonsense!" barked an irritated Holmes. "Timing is everything! And we haven't a moment to lose!"

He turned to Moore. With his intent eyes separated by that long, narrow nose, Holmes created a rather menacing image of himself, one I had seen many times.

"Timing is everything," said Holmes, delivering the line with a soft, yet extremely serious tone.

Moore, in a manner that resembled an obedient schoolboy, looked up at Holmes,

"Yes, sir," he said. "I'll see to it. Exactly as you instruct."

It was a wise move on Moore's part. For surely to respond otherwise would have been like a lion tamer placing his head in the mouth of an untamed king of beasts. It would have been exceedingly bloody.

"Good. Very good!" said Holmes. "Now," he said to me, "Watson, you will return to your home as usual. Tomorrow you will book yourself a flight to Delhi."

"India?" I confusedly asked.

"Is there another?" he snidely replied.

"But why India, Holmes? Should I not be going to—?"

"I merely stated that you will purchase a ticket to Delhi. I said nothing about going there."

"Ah! I see."

"Do you? Both of you? These people are not fools! They will do everything within their power to intercept us, annihilate any aircraft, derail any locomotive, sink any vessel that may transport us, if necessary. If we are to travel to America, we must do so unobserved. In short, gentlemen, we must give them the slip!"

He began to pace about the room. The afternoon was slipping away and Moore and I would have to be returning to London soon if we were to follow Holmes' instructions and leave at dusk. I stepped over to the window to examine just how much daylight was actually left. I was about to pull the sheer back when—

"STOP!" shouted Holmes.

I pulled away immediately.

"We do not want to give the impression that we are aware of

our position," said Holmes. "As far as we three are concerned, we are but three innocent little lambs grazing in a meadow, oblivious to the presence of the hungry wolf. Mr. Moore, as I have instructed, tomorrow you will take your time returning to Washington. Your work in England is done. You are now a simple tourist—You, Watson, when you book that flight to Delhi, you will take care to casually inform the travel agent that you are to attend the annual conference of New Age medicine that is to be held at the Yoghatatama Ashram's Center for the Study of Human and Spiritual Evolution in Delhi. You will not, however, get on that flight. You will take a cab to Heathrow. On the way you will instruct the driver to stop at St. John's Haberdashery to fetch another linen shirt for the Indian heat. Tell the driver to wait. Then, once inside the shop, you will step into the dressing room to try on the garment. The rest you will leave to me."

"But what about you, Mr. Holmes?" asked Moore. "Won't these people, whomever you say they are, put two and two together once they discover you, too, have left England so soon after my visit?"

"I shall not be leaving England," replied Holmes.

"What?" Moore and I cried.

"Gentlemen, gentlemen. Calm yourselves. Of course I will be with you."

"But, Holmes," I began, with a squeaky pitch of confusion. "How on earth can you be two places at—," it hit me. "Of course! The Empty House."

"Excellent, Watson. You begin to catch on."

"What empty house?" belted out Mr. Moore.

"I was under the impression that you had read my accounts of Holmes' cases?" I put it to Moore.

"Yes, I did."

"And you do not recognize the significance of what we are referring to?"

"Mr. Moore," said Holmes, "do you not remember the very overly dramatic report of my return to England after a three year absence, which my dearest friend Watson here had chronicled?"

"Why, yes, sir, I think I do," answered Moore.

"Holmes," I boastfully interloped, "had a bust, an exact replica of himself, made of wax so that it could assume a position before—"

"The window! Yes, yes, I remember! Yes, that was marvelous, Doctor. Yes, Mr. Holmes. Marvelous!"

"This time, gentlemen, I have improved upon that ploy. I shall not need the services of another to turn the figure periodically while I am away. Thanks to the internet, I have established an ongoing dialog with a Mr. Kiate, a master inventor with a certain Japanese company in Tokyo."

Holmes stepped over to a section of his bookshelves that swung out, revealing a small, closet-like hidden chamber. He stepped inside and retrieved a life-sized bust of himself.

"Unlike my last decoy, this one is made of a most resilient rubber, not wax. And, most importantly, it is also robotic and can run on battery or alternating current. It, as was my previous decoy, shall be placed before the window. However, since we will be gone for some days, I shall instruct Hollingsworth to open and close the drapery in the morning and at sunset."

"Holmes," I shouted with pride, "you never cease to amaze me. This is sheer genius."

"Not mine, I assure you. The credit rightfully belongs to my very clever Japanese associate."

He waved us to the door.

"Now gentlemen, I'm afraid you must take your leave. Daylight is diminishing and I want our parasitic visitors out there to be very certain whom it is that leaves this house. I do not want them to have the slightest doubt regarding our whereabouts."

Moore took another sip of Holmes' exceptional Keemun tea and stood revitalized, ready and eager to march off into battle for his beloved general.

"We're off, Mr. Holmes," he said.

I looked at Holmes and saw in his face that familiar expression, the one that had long ago convinced me that the two of us had a uniquely telepathic relationship.

"Three o'clock, Watson, at—"

"St. James' Haberdashery?" I eagerly interjected. "I shall be there."

And with that Moore and I marched to the foyer to make our exit. But just as Hollingsworth appeared ready and in position to open the door, Holmes waved him back, then stopped short and turned to us.

"Watson," he started, "on the way back to your car, do not examine the area. Keep your eyes fixed on one another. In fact Watson, start an argument with Mr. Moore accusing him of misleading you and creating tension between you and I. Initially our surprise guests will find this unbelievable, but when they see that we are all in separate locales, they will let down their guard. It won't be much of a window, mind you, but we must make do with what we have." He patted me on the shoulder, "A demain, mon ami!"

"Yes Holmes, until tomorrow," I said before slipping out, with Mr. Moore in tow.

We scarcely covered ten feet of ground when Moore launched into a rant about Holmes' curmudgeon-like state. It was very good of him to provide me with the necessary motivation to fire back, as Holmes had instructed. Save for Moore having to fight back a guilty little smile, the ploy went off rather well and we remained in character until we were back through Uckfield, on the A22.

The next morning, as instructed, I rang the local travel agent and booked myself on the next available flight to Delhi, explaining, just in case our conversation was overheard, that other plans of mine had fallen through and I could now attend the medical conference I had been looking forward to. Later, as afternoon arrived, I did as Holmes instructed and had Mrs. Gale fetch me a taxi. After bidding her farewell I firmly announced to the driver that I wished him to take me to Heathrow, making a quick stop at my haberdasher's on the way. It all was going perfectly according to plan.

When we reached Noel Street, and began our approach to St John's Haberdashery, the clothiers I have patronized for some seventy years now, I began to grow anxious, a drop of perspiration

or two formed on my brow as I wondered what else Holmes had
up his sleeve. Nevertheless, I pushed on, and when the driver
brought the taxi to a stop in front of the small shop, I took a deep
breath to steady myself, assured him that I'd be right out, and
flung myself out of the cab and strode confidently into St. John's.
Once inside I asked to see a white linen shirt. I was shown several.
From them I selected three and headed for the dressing closet at
the rear of the store.

Opening the door to the little room, I found it fairly dark and
began feeling about for the light switch. Suddenly, I felt something
pull me forward well into the room, while the door simultaneously
closed behind me. Magically the light went on and there, before
my eyes, stood two men I had never seen before. One was a tall,
thin, middle-aged-man with a well-trimmed gray beard, eyeglasses
with very thick frames and a woolen Swiss hiking hat on his head.
He and the stranger next to him, a shorter man of about sixty-five,
and with only a mustache, appeared very professorial in their brown
tweed suits.

"Quickly, Watson," said the tall thin one, in a voice I would
recognize anywhere, "remove your jacket."

"Holmes?" I cried, knowing full well who was behind the very
clever guise.

"Yes, Watson, it is me," he replied. "Now off with the jacket,"
he said just as the shorter man removed his own. "This is a
confederate of mine. His name is Noah. Not only is he a neighbor
of mine, and an exceptional chess companion, he is an actor with
our local amateur theater group. It will be Noah who will be
traveling to India."

"How do you do, Dr. Watson?" Noah greeted me, as he slipped
into my jacket, "I've always dreamed of a holiday in India."

"Here, Watson," said Holmes, "get into Noah's jacket. And
give him the linen shirts."

I did so.

"Excellent! Now, Noah my good friend, enjoy your Indian
adventure."

"Thank you, Mr. Holmes. Thank you."

"Not at all, it is we who are indebted to you. Allow me," said Holmes as he switched off the light and pulled us back away from the door. "Off you go."

With that, Noah slipped out of the dressing room, carefully leaving the door open only an inch behind him. Through that small gap Holmes and I watched Noah's performance as Dr. Watson. It was flawless. He calmly and collectedly acted out charging the shirts to my account then confidently strode out of the shop and road off in the waiting taxi.

"Brilliant, Holmes!" I said. "Simply brilliant!"

"Nothing simple about it, my dear friend," he replied.

"No! I mean—"

"I know what you mean. However, you are quite correct, in a sense. This is certain to be the simplest maneuver we manage to pull off on this adventure."

He looked worried for an instant.

"Our friendly proprietor has kindly packed you a bag. I have taken care of passage and passports. Also," he handed me a matching Swiss hiking hat and some thin, wire-rimmed spectacles, "slip these on. I've a taxi waiting in the alleyway behind this establishment. Our flight departs Gatwick in ninety minutes."

CHAPTER V

Generica

Six hours after I had rendezvoused with Holmes at St. John's clothiers, I found myself in an elegant hotel room at the Essex House hotel in New York City. Holmes had determined that an indirect route to Washington would be far more prudent, since any and all direct flights from London to the U.S. capitol were certain to be monitored by our, according to Holmes, virus-like pursuers, invisible to the naked eye, yet acutely pestilent. Then, after a night in the city that never sleeps, we took the morning train to Washington, where we announced ourselves as a pair of Swiss University professors, in America's capitol to examine that nation's civil war documents housed in the Library of Congress. It all fell together perfectly. But, that was Holmes. No matter the complexity of a particular situation, amazingly, Holmes always made it appear routine. And although I had long ago learned to accept, and expect, this of Holmes, his mastery of any given situation never ceased to astound me.

It had been three days since Holmes had taken on this case, which meant, by some miracle, we were to meet President Clinton in the White House rose garden at two that very afternoon. But I had not seen hide nor hair of Holmes since breakfast that morning. And as I sat browsing through the Washington Post in the Morrison-Clark Inn's garden courtyard, I could not help glancing at my watch, 11:45am. We had little more than two hours till our scheduled rendezvous. Yet where was Holmes? As he left the hotel that morning he had assured me he'd be back and ready to go by noon. It wasn't like Holmes to be late.

Suddenly, a voice broke my concentration.

"Excuse me, sir. But are you Professor Heinz Waltzin?" asked the lad in the porter's uniform standing before me.

"Pardon me?" I bewilderedly replied.

"Professor Waltzin?" the young man asked again.

"Oh, ah, right. Yes! Yes, I am he," I clumsily answered.

"There is a call for you, sir."

"A call for me?" I asked with great surprise.

"Yes, sir. If you will follow me, I'm afraid you must take it in the lobby, sir."

I followed the young man to the lobby where he directed me to a white telephone sitting on a coffee table. I thanked him as I anxiously reached for the phone.

"Are you ready, Watson?" said Holmes' voice as it blasted out of the phone.

"Holmes?" I said, "Where on earth are you?"

"Are you ready?" Holmes firmly repeated.

"I've been ready for over three hours."

"Excellent! Now, exit the hotel and turn to your left. On the opposite side of the street you will see a large, white van. It will have the name *Capitol Landscapers* painted on the side panels. Go now!"

"But, Holmes—"

"Now, Watson!"

The phone went dead. I quickly returned the receiver, and the *Post*, and charged for the exit as instructed. Bursting through the door I spotted the vehicle Holmes described and proceeded directly to it. As I approached the van, I deduced from its low rumble and vibration the engine to be running and waiting command. I walked round to the passenger side window and peeked in. There, behind the wheel, sat Holmes. Although the person sitting at the helm did not resemble my good friend, or the Swiss chap I had been traveling with, I recognized that familiar long nose and stern jaw. He wore jeans, a polo shirt, sneakers, aviator sunglasses and a huge gardener's sun hat.

"Get in, Watson. Quickly!" he said.

As usual, I immediately complied. But as I lifted myself into the van and prepared to buckle my seatbelt, Holmes stopped me.

"Walk through to the back and get into those clothes," he said, pointing to an identical set of Holmes' work clothes neatly placed on a wire hanger and hooked onto the inside panel.

"What's going on here, Holmes," I asked. "Have you forgotten we have a two o'clock meeting with Mr. Clinton?"

"Not at all," he answered in his usual matter-of-fact tone. "As soon as you are properly attired, we will be off to tend to a most *presidential* aphid problem. Now hurry."

"I take it this company, this *Capitol Landscaping*, is responsible for tending the grounds at the White House?"

"You are most correct, Watson."

"How is it they allowed you to borrow this van?"

"I allowed myself."

"Holmes," I shouted, "you've stolen this vehicle?"

"Borrowed, my good man. Borrowed! We'll see that it is returned after our time with Mr. Clinton," he cavalierly replied.

"Do you really think this pretense is necessary? You are at your desk in Eastbourne and I am in India, remember? Are we not beyond the evil watchful eye's field of vision now?"

"And what, pray tell, do you think we are about to enter?" he replied.

"No! Surely they do not watch the president?"

"Who better to watch than the man who initiated the inquiries into this supremely cleverest of thefts? Come Watson, we must hurry."

Again, I did as Holmes ordered and before I could buckle my seatbelt, we were off. While Holmes drove us towards the White House I fretted over everything. Would Holmes be able to get us inside the grounds? Would the police be on the alert for our stolen van? Would Mr. Moore have successfully persuaded the president to meet us? I looked over at Holmes, nerves of steel. I looked at my watch, one-forty. I looked up, there filling the view in the windscreen, as we drove up Pennsylvania avenue, was the mammoth residence itself. Although Holmes was familiar with this American palace, I was not. I had never been to the American capitol. New York was always my haunt whenever I felt a need to "jump the pond", as I remember my American friends saying some years back.

Holmes, on the other hand, knew the mansion exceptionally well. He had been the guest of several American presidents over the years. Roosevelt, during the second World War, had often invited Holmes over for his advice, analysis and critique of the strategic allied campaigns, on both fronts. I dare say it caused a bit of a ruffle in Churchill's feathers. But Holmes donated even more time to Churchill and his generals, as a means of ensuring that the two world leaders would get along more than amicably, which they did until Roosevelt's death shortly before the end of the war. Eisenhower and Montgomery, on the other hand, never seemed to see eye to eye on any issue, in spite of Holmes' aid. This was a great disappointment, and, quite frankly, a disaster for Holmes. For due heavily to the jousting egos of the two commanders, far too many aspects of the great D-Day invasion and battles, like that at the Bulge, went terribly wrong. To this day it pains Holmes to even think of that period. Yet here he was again, this time not as the great strategist, but as an unknown gardener, passing, as always, through the heavily guarded White House gate with the greatest of ease.

"This is beyond even you, Holmes," I said as the guards waved us on through. "How on earth did you manage this feat?"

"Elementary Watson. I rang our Mr. Moore this morning. After all, aphids on the president's precious roses simply won't do," replied Holmes.

"But what about that document you gave the gate guard?"

"A facsimile to our hotel from Mr. Moore. Which, by the way, is the reason we will be taking our leave of Washington as soon as we are finished here."

"But why? I thought—"

"No! You do not think at all, Watson," blasted Holmes. "This thief of ours, this ruthless predator, is certain to be monitoring every communication going in or out of America's *first home*. And I would venture to say he has an especially keen eye on young Mr. Moore. I know I should, if I were he. Therefore, if we are to have even the slightest of chances, it is absolutely imperative that we stay on the move. Understand?"

"Completely," I answered, feeling as I had as a lad on the first day of the new school term.

After parking the van, Holmes and I retrieved the insecticide spray gun and tanks from the rear of the vehicle and lugged them by means of a folding wheeled cart into the rose garden. It was smaller than I had imagined. Nevertheless, it was astutely arranged and filled with exactly the right type of roses for the city's zone 6 climate coding. Acting the part of gardener was not out of Holmes' range. He truly was a master horticulturist. And like I had done when I acquired a new patient, Holmes proceeded to give the flora in the vicinity a thorough examination. From top to bottom, Holmes looked them over, poking and feeling at will. His focus was so amazing I began to wonder if he had forgotten the very reason for our visit. But knowing Holmes as I did, that was most improbable.

Suddenly, there was a commotion. Secret Service men began to scurry about and quickly take position, all the while talking into, it appeared, their lapels and cufflinks. They were so rigid, so serious, so machine like, I felt as if I were watching some sort of futuristic group of navy suited, dark sun-glassed soldiers falling into formation. I probably was. Behind them appeared Mr. Clinton, with a small group of underlings at his side. He was taller than I had expected. With that full head of white, wavy hair and those round, rosy cheeks, he conjured up the image of a cherub to my mind. Like sheep's clothing for the wolf, an excellent camouflage for the master politician. And, whether friend or foe, you clearly had to give him that. Then, to cement the image of the gentle seraph, the president included Buddy, the nation's *first dog*, in his entourage.

"Watson, you'll find a pair of sunglasses in your breast pocket. Put them on," I suddenly heard Holmes whisper to me, without looking up from the physical check-up he was performing on the roses. "Now!"

The instant I had complied with his request, we were surrounded by a horde of press people. Cameras and the relentless bright bursts of light they projected were everywhere as a besieged

Mr. Clinton made his way into the garden. I followed Holmes' lead, kept my head low and ignored it all by feigning an intense interest in the rose bushes. Like chicks in the nest, reporters were crying out for something, anything, from the president. I found it rather pitiful. Given the opportunity, I was absolutely certain each and every single reporter present would not hesitate in the slightest to follow the president into the nation's first lavatory for an interview. Suddenly it all came to an abrupt halt. Mr. Clinton, with his left hand tightly grasping Buddy's leash, raised his right arm as a means of requesting a momentary pause from the restless assemblage.

"Please, everyone. Please," he began, "I know y'all have questions you'd like to ask, and I'd like very much to answer them. But the plain fact is this. I have been in conference all day and I have come out only for a chance to take a brief stroll with Buddy. So, if you don't mind, I'm going to ask security here to see that everyone is escorted safely and courteously out and away from the rose garden. I'm sure y'all understand. I thank you for your patience and understanding. It is greatly appreciated."

And with that an increase in security people, who seemed to come out of the woodwork, proceeded to do, with great proficiency, exactly what their president had announced. Suddenly, we were alone in the garden with the most powerful man in the world. Or were we, I wondered as the thought of the thief and the purpose of our visit forced its way back to the forefront of my mind.

"Hello there, gentlemen," said the president in our direction. "What's the diagnosis? Will surgery be required?"

I stood frozen, not knowing what to say, and feeling a little ridiculous in a getup he surely knew was a false front.

"Well, Mr. President, the jury is still out on that just yet," Holmes quickly replied. "I'm afraid I shall require more time to examine the situation at present. I hope that is convenient?"

"Absolutely, sir," answered Mr. Clinton. "Take what time you need. Can I be of any assistance?"

"Why, yes, I believe you can, sir," said Holmes as he continued looking over the Jacqueline Kennedy rose. "When did you first notice this very alarming condition?"

"Quite some time ago, actually. I'd say January of ninety-eight, if I had to pinpoint a month," the president returned.

"I see. Well you are correct in your initial observation. It is definitely a virus that has attacked."

"I see."

"I could be more certain in my diagnosis if I were certain you had gone to great lengths to rid the area in and around the garden from *other* intrusive *bugs*."

"I have indeed, sir. I have indeed. I know for a fact, my men swept the area not but ten minutes ago," Mr. Clinton confidently replied.

"You are certain of this, sir?" Holmes boldly asked.

"I am, sir. I am, indeed."

"Very well then, I shall dispense with this round about dialog and come directly to the point."

"Please do, sir."

"This is an extremely grave situation, even more so than you suspect. Therefore, I must insist that you speak to no one, save Mr. Moore regarding this matter."

"As you wish, Mr. Holmes."

"What you have here, Mr. President, is the severest case of, what I call, *Eloisyndrome* that I have ever had the misfortune to witness."

"What, pray tell is that, Holmes?" I burst in with a shout.

"Yes, Mr. Holmes, please explain?" asked the president with a deep wrinkle of concern in his brow. Holmes clipped off a branch from the Jacqueline Kennedy rose bush and examined it as he spoke, making certain to move his head up and down and side to side. For despite Mr. Clinton's certainty of the area's safety from electronic eves dropping, Holmes knew that even the most sophisticated electronics were no match for a good pair of binoculars in the hands of a master lip reader.

"Well sir," began Holmes, "have you read Wells' Time Machine?"

"Yes, Mr. Holmes, I have," the president answered with a look of perplexity on his cherub-like face.

"Good, then you must remember the Eloi? You will recall they are the people the time traveler discovers when he reaches the year eight hundred and two thousand, seven hundred and one. The meek, small in stature, ignorant, childlike people who inhabit the land in that year."

"Yes, yes, I do. But what has this—"

"This, sir, is what the populous of your country is on its way to becoming, with far too great a number of them already having passed the point of no return. A very serious situation, Mr. President, very serious indeed."

"Surely you exaggerate, Holmes," I interrupted, annoyed with what seemed to me to be a generally condescending remark.

"Excuse me, Mr. President, allow me to introduce my good friend, confidant and sometimes impetuous assistant, Dr. John Watson."

"It is an honor, sir," said Mr. Clinton as he shook my nervous hand.

"I'm afraid you have that backwards, Mr. President. For it is I who is greatly honored," I stammered in return.

"No gentlemen, the honor is all mine. I look upon your presence here today as a gift, a token of your generosity and devotion to humanity. Do not fear, I understand what we discuss here today is an ugly subject. But against all evil in the world we must unite, work together and remain strong in order to defeat it," responded the president, as if he were delivering the State of the Union Address.

"Then you do not mind if I speak frankly, sir," asked Holmes.

"No, I do not. In fact, I insist upon it," said Mr. Clinton, as he waved his hand toward the pathway. "Let us walk a bit, shall we?"

"Very well, then," replied Holmes as he and I joined the American president for a stroll between the soft, yet vibrantly colored field of freshly blooming roses. They were just the thing to ease the sting of what was to be a very disturbing conversation.

"Mr. President, as I said, the problem is quite severe. Far more so than you or Mr. Moore had perceived it to be," said Holmes with a slight hint of sympathy.

"Go on, Mr. Holmes," the president anxiously pressed.

"This was a raw, relatively young country. Thus, it was ripe with opportunity. And like the first opportunists that settled this land and brought disease to its native populations, this villainous thief has delivered the *Eloisyndrome* upon today's inhabitants with his arrival. But unlike the ruthlessly tyrannical egotists of the past, this man does not intend to follow a path of mass annihilation. Oh no, no. He is far too clever for that. His plan is to gradually reduce the intellect until, like the Eloi, the great flock will perform at his command and, metaphorically speaking, *feed him.*"

"This is horrible," Mr. Clinton responded with fright now taking a firm hold of that gray head with the boyish face.

"More than you realise," said Holmes. "For he has very nearly succeeded. If I had to, I would venture to say his scheme is approximately ninety-four percent complete."

The president and I stood aghast at this revelation.

"You see, sir," Holmes continued, "in order to amass power and great wealth, begetting greater power and greater wealth, one needs a devoted and dutiful flock. Not one ruled by means of physical brutality, intimidation, low wages, poverty and deplorable working conditions as was inflicted upon those spinning the great wheel of commerce for the industrial barons of the industrial revolution. No sir, what you must have, first and foremost, is a happily duped herd. Thus, it would appear, this man, this most ingenious of all thieves, like the late Moriarty, seldom, if ever, commits an actual crime, according to those on your books. His crimes are crimes against the very fabric of the American, against the very heart of humanity. Yet, ironically, this man is revered."

"What? How? Why?" pleaded the president.

"Manipulation, of course!"

"How do you come by this intelligence, Holmes?" I insisted.

"Who the hell is this man?" demanded the president with a swelling rage in his voice.

"I am unable to say," Holmes rather coldly answered.

"Why not?" both the president and I cried out.

"I regret this. But, it would not be wise for me to reveal this to you quite yet, sir. For, begging your pardon, I cannot risk any advantage I may have by chancing someone overhearing you in conversation, even with the very trustworthy Mr. Moore."

"Ah, I see," Mr. Clinton said, sounding rather disappointed and slightly offended. "Well then, what can you tell me?"

"May I tell you exactly what has taken place?" Holmes confidently replied.

"Yes!" both the president and I, again, eagerly shot out.

Holmes flashed us a serious look, took a deep breath, then began to explain.

"Like the *Spanish Prisoner*," he began," the *Ugly Sister* scam and the *You May Already be a Winner* cons, I've given a name to this most original of swindles. This one I call *Generica* because it yielded exactly what it intended, a bland, monotonous, perfectly generic land of plenty. For you see, America may be the land of everything, the land of the colossal shopping mall, the mini and strip malls, the land of absolute abundance, yet it is a wasteland."

Holmes sank into a momentary silence as he paced about, pretending for the distant onlookers, to be checking every single rose bush in the garden. Mr. Clinton and I waited impatiently for Holmes to resume his explanation. But I could see that it gave Holmes no pleasure to throw a mountain of trouble at the American president, a man who has had his share of trouble and controversy ever since launching his initial campaign for his present position back in nineteen hundred and ninety one.

"Mr. President, you are to be highly commended, sir," said Holmes. "For though you are a gentleman and a scholar, you, sir, are a product of the American South, where, I dare say, the outbreak of *Eloisyndrome* is far more severe. In all honesty, I would not have expected a Southerner to notice the theft."

Mr. Clinton's face immediately tightened. He looked like a man who had stubbed his toe and was trying to ignore the pain.

"Though that does not feel very much like a compliment, I

will acknowledge it as one. For I'm sure that is how it was intended," the president proudly countered.

"I pay you the sincerest of compliments, sir," replied Holmes.

"Holmes!" I said, giving him a look that shouted 'get on with it'.

"Yes, you're quite right, Watson."

He took a breath, then turned and looked the world's most powerful leader squarely in the face.

"Mr. President, what occurred is this. Over time, this master of thieves, as any con men worth his weight would have done, gradually and subtly introduced vulgar, crass and appallingly cheap imitations of real cultural elements into American society by capitalizing on periods of depression, frustration and rebellion. By very cunningly reducing things to their simplest of forms, our man targeted the naïve, the uneducated and the very, very impressionable. He encouraged defiance of the old, richer elements that make up a resplendent culture and cleverly dubbed this subtle movement as *breaking the chains that bind*. In short, as *hip*. And, as you now see, it has worked splendidly. Then, day by day, year by year he gradually removed any and all cognitive challenges to the individual's cultural intellect."

"Can you cite an example, Mr. Holmes?"

"Many, Mr. President. Far too many, I'm afraid," Holmes replied. "Let's take beer for example. In truth, there is really no such thing as beer in this country."

"What do you mean?" remarked the astonished head of state.

"Well, sir, what you have here may be referred to as beer, but it is the laughingstock of the rest of the civilized world. Surely, you've noticed that American beers are shockingly watered down and rather bland in taste."

"Why, now that you mention it, I have noticed that I myself have been gravitating over to Czech and German beers because I found them to be heartier and far more satisfying. But I nev—"

"You weren't supposed to, sir," Holmes cut in. "Like most things in America these days, the simpler the better all round. The art and the passion of a product are gone. Why? Simpler is less costly for the manufacturer to produce. Sure, it is also less tasty, less substantial, but that is conquered by fast paced slogans that suggest a carefree, whimsical attitude. The old taste is heavy and overbearing. So forget the old, the real. It's a ball and chain—It is not a very pretty picture, I'm afraid."

"No, sir," said Mr. Clinton, "it certainly is not. But please, do continue, Mr. Holmes. Please, cite another example if you would, sir."

"Have you ever noticed how one major American city, and its suburban communities, resemble that of another?" Holmes asked.

"I'm not sure I follow, Mr. Holmes," the president answered.

"Tour your nation with a more critical eye, sir, and you will soon see that every city will resemble every other. Each one will have the same shopping mall with the same shops, department stores and restaurants, food parks and eateries. *J. Crew, Macy's, Sears, Robinsons/May, The Limited, The Gap, GNC*, which I may say is an absolute joke of a vitamin and mineral chain. Do not forget *JC Penny, Banana Republic, Victoria's Secret, Barnes and Noble, Applebee's* and the twenty-five movie theaters housed in every mall. Everywhere you travel in America will feel like every other part of the country. When in actuality the landscape should be diverse, regional, making each city, and its *banlieues,* unique not generic, which is what they have become. Hence, *Generica.*"

"My God!" cried Mr. Clinton. "I think I am beginning to see what you mean, Mr. Holmes. We have become an insatiably gluttonous society. We have enough, yet we want more, more of everything. More and more and more and more! Oh, the magnitude of this horror makes me quiver."

He took a pensive presidential pause to develop his thought, before continuing on.

"Did you know, gentlemen, and I know you'll find this quite laughable, but we actually have a chain of stores in this country that sells nothing but storage containers? Yes, that's right, containers for storing a consumer's dutiful haul? So, if all your *stuff* is starting to take over your home, fear not. Store and stack it away in containers. Then, lucky you, you'll have room for more *stuff.* Can you imagine? Buying just for the sheer thrill of buying. Good Lord, what have we become?"

"You have a keen eye, Mr. President," complimented Holmes.

"Yes," I felt compelled to concur.

"Thank you, Dr. Watson. Thank you both. However, this new understanding only places a greater weight on my already overburdened shoulders," replied a very dejected American president.

"It is a large pill to swallow, indeed," said Holmes.

"What do you propose we do, Mr. Holmes?"

"There is but only one recourse, Mr. President," replied Holmes.

"And that is?" I quickly asked, accidentally beating Mr. Clinton to the question.

"Track down this thief and eliminate him," answered Holmes with an icy callousness that left both the president and I not only flabbergasted, but chilled to the bone.

"Holmes," I blasted, "surely you mean to suggest that we apprehend this scoundrel, convict him in a court of law and put him out of business."

"No I do not!" Holmes quickly and very curtly answered.

"Mr. Holmes," said the president, "I cannot and will not be a party to any such action. Can we not just seize this pirate and retrieve our culture?"

"Impossible!" barked Holmes. "You might as well construct a home on Jupiter. If it were only the theft, perhaps. But your stolen culture has been infected and must be cleansed."

"Cleansed?" the president and I simultaneously scoffed.

"Exactly!" Holmes said sharply. "Reintroducing the reclaimed culture directly into the American mainstream is certain to send the whole of the populace into such a severe state of shock, I am certain it will not recover. Thus, if we are to attempt even the hope of a recovery, we must REMOVE the very source of the corruption. Like the blood that flows through the dialysis machine, the reclaimed culture must trickle in just as the tainted culture is slowly extracted. No gentlemen, the instant cure we cannot effect."

Mr. Clinton and I looked at one another in horror.

"Yes, my good men," whispered Holmes in that perpetual matter-of-fact tone of his, "In a word, *remove!*"

CHAPTER VI

The Machine

"This nation uses two-thirds of the world's resources, yet its own population is a mere one sixth of the global populous," fumed Holmes, as he gazed out the window at the American countryside whizzing past us as we sat on the train back to New York.

Though our meeting with the American president was a bonding experience for all, our discussion amidst the roses weighed heavily upon our moods, especially so for Holmes. As if concrete blocks had been fastened to his spirit, he rapidly began to sink within himself. For Holmes, the task at hand was growing more daunting by the second, a rising tide he viewed as virtually unstoppable. Having last visited the United States only nine years earlier in the year nineteen hundred and ninety one, Holmes could see just how rapidly the cultural infection in this country had progressed. The odds against defeating the bestial bacteria were miniscule. With odds at only forty million to one against, playing the state lottery appeared much more promising. Thus, for the first time in his life, Holmes was beginning to consider a situation hopeless, a notion that infuriated him very nearly to the boiling point. To counteract this despair, Holmes increased the number of breathing and meditative exercises he would perform throughout the day. For despite a feeling of futility, Holmes was a man who fought to the bitter end. He had never learned to accept defeat, and he wasn't about to attempt to acquire that skill, not without one bloody hell of a fight.

As the train carried us to our destination, I sat studying Holmes' facial expressions. All shone torment, which lead me to conclude that Holmes was beginning to feel a little like David, going up against Goliath. But, I was confident Holmes, like David, always had a few good rocks up his sleeve.

"Watson," said Holmes, still fixed on the view through the window, "have you noticed how the scenery appears to repeat itself? The same fast food restaurants, the same shoe stores, the same super markets and the same banks. Each and every one reappearing approximately every three miles."

"Yes, I have noticed that," I replied.

"One could almost argue that the window is nothing more than a video monitor projecting a looping video tape," he suggested.

"Yes, I see what you mean. The landscape is rather constant, as if it were just one long, continuous city."

"Exactly, Watson! Exactly! Everything is uniform. One city, one suburb, each a mere clone of another, precisely as I had discussed with Mr. Clinton.—Oh I tell you, this is a masterpiece of an assault!"

He took a long, deep, heavy sigh.

"It began with the infiltration of the simple," he continued, "the mundane, the tasteless. Then, once the distractions were in place, came the theft of the richer, more diverse culture. This man is cunning, Watson. Very cunning, indeed. You see, by replacing the stolen culture with a disposable one, the swindle culminates with the heisting of all aspects of individualism, as well. Thus, the citizenry itself becomes generic, nothing more than a sea of worker ants straining themselves to build the mound of commerce—And for what?" asked Holmes, sounding like a vicar before the congregation.

"I don't know, Holmes," I eagerly responded, breathless with anticipation for the answer.

"As they say in the lowest form of vernacular," said Holmes, "*the man*, Watson. They do it for *the man*."

He took another deep breath.

"We have our work cut out for us here, my friend."

"Where do we begin?" I spiritedly asked. For by now, I was ready to lead the charge myself.

"We are going to have to throw a wrench into the machine, my good man," he replied.

"You are speaking metaphorically, I take it?" I asked.

"If only I were," replied Holmes.

"Do you mean to say there is some sort of actual machine in all of this business?"

"Ah, now that is a question," Holmes excitedly replied. "Money, Watson, money is fuel," he continued. "And with such fuel, one can propel oneself into a position of power. Thus, affording themselves the opportunity to acquire more fuel and thus, more power. To do this, however, one needs a clever scheme. A very clever scheme! One needs a *mechanism* in place that will generate the necessary fuel, and keep on doing so, relentlessly. But a mechanism of this type is very complex and requires many parts. The more ambitious the mechanic, the more parts he will require, making the mechanism even more complicated."

"I am not sure I take your meaning, Holmes," I quickly stated, with an obvious and total confusion painted on my face. "Then you are speaking metaphorically? Or are we talking about a machine that makes counterfeit money?"

"No, my dearest friend, I do not speak of a money making machine. Yet, on the other hand, I do."

"You confound me, Holmes."

"Do you remember the opulent German movie palaces of the early part of the twentieth century?"

"Of course. I made several trips to Berlin in the twenties. They were spectacular," I answered.

"They were constructed for use as a tool to appease the proletariat. The tired, underfed, underpaid mass whose lives were nothing more than a dismal existence of poverty, or on the fringe of it, overwork and despair. They, in all their misery, existed solely for the sake of commerce. Not theirs, of course, but others. They existed to feed the machine put in place by the factory owners, merchants and politicians. In actuality, each worker was a part of the machine. In fact, they were the very engine. And like any engine, it required lubricant. Thus, the movie palace was created," he said with a hint of sadness in his delivery. "The palaces were created to provide a means of escape from the inescapable."

I looked at Holmes. His melancholy eyes were transfixed upon the countryside on the other side of his window.

"Inescapable?" I curiously asked.

"Yes, Watson," he resumed, "each week the worker would take the family to a new movie, which was most certainly a movie about hope, a movie with pretty people, lovely towns and beautiful homes. A movie that contained everything the fatigued, underpaid and underfed soul dared to dream of. Everything he would never in his life obtain. Yet, he refused to believe the reality of his predicament. He had his dreams, and if only in the back of his mind, vowed to effect an escape from the doldrums, one day. One day he would lead a life like those on the screen. Possess all the niceties the movie characters owned. One day. But until that day, he could sit and watch an uplifting movie at week's end and not feel so bad about his particular station in life. Maybe even rethink his situation, fool himself into thinking that he actually had happiness, something the rich on the screen were perpetually in search of. In the end, as it had all been designed, he would feel fortunate, refreshed and ready to drudge on another week, then another, then another. Oh, it was a brilliant strategy."

"I think I understand the analogy you draw, Holmes. But surely the conditions here are not so desperate. This is a prosperous nation. The majority of its citizens are very, very fortunate," I offered back.

"True, Watson. That is very true. But *that* is what separates this scheme from the others. Here the people believe they are happy. Their needs, for the most part, are satisfied. How is that? Simple. Keep their needs simple. Get them to love the simple, the mediocre and the task becomes simple, and very, very profitable. For example, on our way to return the van I borrowed in Washington, you and I stopped to refuel at the petrol station, that was housed in that rather disgusting mini food market, to change our clothes in its WC. Do you Remember?"

"Of course, that was only hours ago," I answered.

"What was your impression of that facility?" asked Holmes.

"It was appalling. Rather *plastic*, if you will. It was filled with nothing but processed, pre-packaged food products, a plethora of soft drinks, cheap beer and candy. Absolutely nothing of good taste, quality or of genuine nutritional value could be found in that establishment," I replied.

"Very good. A most excellent and accurate assessment."

"But one can find similar petrol, slash, markets in England and France. In fact, they dot the globe these days."

"Yes! But here it is quite different. Here there is also an abundance of excellent, healthier foods readily available. Yet few people pay thought to whether they should or should not partake of that *'big gulp'*. Why? Because the people in this country actually look forward to such empty products."

"And why is that?" I interrupted.

"Because, my good man, the products have been portrayed as not only quick and easy and ready when you are, but as exceptionally *hip*. You see *hip* is the essential selling point. You will stand out if you are seen partaking of this *very cool*, as it is now said, product. Want to be part of the cool sect? Want to be with it? Then these products MUST be an essential part of your life."

"But Holmes, that makes no sense whatsoever. Being unique by being part of the mass is rather an oxymoron, is it not?"

"Precisely! But never mind that most of the nation is already part of that supposedly very select faction, and that you will not actually stand out, as had been suggested, Watson. You are unique because you are able to exhibit your individualism by being part of the *hip* crowd. *Hamburger Helper, Turning Leaf wine, Wonder Bread, Twinkies, Pop-Tarts, White Zinfandel, Velveeta cheese spread.* Life is marvelous! Life and *you* are exceptionally *cool*! *Cool*, like *hip*, is a very big issue here, Watson."

"Yes, I am getting that."

"Unfortunately, very few of these people actually know what *cool* really is."

"Then this is the machine you speak of? This *cool*?" I said, thinking out loud. "How on earth can we possibly contend with this, Holmes?"

I received no reply, nor a glance. Holmes just kept staring out at the countryside. In actuality, I needn't have bothered asking that last question, for what else could have been possessing Holmes' mind? And though this present mood of his was far more morose than any I could call to mind, it reminded me of the time we battled the evil Reverend Pilpher.

Though I have yet to chronicle that chapter in Holmes' career, Pilpher was a man who had wantonly duped thousands of people out of every single jot of property they held. Be it stocks, bonds, land, even the very clothing they wore. By incessantly preaching that possessions were the way of sin and that salvation was to be found only by ridding oneself of all worldly goods, he bilked an army of followers out of house, home and future. An exceptionally ruthless and unscrupulous man, Pilpher managed to amass a king's fortune by spreading his message via televised sermons where viewers were encouraged, browbeaten, I dare say, to phone in and pledge their wealth in the form of what he termed as *love gifts*. An act he liked to assure his patronage was in fact tantamount to *bondage freedom*. It, he claimed, was the only true method for obtaining a sincere and exceptionally close personal relationship with Christ, the almighty, and his fellow Christians.

The funds accumulated through such an outrageous swindle would be used, Pilpher repeatedly proclaimed, to aid him and his organization in spreading the word of Christ throughout the known world and beyond. To accomplish this goal, the good reverend found it necessary to purchase homes in various countries around the world. One in Bermuda, where sin he said was found in the abundance of relaxation and pleasure. Another purchase took place in Fiji, where the "*unschooled*" inhabitants required rescuing from their heathenish beliefs and rituals. Then, the selfless reverend acquired properties in the South of France, Italy, Greece, Argentina and in Honduras, where he very wisely resides today, thanks to that country's lack of extradition treaties with the world's super powers. But worse were the scars the man inflicted upon his victims and their families. Though most of his followers were successfully deprogrammed after Holmes' vanquishing of the charlatan, a great number of Pilpher's followers remain convinced of the man's innocence. To this day, those sadly lost and confused souls continue to send money to Pilpher, believing they must maintain the man whom they are certain is the very reincarnation of Christ, living in wrongful exile, a modern day form of persecution.

Such a diseased twisting of the mind Holmes could not defeat. And for the first time in his extraordinary life, Holmes felt powerless and wholly inept. It ripped into him like nothing I had ever seen. Fortunately I was able to talk him through by pointing out all that he had accomplished and by reminding him of the many lives he had saved. Now, studying his anguished face as we sat on the train these many years hence, I determined that I would have to take that task upon myself once again. For in Holmes' grimacing brow it was evident to me that the great, unflinching warrior was battling the fear of impending failure, much like the one he, quite incorrectly I will forever argue, believed was the end result of his dealings with Pilpher. So, to begin, I thought it best to distract him from this current episode of brooding.

"Holmes," I said cautiously, "I understand the whole concept of making cheap, disposable and tasteless products overly available to the mass which you have laid before me. But I regret to say that I am finding it rather hard to believe. Surely these people are not so easily *duped*, as you say. Certainly many, if not most, of the targeted consumers are well educated. After all, there is quite an abundance of quality universities in this country."

"Is there?" Holmes replied with that famous biting sarcasm of his while still locked on the monotonous countryside filling his window.

"Oh, come now, Holmes. You know there are," I challenged.

"Perhaps you are correct. I can think of a few worthwhile institutions. But after all, the view of education in this country is quite different from that of a country in possession of a much richer culture," he shot back.

"Come now!" I protested.

"I would wholeheartedly love to agree with you, Watson. But the facts speak for themselves. American colleges and universities have become more *vocational*, rather than *educational*. By that I am speaking of a full, well-rounded education. Far too many, so-called, educated people in this country have no sense of geography, art, music, architecture and even science. Many of them, shockingly, confuse astronomy and astrology. They know little of geology and meteorology. They could not differentiate between Chopin and Wagner. You may even hear them use the term *expressionist*, when referring to *impressionist* painters. Do you know, I actually witnessed one American, a man well into his fifties, point to copy of Van Gogh's '*irises*' and promptly announce it to be a work by Rodin?"

"No!" I shrieked in horror.

"Yes, Watson, a very sad state of affairs, to say the least. But, of course, this is exactly what was supposed to have occurred. And although a crime of great inhuman proportion has been ruthlessly perpetrated upon this society, you must tip your hat at the supreme execution of this most ingenuous of master plans."

"But Holmes, all of these institutions have courses of study in each of the very areas you have mentioned?" I argued.

"Well of course they do. But you must understand, here the goal is to push through the course as fast as possible, if it is not the chosen field of interest. In this society the focus is on business and information technology. Both honorable fields, I grant you. But if all you know are ones and zeros, or acquisitions and mergers, you are *not* an educated person, regardless of your diploma."

"Really, Holmes!" I said with great annoyance at his impossibly high standards.

"My case is easily substantiated. For example, if you possess a so-called education yet cannot tell me where Nepal resides on the globe, you are obviously lacking in some educational basics. If you cannot identify the authors of *The Grapes of Wrath, Crime and Punishment, War and Peace, The Snows of Kilaminjaro*, to mention a mere few, then, again, you are sorely missing the essential basics of the fully educated individual. And it is for this very reason such rubbish as tabloid journalism and television programming are so popular in the U.S."

"Ah, there I have you," I interjected, "the British tabloid press has long been recognized as exceedingly popular."

"That is true," Holmes quickly bounced back. "But Britain is a society of classes. The rags you speak of, are usually purchased by individuals lacking the very thing we speak of, a quality education. Here, in the earth's most powerful nation, you are taught to believe you are an educated individual if you have attended *any* college or university. Yet this is simply *not* true. Why, in this country, funding for the arts is a never-ending battle. The casualties of that battle, deprived of a richer sense of themselves, are America's children. Most, you will find, cannot explain history in terms of periods, such as Renaissance, Baroque, Rococo, Classicism, etc. And we are speaking not only of art and music when these periods are discussed, but of life, human history and the impact art had on the state of history and the development of society, as well as the human being. Instead what you have are people buying newspapers, pulling out the sports section and reading only it. And even if you were to read the rest of the paper, you would be reading articles strategically written at a grade eight level to assure that at least sixty percent of the US's proletariat will be able to comprehend the basics of what is being told to them—No, no, no! A university degree in this country is nothing more than a mere permit, granting the individual permission to mount one of those ridiculous alumni-license-plate-frames onto their vehicles."

My ploy was working. Holmes' passion for the subject was clearly distracting him from his brooding.

"Are you suggesting that our man is an educator or a member of the board of regents, perhaps?" I eagerly jumped in.

"If only that were the case. Our task would be simple. But alas, it is not. Like the noble mass, professors and teachers have fallen victim to the great sabotage themselves. Take a look around us, Watson. Now although I agree with the great writer Theodore Sturgeon's assertion that ninety percent of everything about us is rubbish, I'm more inclined to believe the figure is actually ninety-four percent. For none of it will endure. And why? Because it is *not* intended to! Use it up, toss it away and *buy* more. Much more! You see, to achieve this devolution of culture, a great deal of conditioning must occur. To accomplish this, manufacturer and merchant must praise the consumer relentlessly. By repeatedly informing the consumer of the astute manner in which he selects a product, they interfere with his cognitive process.

Understand! Buying is an emotional process, not a cognitive one. Therefore, it is actually the consumer's ego that is initially targeted, not his pocket book. Thus, in addition to praises of consumer acumen, insinuations of *hip* and *cool* and *uniqueness* make their way into the marketing strategies, out gunning the target who, in no time, falls victim to the flattery and begins to believe wholeheartedly in the rhetoric. Subsequently the cravings for the product become insatiable. '*Stand out*! Be *cool* like the rest of us and purchase this empty product'. Ego, Watson! The contradiction is evident. Everything, particularly the words of praise, is rubbish. I suggest you read my monograph on the subject. It is entitled, *C.R.A.P.* It speaks in detail about this insulting assault being perpetrated on the individual intellect, citing such examples as nightly news broadcasts that lead off with stories of celebrities that have married or divorced, award programmes, a cat in a tree, rescued by a ninety-year-old blind woman, anything sensational. Anything but boring *real* news! Anything that will keep the viewer *entertained* more than informed, save for one area."

"What is that?" I asked, sitting on the edge of my seat.

"Knowledge of empty products, the famous who partake of these, and current fads sweeping the nation."

"I see. By the by, what does your acronym, *C.R.A.P.* stand for?" I asked, feeling a bit hit over the head myself by this latest rant of his.

"Cretin-istic rubbish approved for plebeians. I hesitated to use the word *plebeian*, but after some thought on the matter, it occurred to me that those most likely to take offense were also more than likely to be unfamiliar with the word, as well as with myself and my monograph." Holmes answered with a great disgust in his tone.

I, too, was disgusted. But not so much with Holmes' examples, but with the ease at which he could throw insults at the very people we were there to help.

"Holmes!" I cried out with a vengeance. "How can you be so callous and insensitive towards the very people you have come to rescue?" I scolded.

"You are very much mistaken in that regard," he calmly stated. "In actuality, I am honestly stating a fact, which, by the way, I can support."

"Then I suggest you do so. For I can see no reason to attack these people so viciously. I am certain the word *plebian* is not foreign to them in the slightest," I firmly insisted.

"As usual, my dear friend, you are far too kindhearted. Nevertheless, your challenge is happily accepted. Let's see, which episode shall I present? Ah, I know! Let me recount an episode regarding the naming of the nineteen-eighty-nine release of a James Bond movie, shall I?" Holmes all too confidently offered.

"A Bond film?" I confusedly asked.

"Quite so. The film, the second and last staring the Welshman, Timothy Dalton as Bond, was originally to be entitled, *License Revoked*. However, the producers of the film had reservations about the use of the word *revoked*. They were uncertain as to the American mass' familiarity with the word. So, to avoid any confusion which might adversely affect box office receipts, they, and quite wisely in my opinion, opted to change the film's title to *Licensed To Kill*."

"No! Surely you jest!" I scoffed.

"Regretfully, I do not," Holmes replied with a genuine sadness and disappointment in his voice. I too felt the sting of our conversation.

Suddenly I noticed we were approaching New York and I wondered what our next move was. When out of the blue, Holmes' old determined self returned.

"We shall hail a taxi and take it to Wall Street, Watson. That is our next step," he said, quickly answering the question he had correctly read in my expression.

He was amazing.

"Why Wall Street, Holmes? Is this villain some sort of corrupt corporate mogul? A sociopath of an investment banker or something or other?" I foolishly asked.

"Come now, Watson!" Holmes barked. "That is too immature an observation, particularly for you. The head of a large corporate enterprise is exactly where the amateur sleuth would begin his search. This is greatly beneath you."

"Holmes!" I protested. "You go to far there."

Holmes caught himself and took a pause.

"You're right, my friend. As usual, you are right. Please, forgive me this insulting outburst."

Always the pushover, I took a breath and calmly retreated.

"Of course, Holmes, of course. The strain this case is placing upon you is clearly beginning to show. Please, tell me, how can I help?"

"You are too good to me, Watson. Too good, indeed."

"Nonsense! How about some food? I know I could eat. I'm absolutely famished."

"After our stop on Wall Street, we shall dine wherever you suggest."

Once in the city, we began making our way to Wall Street by taxi. I still had no idea what Holmes was up to, but I possessed one power that Holmes did not. Patience. I knew he would enlighten me in due course. But at that moment our course was due south, south from Grand Central Station to Lower Manhattan, where we would inevitably run into the famed financial district. As we proceeded along Broadway, a route I had always enjoyed, I wasn't the least bit frustrated by the unceasing traffic. It was part of the experience. Throngs of pedestrians, legions of taxis, Alps of steel and glass, boundless energy. One could never tire of visiting this thriving metropolis. Past Washington Square, past city hall, traveling slowly till we reached our ultimate destination, the very vortex of American commerce.

Upon reaching the renowned avenue, Holmes marched us straight into the Exchange. What he whispered into the ear of the security guard as we arrived, I do not know. But whatever it was, it delivered us onto the famous floor of great havoc with remarkable ease.

"Watson," Holmes said loudly to be heard over the thundering volume produced by what appeared a chaotic frenzy of buying and selling commodities that was taking place all around us, "this, as I am sure you have already surmised, is the very nucleus of the machine. It cares not for what is sold, only that *it*, whatever *it* may be, is *sold*. The frantic people you see before you are only concerned with pushing a product and, obviously, profiting from it. If the product is junk and does not capture the hearts and minds of the great herd, it is forgotten. On the other hand, if the product is junk, yet sells, it is revered. In short, these very, very influential people could not care less about the quality or substance of what is sold, only that it *sells*. Thus, the cultural waters in this country will forever remain murky at best."

"Then you *are* suggesting that this man, whomever he is, is an investment banker or broker?" I reluctantly asked for fear of another rebuke.

"As I stated before, the culprit is not involved with these middlemen. Not directly, that is," replied Holmes.

"Influential? Middlemen?" I asked with great confusion.

"Our man dictates trends, Watson. He sets the fires and leaves the stoking of them to these people."

"Ah, I see. But Holmes, if this rogue we are after is not to be found amongst this horde, then why are we here? Are we not wasting time? Should we not go directly—,"

"Where do you suggest we go?" Holmes quickly cut in.

I drew a blank.

"Exactly!" shouted Holmes. "Where are we to find this bandit?"

Again, I could think of nothing to say.

"In addition to introducing you to this, this cast of characters in this little drama of ours," Holmes continued, "I am hoping to find something which will point us in the direction of the fiend himself. For like the ninety-four-percenters clamoring sheepishly about the nation, the people about us in this very room are also drones. However, they are more closely linked to our man. It is they who transport the nectar, if you will, the seeds he generates. Then once here, in this extremely fertile soil, his ideas and schemes blossom like California Poppies in early spring."

"What should we look for, then?" I energetically asked.

"Imagine Renfield," said a distracted Holmes as he overlooked the hollering crowd of busy business bees.

"Renfield?" I repeated.

"Yes, Watson, Renfield," he answered, trying to hold back that cursed frustration of his he displays anytime his conversational companion, no matter whom it may be, cannot keep pace with his references.

"I'm afraid, I still—," I uttered futilely.

"As in trusted, pathetic, bootlicking servant," Holmes cut in sharply.

"I'm sorry, Holmes. But I do not—,"

"Dracula, Watson, Dracula!" he exclaimed. "As in Dracula's sniveling little sycophant of a manservant. That's what we are looking for. Renfield! We are looking for our Renfield."

"Ah, I see," I said with obvious irritation, "how very, very non-agile my mind is today. How could anyone not immediately catch hold of that reference? Please, forgive me."

Holmes fell silent as he examined the faces in the room. We had to have looked very suspicious, the two us of, standing in the middle of the calamity, erect, observing, not screaming out and signaling with our fingers, like the rest of the sardines crammed into the chaotic room.

"Holmes," I said, "do you not think standing here, as we are, we are sticking out like sore thumbs?"

"Yes, Watson, I do," he answered rather aloofly.

"Then perhaps we should—"

"We are exactly where we should be and doing exactly what we should be doing," said Holmes quickly.

"What? I am not sure I understand," I said, just as I caught sight of a rather meek-ish looking man fixed on the sight of Holmes and I. "Holmes!" I cried out.

"I see him, Watson! I see him. Now casually look away."

"What?"

"The intent is to draw them out. Not to show our hand."

"Draw them out?" I insisted. "But we are not ourselves? We are in costume."

"That only furthers our cause," replied Holmes.

"How do you mean?"

"Whomever should react to our presence has obviously been alerted to the possibility of our involvement, disguise or no disguise. Therefore, if we spy an individual who has taken a little more interest in our presence than is expected, we have baited the hook and we should, as any self-respecting fisherman, reel our catch in."

"But, Holmes," I said, "I thought we were not supposed to be recognized."

"A little elbow room to get into the country and speak with the president is all I could have ever hoped for. For it is certain they would have seen through our decoys and disguises very shortly—Quiet!" Holmes demanded as he waved me back behind a group of rabidly shouting investors.

Looking through the animated people before me, I caught a glimpse of our smallish, bespectacled watcher. Like me, he was now using the others in the room to shield himself from view as he spoke into a very nearly microscopic cellular telephone with great rapidity. I turned to Holmes, to get his impression of the sight, only to find Holmes had stepped away and was speaking with a few of the businessmen on the floor. It was an odd looking conversation. While Holmes stood speaking to them, the frantically busy men were waving their hands about as if they were on the Titanic, pleading for a place on a lifeboat. It was extremely surreal. Nevertheless, I could see a hint of a smile break on Holmes' face as he thanked the gyrating group.

"Eureka!" Holmes cried out upon his return. "We have our man, Watson. His name is Jurgen Lesters and his area of expertise is marketing. Yes, Watson! We have our sniveling weasel!"

"How can you be so sure this is your Renfield?" I asked.

"Later. I will explain later. Right now we must get to a telephone," Holmes responded.

"I've my mobile with me," I offered.

"Come, come, Watson! Not only are cellular phones the easiest communication devices to eavesdrop in on, they are also remarkably proficient in revealing one's exact location on the globe. Now quickly, we must leave immediately," said Holmes as he began forging a path through the turbulent human sea.

Out on the street, the greatest of sleuths quickly hailed a taxi and hurried us into it. Very firmly he instructed the driver to take us to the Plaza Hotel. Then came a brief, peripheral glance back at the sidewalk. I followed suit. There, speaking with breakneck speed into his mobile, was this Jurgen Lesters character, as he watched our taxi pull away.

"I should think we have about twenty minutes before they confirm our presence here," Holmes happily announced.

"And what is at the Plaza?" I asked.

"Why we are, of course," he said loudly. "We will check into a couple of rooms, then dine in their very excellent restaurant."

"Yes, all right. But what about this phone—,"

"There is plenty of time," said Holmes coolly.

"Do you not find this Lesters just a little too stereotypical for the purpose you say he serves? Why he appears to be the *very* incarnation of the fictional Renfield character," I suggested.

"Your own question is your answer," Holmes confidently replied. "His camouflage is your doubt."

Arriving at the famed Plaza Hotel, Holmes, keeping his voice at just the right level of decibels to ensure his being overheard, repeated our hotel and dinner plans as we exited the taxi. Inside the opulent lobby Holmes glanced back though the large entry door to watch our taxi motor away. Then, as fast as Jurgen Lesters could speak into that wee phone of his, Holmes bolted back out and on to the street.

"Holmes!" I called out.

"This way, Watson," Holmes commanded.

Naturally I followed.

"The answer to your first question is, 'no'," he said to me as I caught up to him, "we are not staying at the Plaza. As to question number two, I merely wanted our taxi driver to provide this Mr. Lesters, and his brood, with false information when they visit him. Which they are certain to do."

"And question number three?" I asked.

"We shall walk to the Essex House and register there. However, I doubt we shall hold them off for more than a dozen hours or so with this little maneuver of ours," Holmes incontestably answered.

I said nothing. I just took it all in my stride and exercised that prowess of patience I boldly claimed to possess.

Twenty minutes later, I found myself in yet another luxurious room in the Essex House hotel. Holmes had the adjoining room. I was glad to have a moment's peace. It afforded me the opportunity to meditate and perform my yoga and breathing exercises. As if I had finally reached an oasis after crossing the Sahara on foot and had taken that long prayed for guzzle of water, it was revitalizing to resume them in the few minutes I had alone. Holmes was to be by to collect me for dinner in a few moments, so I had precious little time. Even less than I had thought. For right in the middle of performing the Rishi's posture movement, the telephone demanded my attention with a sudden blast. Again it was Holmes, instructing me to meet him at once. However, this time he was several city blocks away at *Basera*, an Indian restaurant of excellent reputation. And it was there that I, with the help of our hostess, found Holmes in the back of the main dining room, enjoying a glass of sparkling mineral water while pouring over several pages from what looked like a packet of business letters.

"What have you there?" I asked as I sat down at Holmes' table.

"Ah, Watson. You made excellent time," said he. "This is some material I had our comrade in arms fax to me at the Kinko's on Fifty-fourth street. Our little Renfield is quite the interesting character."

"So soon?" I said in amazement at Holmes' ability to hone in on the scent and locate the trail. "What does Moore have to say?"

"As I suspected, this Mr. Jurgen Lesters, this very successful, so-called, independent marketing analyst, is just the man to serve as our man's man. He is exactly the breed of *swallow* that could lead us to the scoundrel," announced Holmes.

"How do you mean?" I begged.

"He's a consultant, a freelancer, a man, who by working for several firms simultaneously, gathers and distributes information like a bee collects and distributes nectar. Thus, very astutely manipulating, if not the whole of it, a very large portion of the financial world. The end result being unimaginable influence and profits for himself and his confederates, one of whom, I would very much like to meet up with in a dark alleyway."

"Holmes," I said, horrified to hear him speak of violence once again. "You cannot speak of this. I will not permit you to even entertain the thought of such action. Just imagine what your old friend Mahatma would say if he could hear you now?"

With his eyes still absorbing the information on the pages before him, Holmes answered with such certainty that one would have thought he had discussed the matter with the late Indian independence leader only minutes earlier.

"He would understand, of course."

"What?" I said in shear disbelief.

"I would really enjoy debating this further with you, Watson. But at the moment we have a great deal to accomplish before we are faced with a decision along those lines. For instance, read this list of firms our little, unassuming Mr. Lesters does business with."

He handed to me a page of names and addresses.

"There are quite a few here, Holmes," I said. "About twenty five, I'd say."

"Twenty nine."

"Well, he's a busy man."

"To say the least. He has homes all over the globe. And let's not overlook those he has in nations where labor is inhumanly inexpensive. He makes a few trips each year to Singapore, Indonesia, Hong Kong, the Dominican Republic and Haiti. He is everywhere a dollar can be made, and consumers and workers exploited. And, like his master, he is obscenely rich. So rich, in fact, that both he and his master will never be found on any list containing the names of the world's richest people."

"Holmes," I begged, "this is all sounding a little too fantastic."

"No, Watson. I think the word you meant to use is *despicable*," Holmes passionately returned. "Now, my good friend, what say you to one of these most exceptional baked vegetable samosas? Yes, I did say baked. The good proprietor of this exceptional restaurant will not fry them if you are disinclined to be reckless with your health. I've also taken the liberty of ordering some naan-bread, basmati rice, bhartua, masoor dahl and a wonderful vegetable zamfrezy."

"Sounds absolutely perfect," I gratefully replied.

"After dinner we shall return to our rooms for a much needed night of sleep and be off on the first flight to Chicago in the morning," said Holmes.

"Why Chicago?"

"If you'll refer to that list of companies," said he, pointing to the page he had handed to me, "you'll notice one of the firms in Chicago holds its annual board of directors meeting tomorrow."

"Renfield is a member of the board?"

"No."

"Then I am afraid I don't understand. Surely, if the brute behind this sabotage and extraordinary theft is as reclusive as you say, he cannot hold such a visible position."

"But he most assuredly does."

"Then we have him!"

"Wrong, my good chap. However, you are correct regarding his reclusive nature, for he himself is certain to absent from that meeting.

"Then why—," I tried to ask.

"His man, Lesters, is his proxy."

"Of course!" I excitedly exclaimed. "Holmes, you've outdone yourself this time."

"Elementary," grumbled Holmes.

"Yes, yes, *elementary*!" I scolded. "Perhaps one day you will learn to accept a compliment as easily as you can learn the identity and obtain the dossier of some hooligan like this Lesters fellow."

"Ah, excellent! Our food has arrived," he announced to evade acknowledging my minor rebuke.

"How can you be so certain this Lesters chap will be in Chicago tomorrow?" I said as servers covered our table with half a dozen exotic and healthy dishes.

"With Moore's assistance, I managed to confirm my suspicions with a quick scan of the airline and train reservations available on the internet," answered Holmes.

With a single flick of his index finger, he quickly caught the attention of our server.

"A sparkling mineral water for my friend here," he instructed, "with a *lemon* twist, not lime," he quickly, and quite correctly, pointed out.

CHAPTER VII

Opening Move

Try as we might, here and there, neither Holmes nor myself had been able to partake of either of our regular exercise regimes in the last few days, so we felt it wise to walk back to our hotel after what was surely a meal of utter genius. A most sagacious decision, for the walk set free a massive amount of endorphins that had been imprisoned within us by our inactivity. Their release set loose a flurry of electrical activity in our cerebellums, which hit us like tidal waves pounding the Alaskan coastline. So struck were we that not a single syllable passed between us the whole of the return trip to the Essex House. While Holmes kept busy playing a mental game of chess with the clues in this case, I mulled over all he had revealed to me about this strangest of all our exploits. Although much of it sounded more than a little preposterous at times, I knew that if Holmes proclaimed it to be anything but, it was anything but. For how could I doubt the man who had never, in all the years I had known him, blundered or made an incorrect observation. Holmes, I must say, would not only argue the accuracy of such praise, but label it as mere runaway emotion, or something embarrassingly non-cognitive on my part, most vigorously. But no matter, I stand firm in my position.

Unfortunately, my certainty in that regard did not extend itself to the meaning of a particular term I had heard Holmes use a time or two by then. Upon my initial, as well as subsequent, hearing of the term, I fully expected to grasp onto its definition within the context of my conversations with Holmes. But I was unable to ascertain a complete understanding. Hence, like a temporary mental fixation with a particular melody, the silly thing kept echoing through my mind. A rather irritating episode of involuntary repetition, I can assure you. So, as we headed into our final stretch for the Essex House, I dared risk interrupting Holmes' study of our present position in this game of survival with a question.

"Holmes, what is this term I've heard you use? I believe it was *ninety-four percenter*? Is that it?"

"Yes, that is it," he quickly and rather casually answered, as if the term in question were as common as table salt.

"Just what exactly do you mean by it?" I pleaded.

"Are you familiar with Fred Paulson, the educator and author?"

"Isn't he the chap who wrote those excellent accounts of action during the second World War?" I replied.

"Yes, Watson, that is exactly the man," he said, paying more attention to our surroundings than my need for clarification.

"What has this novelist to do with this case?"

"Nothing."

I felt my patience waning. That cavalier attitude of Holmes' could be extremely irritating at times. I knew he was fully aware of what I was asking of him, and he knew I knew. This was his way of expressing his disappointment in me. His way of saying that I clearly should have been up on a particular subject. But I wasn't in the mood.

"Confound it, Holmes! Just, if you would be so kind, answer my initial question, please," I snapped.

"Very well, Watson, very well," he professorially stated. "Paulson is also the author of an extremely perceptive book on the present cultural and sociological state of the United States of America."

"Then he does have something to do with this case?" I confusedly asked.

"No, old chap, he does not. He merely penned an excellent account of what we have been discussing and what we are here to try and reverse, the stymied cultural depth of this nation."

"What is the name of this book?" I demanded.

"*The Great American Devolution*."

"And in that book you discovered this term?"

"Not exactly."

"What!" I nearly shouted.

Holmes quickly held up his hand in truce.

"Let me explain," he said. "I learned of his book by reading a review of it in *The Economist* about a decade ago. The reviewer, who thoroughly enjoyed the book, summed up the book's theses in this manner, '*Ninety-four percent of Americans are frothy know nothings prone to bragging*'."

"Holmes!" I cried, stunned by the audacity of that comment. "That is most unfair. You cannot honestly agree with this outrageous assessment?"

"Regretfully, the figure appears to be right on the mark," Holmes coldly answered. "Thus, as you have no doubt deduced by now, I have coined the term based on—."

"Must everyone aspire to your absurdly high standards?" I scolded. "You cannot expect everyone to possess an intellect equal to yours."

"You misunderstand me, Watson. I do not intend to belittle Americans inflicted with *Eloisyndrome*. I merely fashioned the term so that I may have a means of recognizing, and referring to, the poor infected group. And since the figure accurately represents the proportion of cultural damage that has already occurred and its number of casualties, I thought it rather fitting. That is all."

"Well, you will pardon me if I elect not to refer to those we are here to aid in such a condescending fashion."

"If that is how you feel," said Holmes. "But you are mistaken to conclude that it is meant in a condescending manner. Think of it as more a medical or psychological term."

"You're joking?" I challenged.

"I honestly wish I were," Holmes coolly returned as he raised his hand to slow down the tongue-lashing he knew was on the way. It worked. For with all my strength, I fought back my outrage. "Seriously, my dear friend," he charged on. "Tell me what other country has made sport out of dragging eighteen wheel commercial trailers through mud? What other nation holds huge, freakish, monster-like truck rallies and races? Tailgate parties? World

Wrestling and Roller Derby spectacles and still has the audacity to incessantly profess itself to be '*number one*'? Number one what, I ask you? In military might, perhaps? I will concede that point. But all the might in the world does not make one nation, or one person, better than the other. Might, as I am sure you are aware, *does not* necessarily make right. I would liken the situation to a particular nouveaux riche couple had I the great misfortune to assist some years back. All the money in the world, yet they preferred Elvis on black velvet to Monet's *Waterlilies*."

"Good Lord!" I involuntarily shouted.

Though it took every ounce of my remaining strength, I elected to reserved comment for the moment and resumed my thoughtful posture for the last half block to our hotel. I had yet to find comfort in any of Holmes' explanations and rationalizing for his cold and unfeeling terminology. But that was Holmes. Most things were simply a matter of mathematics to him. Equations and solutions, they were his world. Distancing himself from the *great flock*, as he often liked to put it, he kept the dreaded emotions from interfering with his examination of the facts. Facts, be they items, people or places, all were mere numbers to Holmes. It seemed cruel at times, but then so, I could not dismiss, is Mother Nature. I also could not dismiss the dire byproducts of Eloisyndrome Holmes had cited examples of. As a matter of fact, as we walked, I began to recall a few horrid aspects of American culture I myself had observed. Bowling shoes immediately sprang to my mind, as did a beer-bellied baseball pitcher with a mouth full of chewing tobacco. That thought led me to the baseball cap as fashion statement, large, fuzzy dice hanging from a rear-view-mirror? The images shook me so, I had to force myself to stop or surely I would have lost that lovely dinner I had earlier consumed. Fortunately, we had reached the Essex House, just the thing to distract me from my downward spiral.

As we entered the hotel, I noticed Holmes studying me as we made our way to the lifts. Reaching them, I could feel that concerned, lifeguard glare of his cast upon me like the rays of the sun.

"What is it, Holmes?" I said.

"Nothing, old friend. Just checking your vitals, so to speak. After our discussion, I was afraid you might have grown somewhat ill. The subject used to turn my stomach. But I've been dealing with the problem for some time now and my constitution and skin have, thankfully, toughened over the years," replied Holmes.

"I must admit, I was feeling rather, seasick a moment ago."

"I don't blame you. It is a rather turbulent current we are attempting to swim against."

"And I am beginning to understand just how strongly it rages," I answered as we stepped into the lift to be hoisted up to our rooms on the eleventh floor.

"During my last visit to the states," said Holmes, "I happened into a lift with two American professional men. Their conversation was of T1 lines, servers and disk drives, so they were obviously in possession of an education, or so one might initially deduce. One of the men had a stack of CDs he was carrying in one hand. On the ride up, the empty-handed one snidely commented on the sight of the discs in the other's hand. I, too, glanced at them and was very surprised to see a collection of classical music in the hands of an office-drone, rather than the usual pop fare. Yet it was at that moment that I realised just how miserably the educational cultivating systems in this country were failing the majority of its citizens."

"But why on earth should a collection of classical CDs dishearten you, you a Tchaikovsky devotee, of all people?" I pressed.

"It was not the discs, but the other man's comment."

"Which was?" I impatiently asked.

"Brace yourself, Watson, for his words were these, '*Still listening to Picasso, huh?*'" said Holmes.

"No!" I screeched. "Holmes that simply cannot be. That is horrific."

"Isn't it, though—," he started to say as a sudden, quick jerking of the lift captured our full attention.

Then, when we had but one floor to travel, the thing came to an abrupt and very harsh halt. I tried selecting another floor, but no luck. I then tried the fat, protruding red emergency button. Again nothing. An awful sensation, a combination of confinement and panic, swept over me as I realised the lift did not contain a telephone for such emergencies. Then, after a few seconds of applied patience, BOOM! A thunderous explosion occurred somewhere out in the shaft, which rocked the small, elevating room. Struck speechless with fear, I looked at Holmes. He raised a finger to his lips, signaling me to remain silent as he tried to listen for clues from beyond the wood paneled walls. From outside the lift, very nearby, we heard a slight crackle, then a very loud SNAP.

Holmes quickly sprung at me and positioned me in one corner of the little room. He then lifted my jacket and filled my mouth with an end of it. Next, he took my hands and locked them onto the brass support railing that traveled along the three solid walls. Afterwards, he bent my knees, then quickly jumped into the opposite corner and repeated the process on himself. No sooner had he braced us for impact, we began to descend. Initially, inch by inch. Then, after another loud snap, SWOOSH! Gravity commanded us downward.

Racing out of control, and waiting for the inevitable cataclysmic collision with the earth, I shut my eyes tightly, hoping to spare myself some of the rapidly approaching anguish. Thus, resigned to what appeared my fate, I found, as the brute force of our plummet mercilessly hiked my cheeks very nearly over my eyes, waiting for the crash unbearable. SHREEK! SHUMP! THUNK! All of a sudden, the lift jerked violently, then traveled about twenty feet upward, then back down twenty feet, as if it were a mammoth sized yo-yo.

"Quickly, Watson, put your hands together and boost me up," ordered Holmes. "We have just a few seconds."

I complied immediately and hoisted Holmes through the escape hatch in the lift's ceiling. Once on the outside, Holmes reached down to pull me up.

"Push off of the support railing," he instructed.

Again, I complied. It made all the difference. Instantly I was out in the smoke filled shaft with Holmes.

"Good God, Holmes!" I exclaimed. "Good God!"

"Onto the service ladder," directed Holmes, as he pointed to a steel ladder mounted to the elevator shaft. "Hurry!"

I quickly leaned forward and simultaneously stepped and reached out for and onto the ladder, grabbing hold with all of my might.

"Climb up, Watson!" Holmes shouted.

I did as ordered. But just as Holmes began to jump for the service ladder, SCREECH! WHACK! POP! A large and very fat cable snapped with such violence, I thought another explosion had occurred. All at once, the vibration and thrust knocked Holmes down on top of the lift and it resumed its plummet. I was horror struck.

"HOLMES!"

But at the very instant his name left my mouth, he successfully performed a rolling dive off the tumbling car and managed to take hold of the service ladder.

"Face the wall and close your eyes!" he shouted up at me.

No sooner had I done as directed, the lift blasted into the base of the shaft with a delivery like the A-bomb. I know this because my curiosity made me slow to close one eye. But the second I saw that plume lifting off like a space shuttle at Cape Canaveral, I quickly followed Holmes instructions and hung on so tight I feared I might rip the ladder lose of its steel anchoring.

After the thunderball of hot air and debris rocketed past us like a two second hurricane, I carefully looked down at Holmes. With only one arm wrapped round the ladder, he was barely hanging on.

"HOLMES!" I hollered, again.

Nothing. His hanging head told me all. He had been far too close to the colossal blast. I fought panic and quickly scaled down the shaft to him. He was caked with dust and debris. His jacket was a shambles and, worse yet, blood was visible at his shoulder.

"Holmes!" I pleaded. "Can you hear me?"

Again nothing. Reaching him, I immediately took him into one arm. I could feel him breathing, but that did not give me cause to breathe any easier. Since I dare not let go of him, I shook him in an attempt to bring him round. Unfortunately, my arms were rapidly growing fatigued and I was not certain how much longer I could manage, but I was resigned to either saving him or going down with him. However, since the latter was not particularly appealing, I gritted my teeth and kept shaking him. Finally, just as I began to doubt my resolve, Holmes started to regain consciousness.

"Holmes? Can you hear me?"

Slowly his head straightened. He looked at me. He still had that look of complete bewilderment, that same look I had seen on the faces of numerous accident victims during my medical career. But I could also see the fog lifting ever so slightly from his eyes.

"Watson?" he asked rather weakly.

"How are you? Are you strong enough to take hold of the ladder?" I asked. "I can't hold on much longer."

He nodded and grabbed hold.

"Good. Now let me check this wound of yours," I said, referring to the gash under that shredded jacket shoulder of his. "It does not look too serious," I said as I peered through the tear in his jacket, "but I will need to take a better look as soon as I—"

Holmes suddenly lost consciousness and fell limp. It was all I could do to clutch him with one arm to keep him from joining the lift at the bottom of the shaft.

"Now what?" I asked of myself, despite knowning our only option was to climb up to the next level and pry open its access doors. But if we were to effect any escape at all, it was all too clear to me that I now had to manage to lug Holmes up the ladder along with me. It was also clear that I needed to do this in a hurry, for neither of us could last very long in that shaft-come-chimney. I admit, albeit somewhat reluctantly, I did succumb to an initial sinking moment of defeat. But the thought of the millions of people whose very freedom and future Holmes was attempting to rescue, shot into me like an injection of *cyanocobalmin*. If I could not first manage to save my good friend, all would be lost and the fate of the good people of that great country would be irreversibly sealed.

Suddenly I was more resolute than ever. Yet, simultaneously, I must say, I felt completely overwhelmed by the responsibility of my position.

Fearful and fatigued by this most dire of situations, I ignored my distress and discomfort and began. First, a step up the ladder, followed by a well timed push off with my other foot, a balancing act while also reaching for the next highest bar. Add to the mix a heave of my good friend somewhere within the sequence and it sounds even more dangerously complicated than I care to remember. Yet step after agonizing step, I forged on. Fourteen excruciatingly brutal steps. And, like the last leg of any endurance event, that final step was infinitely more painful than the others. To this very day I am at a complete loss as to how I ever managed to muster up the strength to cart our two aged bodies up the ladder.

The only remaining hurdle left for us to overcome was getting across the empty shaft, for we had thrust ourselves onto the rear-end of the shaft. Judging from our position within the shaft, I surmised us to be at the fourth floor door. But that means of exit lay about ten feet away. And since the lift and its cables had fallen into the abyss, we were presented with no way to cross the shaft. There were, however, eight inch steel sections of horizontal scaffoldings that were periodically spaced throughout the length of the entire shaft. If one were able, which we were not, one could tight-walk a beam to the door. Once there, if one were fortunate enough to reach it, opening the heavy door from your ending position, approximately forty-five degrees off, instead of dead center, would be another matter. And even if I could manage it all, I could not carry Holmes as I crossed a beam. Yet, again, air suitable only for suffocation was all we had left to us. It was either act or succumb.

By then, at the bottom of the shaft, people were assessing the situation. The dense plume had dissipated sufficiently for me to view the great calamity from above. Arriving emergency medical teams and firemen were horror struck as they sifted through the wreckage for bodies or survivors. Though I could look down, they apparently could not see us through the residual smoke and dust. I was just about to call down to them when Holmes' hand came and over my mouth, his eyes were nearly closed as he looked at me.

"No, Watson, no!"

"Why not?" I managed to mumble from underneath his hand.

"They must think they have succeeded," he mumbled.

I pulled his hand away from my mouth and looked him sternly in the eye.

"You are not going to tell me this Renfield and his people are behind this?"

He nodded confirmation.

"No, I cannot believe that. They cannot possibly know where we are. And besides, we must get out of here. We cannot stay here for very much longer, or surely we will perish."

"A phone," he uttered in a whisper.

"A telephone?" I said puzzled. "All we need do is yell and be rescued."

"No! Phone!" he repeated.

"I've my mobile in my poc—," I began to say before Holmes cut in.

"No!"

"Why the blazes not?" I pressed.

"The number will be identified as yours in an instant. Thus, suggesting we have not perished here tonight."

"Let them, whomever *they* may be, be damned!" I defiantly said.

"No, Watson! We must make our way across that beam and effect our own escape."

"But Holmes, how on earth will we open the door? You are in no condition—."

"I must. I simply must," he said as he stepped out to the beam.

"No Holmes, you are simply too wobbly to attempt this as of yet. Let me try," I insisted.

"We must both go," demanded Holmes. "It will require both of us to open that door. Here, give me your belt."

I looked at him an instant, but did as he asked and removed my belt and handed it to him. He then removed his own and fastened the two together, making one sixty-eight inch strap. Afterwards, he stepped over to the closest crossing beam. Once on it, he knelt down, then quickly fastened the belt around himself and it.

"Holmes," I pleaded, "that, I fear, will not hold, if you should slip."

"Then pray I do not," was his determined response. "Come, Watson, it will require both of us to pry open this door."

Nervously, I approached the beam and followed Holmes' lead. I felt fortunate to have never feared heights as a great many people do, for I could not fathom being more frightened than I already was. Nevertheless, I inched my way cross the beam behind Holmes.

Owing a large debt to the devoted practice of Yoga for providing us with a heightened sense of balance, we successfully reached the door at the other side of the shaft. Now the challenge before us was to position ourselves in some way that would allow us to accomplish our goal without losing our balance and taking the final plunge. I reached around Holmes and gave the steel door a heavy yank. Nothing.

"Have you a knife or anything flat and strong?" asked Holmes. "In my haste this morning, I neglected to bring along my Swiss Army knife."

"I do, as a matter of fact. Here," I said as I handed him my own Swiss Army knife. "What, by Jove, can you do with this little knife, Holmes?"

"Observe and learn, my good man. Observe and learn." And with that he stood, strapped his left hand to a vertical scaffold with one belt, then stretched himself out before the door, placing his right foot on a remnant of the threshold. He then inserted the blade up into a seam at the top of the door. There was a clank of metal to metal and presto! Like magic the door opened just enough for Holmes to grab hold and pull it in our direction. I stood dumbfounded.

"I thought it would have taken the pair of us to achieve this?" I happily stated.

"It did, Watson. It did," Holmes replied as he ignored the pain and hoisted himself up and out through the door.

A long time ago I learned there was no sounder advice than to pay heed to whatever passed from Holmes' mouth. Therefore, I did not hesitate to stretch myself over, like he had done, and effect my own escape from the now chimney-like shaft.

Exhausted, we laid on the corridor floor a second or two to catch our breath. The corridor itself was a chaotic mess of frightened hotel guests scurrying about for answers to the loud commotion and great plume of smoke. Along with us from the shaft came a light, yet steady, stream of smoke, which did not help ease the tension in the faces of the hysterical crowd. A chambermaid, panicked at the sight of us, lost control of the cart she was steering the instant we appeared. So, to defuse the panic, we immediately set about closing the door we had just come through. It did not help much. As a matter of fact, our arrival only served to set off a great stampede for the stairwell, with several of the, what appeared, spooked bison, leaving the doors to their rooms wide open as they bolted out, leaving Holmes and me standing in an empty corridor.

"It would appear the event was even more horrifying on this floor. How very fortunate we were to have missed it," Holmes said sarcastically.

"Most extraordinary," I added.

"Come, Watson! There is not a moment to lose," said Holmes as he handed me my belt and Swiss Army knife, before rushing into one of the abandoned rooms.

"Holmes! What on earth are you doing? You can't—," I tried to no avail, as usual, to insist.

Having no choice, I followed after Holmes, where I found him dialing a number on the room's telephone. As he waited for his party to answer, Holmes turned to me, with a look of shame.

"I blame myself, Watson. Forgive me. It was a mistake to choose a hotel so close to the Plaza. It was also a mistake to use the Kinko's on 54th street. Added up, these things gave a reasonable fix on our location. This should have been expected. Are you sure you're all right?"

"What do you mean? Are you saying they really tried to kill us tonight?" I asked, picturing Holmes and I as goldfish in a glass bowl, our every move watched.

"I am afraid so," he managed to say before the party picked up on the other end of the line. "Moore!" he screamed into the phone, "say nothing and pay attention! We haven't much time. I want you to make sure the word gets out that two Swiss gentlemen did in fact die in the lift crash at the Essex House hotel tonight.—Oh, excuse me, the *elevator* crash.—Yes, just now.—Stop! Listen and say nothing! Obviously, as you can hear, we have managed to escape. But such attacks will no doubt continue. Therefore, it is imperative that you buy us some time. Get some people you can trust over here to pronounce us dead at the scene.—Immediately!—Say the bodies have not yet been recovered from under the very weighty debris.—Immediately!—Yes we are still to meet at the Four Seasons in Chicago.—Yes, tomorrow, 9:30 am," Holmes firmly stated before hurriedly disconnecting and turning to me. "We'll have to do our best to clean ourselves up, before we grab a taxi to the airport," he said as he proceeded to wash himself in the bathroom basin.

"This is not our room," I reminded him.

"There is no time to hike up to our rooms. Besides, I am certain they are being *staked-out*, as they like to say these days," he explained. "By the way, thank you Watson. Thank you for saving—," he attempted to say, with an extremely rare, though genuine, humility.

"You never need express thanks to me," I replied. "We are beyond that, Holmes."

"I owe you everything."

"Nonsense! It is I who owe you. Now, let me have a look at that shoulder," I insisted.

The slice into his shoulder was more severe than I had initially thought.

"Holmes! This is not good at all. I am afraid it will require suturing."

"We haven't time!" he argued.

"We do not have time for an infection, either."

"Fine, we'll stop at a chemist's on the way. But right now we must freshen ourselves and be off. There is no time to waste."

I knew it was pointless to argue with him in this, just as he knew it was futile to fight me over tending to his wound. I was the medical man, and he had always deferred to my judgement in matters of health and injury. So, without further delay, we scrubbed our faces and hands, dusted and damp wiped our clothes then raced into the corridor where we found the stairwell and joined the ensuing panic that was rushing downward like a colossal avalanche. Within that human torrent, Holmes spotted one man holding a blanket over his head and asked if he might share his cover with us, two elderly gents needing to escape the hotel fire and the panic stricken horde, thrust into that state by a few speculators within the stampede bellowing out that the events of the evening were the result of a terrorist bombing attack. Then, just as we reached the lobby, which then resembled more a corral than a vestibule, Holmes and I crowded under the blanket with our generous neighbor and made our way out of the stairwell, through the unleashed mayhem, past the skittish human livestock and out onto the street, where fire trucks and police cars filled the street like so many pieces on a checkerboard.

Paramedics on the scene inquired as to our conditions. Keeping our heads covered, Holmes assured them we were fine as we pressed on, discarded our friend and his blanket to quickly blend into the crowd of curious onlookers. In an instant we had rounded the corner, where we hailed a cab and made our escape.

"La Guardia," Holmes instructed the driver.

"Would you mind stopping at a chemist's on the way, please," I quickly added.

"A what?" asked our driver.

"A drug store, if you would be so kind," Holmes quickly explained to the driver, who, by now, was looking us over with a very suspicious eye.

"Hey, if you in some kinda trouble—," the driver attempted to say, as he spotted Holmes' torn jacket.

"There is no trouble, sir," I shot back.

"I don't want any trouble," the swarthy driver reiterated.

"Sir, do we actually appear to be troublesome or criminals, if that is what you infer? Well you are incorrect in your initial assessment," said Holmes sternly, before the man could answer. "We are two men of some obvious years who have been shamefully accosted in this city of yours and we merely wish to leave it without delay."

In much the same manner in which my father had whenever I had been caught red-handed in some mischief, Holmes leaned forward and delivered a firm glare to our driver.

"Now sir," continued Holmes, "will you drive my doctor friend and I to the airport, or shall we take our business elsewhere?"

"Oh! Ah, okay, sure. No problem, no problem," the driver nervously replied, just as I had, when I was the recipient of my father's stern scowl.

And as our rather anxious and unsettled driver hurriedly went about his duty and sped us away, I kept an eye out for a chemist.

"Watson," said Holmes, distracting me from my task, "after our *Adventure of the Empty House*, as you so well coined it, do you remember my asking you to fetch my index of biographies?"

"Of course. I shall never forget it," I answered. "Colonel Sebastian Moran, the second most dangerous man in England. Yes, I remember all too well."

"Well, I do not have my index with me this time. However, I do have my Palm Pilot with me, which also contains an index of biographies. Here," he said as he lifted the palm pilot out of his outer side jacket pocket and handed it to me, "bring up the *E*s, if you would, please."

I sensed I knew where he was going with this and eagerly did as asked.

"Tell me what you see," he asked.

I scrolled until there it was on the tiny screen before me.

"Well?"

"The Engineer. The most dangerous man on earth," I answered as a fearful chill knifed through my body.

"Quite right, Watson. And I'm afraid he has just made his opening move," he said collecting the palm pilot from me. "The game is afoot, Watson! The game is very much afoot!"

CHAPTER VIII

The Undertow

Prior to catching a "red-eye" flight out of New York's La Guardia airport, bound for Chicago, I had quickly taken to the task of suturing Holmes' ghastly shoulder laceration whilst en route to the airfield. Obviously, a speeding taxi is not the ideal setting for such a procedure, but seeing how time was of the very essence, we had little choice. So, with a quick stop at a late night chemist our taxi would conveniently pass, I grabbed the essentials for the procedure in a matter of seconds. A rather chaotic evening, to say the least. Though even that portrayal fails to fully capture the intensity of the actual havoc. Once aboard the craft, I welcomed with opened arms the chance of a brief reprieve while we sat in flight. Apparently, so had Holmes, as he had, not surprisingly, already given way to the body's demand for sleep. After having had that vicious wound of his closed with very little in the way of anesthesia, in addition to everything else that had occurred that evening, a momentary break in the action, as it were, was just what he needed. I, on the other hand, was lit up like Krakatoa, adrenaline flowing lava-like, hot and unstoppable. For the reality of this brutish criminal's evil nature was now sinking in. No longer would I even think of challenging Holmes in the slightest. No longer would I question the plausibility of the evil one's schemes or motives, no matter how fantastic they appeared. I now considered the glove tossed. And the duel, I understood, was to the death, a circumstance I now accepted willingly and wholeheartedly.

Arriving at Chicago's Four Seasons Hotel in the wee hours, we managed to register and catch a few winks before our scheduled rendezvous with Mr. Moore at 9:30am. As the hands of my watch crept toward that position, I noticed Holmes busily sketching out what looked like an organizational chart of some sort. I made an attempt to inquire as to the meaning of it, but my words could not penetrate that singular concentration of his. So, while he charted away, I availed myself of the large pot of Assam, nine grain toast, *sans les confitures*, save for honey, figs, dates, strawberries and a bowl of piping hot porridge I had room service deliver for both Holmes and myself. It was just the thing to enhance my spirit. But then a good cup of tea alone has always had the strength to lift my mood. I am convinced this is due to the high antioxidant content in teas rather than merely the quality of the tea. Not that I would ever consider keeping Lipton or fruit flavored teas in my home, but even a tea of appallingly poor quality could revive me at times. But thank God the hotel produced a civilized blend, an occurrence I had learned not to expect in America.

What I was expecting, however, was further insight into this man. This extremely dangerous man Holmes had labeled *The Engineer*. Judging from our narrow escape, as well as Holmes' index notation, this was, no doubt, merely round one of what was going to be an extremely bloody bout. But I was also certain that this Engineer fellow, like many before him, had mistakenly underestimated Holmes. You see, for Holmes, there exists nothing better than a match-up with a worthy opponent. Sharp intellect pitted against sharp intellect. Why the very challenge itself fuels Holmes. Going the distance, be it twelve or fifteen rounds, is of no consequence to him. For not only has Holmes been blessed with a jaw of granite, his jab is as lethal as his right hand. But finding this mysterious opponent, it was clear to me, was another matter. It was evident that this fiend was a supremely skilled dodger, bobbing and weaving, while pounding an opponent's body. A very dangerous opponent, indeed. One who moved dreadfully well around the ring, this three million, five hundred and thirty five thousand, nine hundred and thirty five square mile American ring.

KNOCK! KNOCK! KNOCK! The sudden, forceful sound of knuckles striking the door to our suite interrupted my thoughts. I looked over at Holmes, no reaction. He was still engrossed in his diagramming. I reflexively looked at my watch, half-past-nine. So, without further hesitation, I answered the door. There, as expected, stood Mr. Moore, overly hyperactive, almost childlike in his anxiousness.

"Good morning, Dr. Watson. Good morning!" Moore greeted me as he rushed in, quickly closing the door behind him. "I'm quite sure I was not followed, sir. I am really quite sure," he announced, appearing very pleased with himself.

"That is very good to hear," I said somewhat tongue in cheek as Moore turned toward Holmes.

"Are you gentlemen all right? My God, what have I gotten you two into?" he asked, speaking as rapidly as he had glided through the door.

"As you can see, we are fine, Mr. Moore," I answered for Holmes, who was still lost in his chore. "However, I dare say it, was rather a close call, though."

"Close call, indeed!" he said, projecting his voice in Holmes' direction. "Good morning, sir."

But, like my own earlier attempts, he received no reply.

"Sir? Emmm, Mr. Holmes?" Moore went on.

"I'm afraid Mr. Holmes is somewhat occupied at the moment," I broke in. "He shan't be a moment, though. Would you care to join me in a cup of this quite excellent tea?"

He looked at me with perplexity etched onto his square face, an expression I was quite familiar with by now. For over my many decades as Holmes' closest friend and assistant, I have witnessed a countless number of faces falling still when introduced to Holmes' catatonic-like concentration. Initially, Moore, like all the other victims of Holmes' strange unresponsiveness, was uncertain as to what his reaction should be. He peered at Holmes, then returned his sight on to me. Should he be miffed by what appeared to be a complete disregard for his presence? Or should he express concern over what he considered might be some type of physical or emotional abnormality? He thought to speak, yet held back.

"Not to worry. Holmes will be with us straight away," said I. "Please, have a seat and join me in a cup of tea."

But the instant I began to pour two cups, a familiar voice commanded my attention.

"Make that three cups, if you would be so kind," ordered Holmes, who had awakened from his self imposed trance. "Very good of you to be so punctual," he complemented Mr. Moore. "I greatly appreciate that in a comrade."

Moore took an involuntary step back, as he was more than a little startled by Holmes' sudden return.

"By the way, I can assume you took care to handle the events of last night in the manner in which I suggested?"

"Of course, sir," responded Moore. "Per your directive, I had it reported to all forms of the media that two victims were found in the elevator wreckage, two elderly foreign gentlemen, whose identities are being withheld until family members in their country of origin can be contacted. I think that should produce the desired effect—I know some very reliable media-people, sir," he cockily added.

"No doubt you do, Mr. Moore. And, as it happens, we shall need all the reliable people you can round up very shortly," added Holmes, as he took the cup of Assam I handed him. "Now, gentlemen, it is time I presented you with an overview of our situation."

He paused to sip his tea.

"This is quite pleasant," he said to me, before resuming the briefing. "As I have already shared with Watson," said Holmes, directing himself to Moore, "we have entered into a contest of wills with *the* most dangerous man on this very planet. His name I do not yet fully know. Therefore, I have adopted the use of his nom de plume, *The Engineer*, which his confederates have affectionately christened him."

Moore sat up, very stiff on his chair. The seriousness with which Holmes spoke held us both clinging on to his every word.

"I have been aware of his presence for a good many decades,"

Holmes went on. "And I assure you, what Watson and I had the misfortune to have experienced last evening was a mere stroll in the park in comparison with his other deeds."

I caught myself biting my fingernails as I listened, something I had not done in all of my years.

"A beheading, I assure you, would be more to your liking than some of his preferred methods of assault," added Holmes.

Moore and I looked at one another, fear stricken.

"It is the usually dismal story," continued Holmes. "The cruel, overbearing sovereign forcing his subjects to turn the wheels of commerce, rewarding him handsomely for the mere privilege of working themselves to the bone for the greedy ogre. Poverty, sickness, starvation, all forms of misery meant absolutely nothing to the king. Taxes and profits were paramount. However, unlike such brutish rulers, the Engineer camouflages his machine by showering his serfs with an abundance of goods and supplies and praise. Gone are unregulated hours and deplorable working conditions. Gone are most of the abuses perpetrated on the laborer. In their stead are health benefits, minimum wage guarantees, 401K savings plans. Today's drones want for nothing. Thus, the reality of their own repression, for the most part, is not visible to them."

"Forgive me, Mr. Holmes," Moore interjected. "What you describe does not sound very much like repression to me."

"Ah, but that is the brilliance of it!" Holmes excitedly cheered.

"Holmes!" I cried. "A dastardly offense has been committed here and you sound as if you are pleased by it."

"Well I am pleased," he shot back. "One may not agree with this man's results. However, his strategy is nothing short of genius. And one must *always* appreciate genius."

He quickly held up his index finger to halt me from uttering another objection.

"That is not to say I shall not attempt to put this reprobate out of business. For as exceedingly clever as his actions have been, I have not forgotten that a theft of an unprecedented magnitude has been committed."

As he spoke, Holmes dropped the sketch he had been working on onto the coffee table before Moore and me.

"It is quite an elaborate schematic which this cunning thief of ours has constructed. Therefore, gentlemen, to assist you in your understanding of its complexity and function, I have produced this rendering of the Engineer's mechanism. A bird's eye view, if you will. I am confident you will find this visualization of immeasurable benefit."

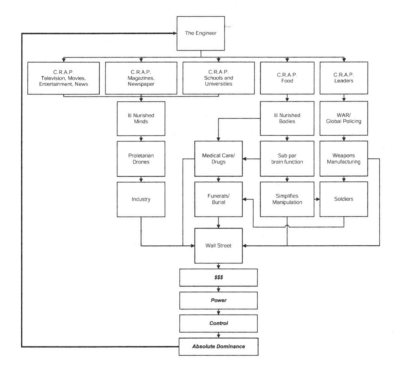

Moore and I carefully examined the document. I needn't tell you it took our breath away. For it laid out the vast web of deception, control, manipulation and profit this Engineer scoundrel had put into place. It was astonishing! To me, it appeared more than simply a machine. It was a factory! It immediately conjured up memories of Moriarty, the mastermind conceiving and hatching elaborate plots, like a grand general, far removed from the actual frontline. Deep in the background, in the dark study of his burrow, he developed his schemes and issued directives to his small army of thugs and miscreants. But this time, unfortunately, we were not facing the villainous professor. He was a thing of the distant past. This modern-day breed of evil we were confronting was a man far more sinister, far more intelligent, which was extremely difficult to fathom. And though my blood was boiling with an eagerness to lead the attack, I could now better understand that haunting sense of futility and hopelessness I had read in Holmes' face. But like Holmes, fighting that reaction would be my first battle in this war. For war it surely was, a war against one single man. One lone, ruthless individual who possessed the cleverness, callousness and audacity to take an entire population under his control. One solo member of a species who thrived on manipulating its own kind.

How was it possible to be so unimaginably inhuman? The realization of such a circumstance was frightening. More so than any horror or science fiction thriller I had ever read or had seen on the screen. Not even the great visionary H.G. Wells, I am certain, could have imagined this unseemly turn of events.

"So, what you're saying here is," Moore put it to Holmes, "is that this Mr. Engineer influences all these areas of life in the U.S., then reaps the rewards of this cultural poisoning by investing rather astutely on Wall Street?"

"You understand it perfectly! That is exactly how it functions, Mr. Moore," answered Holmes. "This exceptionally adroit foe of ours, by indirect means, directly, steers the market by influencing American culture to favor things that favor his particular financial positions."

"*Corrupting* would be more accurate a choice of term," I could not help but heatedly assert.

"You are too emotional, my good friend. But that, no doubt, is what makes you so successful a writer," quipped Holmes, knowing full well I greatly resented that tone of his, the one which always accompanied the insinuation that the accounts of our adventures, which I had painstakingly chronicled, were mere romantic pulp fiction, as he has always categorized them.

And yet, despite being a writer of some competence, I could think of no retort. Nothing! Absolutely nothing! That fact, on top of another of Holmes' condescending verbal shots, positively infuriated me. Paralyzed by this silent rage, I could do nothing but feign a proud, thick skin and glare back at Holmes, which I have no doubt he saw right through.

"Yes, but how can he not be known then? How can it be that I, nor anyone else for that matter, has never seen this unbelievably powerful man?" pleaded Moore.

"I did not say he is a recluse. In fact, I am quite certain of the contrary and suspect he is actually quite well known," replied Holmes.

"What?"

"Dear chap, do not delude yourself. He has not managed to perfect a formula for invisibility, though I grant you, it would appear so on the surface."

"Then you know his face?" Moore excitedly cried out.

"We may all know it."

"What!"

"Put aside your initial impressions and consider this. Our man does not confine himself to a dingy room, as you no doubt perceive. No! He walks freely, and very proudly, among us. An absolute must, if he is to observe behaviors, pinpoint weaknesses and susceptibilities, and measure the success of his labors. No Mr. Moore, he is not unknown. As a matter of fact, I would wager my entire career that his face, though not recognized as *The Engineer*, is known to many, if not all."

"A concealed dual identity!" Moore exclaimed.

"Exactly!" Holmes answered. "But at present, our focus must be on our Renfield."

"Who?" asked a befuddled Moore.

"A rather unkindly reference Holmes likes to use in regard to this Lesters chap," I broke in.

"Ah, I see," Moore replied, even though his expression had given away his inability to grasp the reference.

"Now, as you both are aware," said Holmes, "Our identities are known to Lesters, making it difficult to—,"

"You're wrong, Mr. Holmes. He's seen only the pair of you," Moore, all too eagerly interposed.

"Really?"

"Yes."

"Whom else do you believe Lesters and his criminal brood think I attempted to reach by ringing your private White House office? Whom else did they spy traveling to England, visiting Watson's home, my home?—No, sir, it is you who are incorrect," chastised Holmes. "You forget, my good man, we three are the proverbial goldfish in a glass bowl here."

Moore's square jaw immediately fell open upon impact with the blow produced by this truth.

"Now, as I was about to say, not a single one of us can be seen anywhere near MYND Corporation headquarters this morning. For as you may have heard, the greatly respected Dr. John Watson and his sidekick Mr. Sherlock Holmes have met their demise in the crash of the Essex House hotel lift last evening. And you, Mr. Moore, what would a Washington bureaucrat, particularly after the deaths of the very two men he was responsible for bringing to America, be doing in Chicago at the very time the MYND Corporation board of directors is set to convene? No, sir, it will not do!"

Moore's highly animated mood evaporated at the speed of light.

"Therefore," Holmes went on, "this morning, while friend Watson slept, I made a couple of telephone calls."

He retrieved his pipe from the large Chippendale-like desk in the room, stuffed it with his herbal concoction and began to stroll about the room as he spoke.

"Over the last several years I have formed and association with two very intelligent American gentlemen. Via the internet, I had the good fortune to make the acquaintance of two exceptionally observant and reputable gents in a chess academy—You can deduce quite a lot about the character of an individual by the manner in which he conducts himself during a game of chess.—As a result of our increasingly free conversations, which extended far beyond the subject of moves and counter moves, we found ourselves entrenched in conversations about the rapidly dissipating American culture. You can imagine my surprise and great relief upon finding two individuals in America willing to acknowledge their great country's shortcoming. And, as good fortune would have it, both men are presently in Chicago. The first, a Mr. Kevin Vandenbolt, is a businessman who makes his home here in Chicago. The other, a Mr. Andrew Duzinski, is, very conveniently I might add, in Chicago visiting his father. They, gentlemen, shall be our ears and eyes this afternoon."

"Holmes!" I cried out. "We cannot involve ordinary civilians in this dangerous affair."

"Yes, Mr. Holmes! I agree. This is far too serious a matter for civilians. Besides, I have several very experienced and trustworthy people standing by," added Moore.

"Your people are very nearly no better than any one of us walking straight into that board of directors meeting, shaking a fist at Lesters and asking him where he is off to next. Or, if he would be so kind, as to put us in direct communication with the Engineer. No gentlemen! We cannot rely on the standard methods of conducting a campaign. We must make this a grassroots effort in order to succeed. Anything else is obvious and will show our hand before we are ready," said Holmes with a delivery style that was no doubt inspired by Churchill, Ike or Monty, or the myriad of world leaders he has known during the course of his career.

"But Holmes, these are common citizens. You cannot put them in such jeopardy?" I reiterated.

"They are not common, nor ordinary, by any measure," he countered.

"I don't doubt—,"

"They shall not be in any danger. They are merely to enjoy a brown bag lunch in front of the MYND building. Later, after the board meeting, and Lesters appears on the street, my men will follow him and report back to me. That is all," announced Holmes.

"That's all? What if they're spotted?" asked Moore.

"They have been instructed to back off and report to me the instant they suspect they have been noticed, or *made*, as I understand the slang to be these days."

"But then they will have lost Lesters," Moore challenged.

"That is where you come in. I assume you have hired a car?"

Moore nodded in the affirmative.

"Excellent! You, Watson and I will be parked several blocks away from my two associates and their charge. They are to keep in constant contact with us by means of this number," explained Holmes as he removed a small cellular telephone from his jacket pocket. "I borrowed this, so to speak, from a member of the hotel staff this morning."

"Holmes!" I shouted. "I already have a phone—,"

"We have had this conversation before, Watson."

"Yes, but first the van in Washington, and now this. You cannot go on *borrowing* anything you like."

"There is not sufficient time for such a debate at the moment," Holmes firmly barked back. "Come, gentlemen, we've no time to lose," he commanded as he led the charge for the door.

Thirty minutes later I found myself crammed into the rear seat of a small Japanese hired compact. Moore, the ever devoted government employee, made a habit of hiring only, as he put it, the most 'cost effective' rental cars. Holmes, in the passenger seat, was too absorbed in the view through a pair of binoculars to notice the extremely harsh conditions I was enduring. He had instructed Moore to park on Clark Street, out of sight of his two American volunteers stationed at the corner of Clark Street and East Jackson boulevard, but close enough so he could keep an eye on them with a pair of eighty-millimeter-lens-binoculars.

That morning, prior to our little stakeout, Holmes slipped a local cabby two hundred and fifty dollars to remain off duty and service only his volunteers. He promised the driver another two hundred and fifty, in addition to cab fare, when services had been rendered. For his part, Moore had acquired a rather detailed list of the MYND Corporation board members. It was a rather comprehensive job. And although Holmes was greatly impressed with the efficiency behind the list, it had failed to provide him with any new insights into the case. Moore, on the other hand, was still fascinated by the graphic of the Engineer's machine Holmes had mapped out, letting slip the occasional '*Oh, I get it*', or the '*Ah, I see*' sigh as he studied the mind opening illustration. As for myself, I had been attempting to use the time to meditate. I knew the stresses of our predicament and the discomfort presented by my confining surroundings would evaporate if I could remove them from my conscious mind. Unfortunately, acquiring the desired state became an impossible task as Moore became more inquisitive and debate-thirsty. Like a child who automatically asks '*why?*' to every explanation given to it, Moore's curiosity with Holmes' flowchart was annoyingly insatiable.

"I can see the correlation you purport to exist between the Engineer and entertainment and education and industry, and most of the areas you mention," Moore stated to the profile of the master sleuth whose focus was still fixed upon his two volunteer operatives. "The area I find somewhat cloudy is the pathway beginning with C.R.A.P. Leaders. Surely you cannot believe that our country's leaders have fallen victim to this Eloisyndrome?"

"And what do you base this challenge upon?" Holmes answered, moving only his mouth, as his focus remained its usual granite.

"Our elected officials would never allow themselves and their actions to be dictated by one individual. Our leaders have to answer to the people," replied Moore with a rather embarrassingly juvenile timbre.

A long unnerving silence swept through the car as Moore waited for a reply to his statement. I knew Holmes had already formulated one, but was as yet unable to deliver it, as he was stunned to discover how viciously the virus had progressed in Moore himself. After all, there we were, in enemy territory, so to speak, and our only ally was himself unwittingly fighting infection. The realization washed a cold, frightening wave of futility over me. I was positive Holmes was overtaken by the same undulation when he lowered his binoculars and exasperatedly turned to our rather naïve ally.

"What time do you have?" he softly asked of Mr. Moore.

"Eleven-thirty-two," Moore answered.

With his masterful concentration broken, Holmes' surprisingly subdued demeanor reminded me of that belonging to the wounded soldiers I had tended to in India during my military service. Like theirs, Holmes' face revealed the kind of shock that comes from the sudden realization that war exacts a hefty price from each and every one of us.

"Now then," began Holmes with an uncompromising seriousness overtaking his expression, "we do not have much time. Therefore, *I* shall speak and *you* will remain silent and listen *very* carefully. Understand?"

Moore, the ever-obedient schoolboy, nodded agreement.

"Good."

Holmes paused to collect a breath.

"Your sense of devotion is admirable," he continued, "but its blindness can be an extremely dangerous liability. Therefore, it is imperative you learn to separate fact from fiction and truth from propaganda or you, like those we are here to rescue, shall be nothing more than a corralled sheep."

Moore's body language was like that of a windscreen-wiper frightened puppy, wanting, somehow, to seek safety by diving under the passenger seat the instant the blades were switched on to combat the dropping rain.

"You must learn to seek the motivation behind an action or statement," Holmes continued. "For motivation is the key. It, and it alone, will always reveal the true purpose behind the act or the choice of words. '*Doing the Lord's work*', for example."

"WHAT?" Moore and I simultaneously cried out in horror.

"No, gentlemen, I assure you, I have not lost control of my faculties," said Holmes, nearly chuckling at our reactions, a reaction that informed us that Holmes had almost forgiven the interruption. But then, like a professor who glares into the face of a problem student, he looked to Mr. Moore and resumed his homily.

"Visiting soldiers in the Saudi Arabian desert, during the Gulf War of nineteen hundred and ninety-one, Mr. Bush, your former President, informed the great mass of dutiful young men and women eager to police the globe that they were, and I quote, *'doing the Lord's work'*. When in actuality, absolutely nothing could have been further from the truth. I like to refer to this method of manipulation as the *praise the Lord and pass the ammunition maneuver*. For you see, the brave soldiers of the armed forces were in Kuwait to secure oil for the western world, the sport utility vehicle crazed United States, in particular. That is all. Nevertheless, as usual, the ploy worked. The troops, and the general public, bought into the rhetoric. Thus, like the Engineer, Mr. Bush, generating his own undertow, successfully manipulated the beliefs and actions of the populous to suit his own needs. Needs, I might add, that were not only indirectly fueled by Mr. Bush's own connection to the oil industry, but by the Engineer himself."

"Undertow?" asked Moore, before realizing he had broken his promise to remain silent.

Holmes, projected that all too famous authoritative glower of his at the offender. As usual, it worked to perfection. Mr. Moore quickly pulled himself back and, without thinking, cupped a hand over his mouth as a startled child might.

"Yes, that is the term I had used. By it, I am referring to a strong current of manipulation that sucks people in and pulls them along for the ride, tossing them about in any which direction it so chooses as it flows along," answered a thoroughly exasperated Holmes.

Then, altering the tone of his voice to portray some sort of ruthless businessman, he continued.

"This week the *Godzilla* remake hits the screens. It's exceptionally deplorable CRAP, so let's toss these empty headed guppies in its direction before they have a chance to discover what rubbish it truly is. And let's also toss them in the direction of McDonald's so we can clean up on the Godzilla action figures, as well."

As an ophthalmologist peers into the workings of a patient's optical function, Holmes flung a concentrated gape into Moore's eyes to measure the penetration of his words. Then, after an instant of calculation, resumed his normal manner of speech.

"And, as you can see, it works to perfection. Everyone is happy. The CRAP restaurant chain is forever indebted to the studio for increasing its sales of CRAP food, the film studio has another blockbuster on its hands and the *ninety-four-percenter*, who hasn't the faintest idea he's caught in the vicious undertow, is thrilled. CRAP movie, CRAP food and CRAP action figures. A thoroughly *CRAPpy*, if you will, experience. Yet the victim revels in it."

"That's horrible!" I could not help but bellow out.

"Leaders, like Bush, be they politicians or corporate moguls, or merchants, create their own undertows," added Holmes. "Yet they are all actually parts of the same great current generated by hurricane *Engineer*. A "trickle down effect", if I can borrow another unbelievably insulting line from the former president."

I felt myself deflating as the realization of the nightmare Holmes had just described planted itself firmly into my conscious mind. Moore, had also been caught dumbstruck by the unexpected power of Holmes allegation. His shoulders now drooped and his head hung low.

"Remind me, Mr. Holmes, never to swim in the US. Its waterways, I now see, are far too treacherous."

"It appears so," answered Holmes.

"And it is this undertow that transports the Eloisyndrome?" asked Moore, sounding much the broken man.

"By Jove! I think he's got it, Watson."

"I think we are both beginning to grasp, as Conrad coined it, '*the horror*' of it all," I returned.

"Yes, indeed it is horrible," confirmed Moore. "But how does just one man amass so much power, gain so much control over vast numbers of people?"

"Regretfully, that is a circumstance more common to our species than it would care to acknowledge," said Holmes. "Why just think of the millions of people, in this century alone, who have fallen in league with psychopathic leaders or have been duped by a plethora of money grubbing televangelist mountebanks. It does not require a mastery of deductive reasoning to discern that we, on the whole, are a fearful, highly insecure species that is perpetually on the lookout for someone to allay its fears. Someone who will take charge of its care and protect it."

He let out a slow, deep and deliberate sigh then softly continued.

"It's been a very dark and gloomy road—," BEEP-BEEP! BEEP-BEEP! BEEP-BEEP! Holmes' dubiously procured mobile demanded attention.

"Block Buster video" Holmes announced into the little phone, while simultaneously placing his binoculars back before his eyes. "Yes, I have that video in sight," he continued, to our confusion. "No, I do not yet see that title—Ah! There it is.—Yes, the one on the left. Well done! Off you go, then," Holmes instructed with a hint of excitement in his speech. "Let's go!" he ordered Moore, who swiftly turned over the engine and stomped on the peddle, launching us on our way. "Slowly!" scolded Holmes. "Our goal is to observe, not to be observed."

Moore quickly shot back an expression that was a combination of concern and confusion.

"Rest assured, this fox will not get away. Our enlisted American bloodhounds have taken hold of the scent."

Poking slowly in the distant obscurity, we could barely see the yellow taxi Holmes' *chess buddies* were riding in. From our perspective, it appeared a mere one half inch in size. With such distance between us, and our subject, it seemed to me a painfully inept manner in which to tail someone. However, despite the reservations I had with this method of observation and with Holmes' recruitment of civilians, if you will, for the frontline, I had to admit, Holmes, as usual, appeared to have the matter well in hand.

Maintaining a constant telephone connection with his two confederates, it soon became clear our fox, and subsequently our little hunting party, was headed for Meigs Field, a pint-sized airport located in the very heart of Chicago. Thus, without setting an eye on our prey, Holmes had a fix on his man's position.

All was proceeding swimmingly. A full detailed account of every move Lester's limousine made spat out of the tiny phone Holmes had availed himself of. A right turn here. A left turn there. It was all very confusing to one so unfamiliar with the Chicago area. Nevertheless, as the directional road signs began to make perfectly clear, we were two miles away from Meigs Field when—

"WHAT THE—?" blasted out of Holmes' miniature phone. "MY GOD! BLOCKBUSTER, ARE YOU THERE?"

"Blockbuster here. What is the matter? Are you—," Holmes attempted to inquire.

"THEY JUST CUT US OFF!

Another voice joined in to add harmony to the great panic being projected through the airwaves.

"THEY'RE BEHIND US, TOO!" THEY'RE COMING!"

"BLOCKBUSTER! THIS IS 'A', WE ARE BLOCKED AT FRONT AND REAR! I DON'T KNOW HOW THEY SPOTTED US. BUT THEY ARE COMING. FIVE MEN. FIVE VERY LARGE MEN! NO! MAKE THAT SIX!"

"MAKE THAT SEVEN!" yelled the chorus section.

"Pray, what is your exact location?" demanded a worried Holmes.

"HEY! I WANT NO PROBLEM!!! I DO NOT CARE YOU OFFER ME MUCH MONEY," we could hear the horrorstruck taxi driver scream in a heavy Russian accent. "IS MY TAXI!"

"Quickly, 'A', what is your exact location?" demanded Holmes.

"I DON'T—,"

"SOLIDARITY DRIVE!" Mr. Vandenbolt loudly interloped. "WE'RE AT THE CUL-DE-SAC!"

Moore pounded his foot on the petrol peddle with such force, I thought he would push it right through the floor of the car.

"We are on the way!" Holmes shouted back.

"HOLY SH—!!!"

The phone fell silent. As did the three of us. We knew nothing good was to come of this latest development. And although I knew it had crossed Moore's mind, as well as my own, to remonstrate Holmes for involving his two chess chums, we refrained from such embittered action. We both knew failure was more of a blow to Holmes than any harsh words we may have flung at him.

"Hurry, man! Hurry!" Holmes anxiously shouted at Moore whose focus was already totally on the task at hand and pushing the capabilities of his small, miserably miniscule motoring machine.

Suddenly, there it was. East Solidarity Drive. Like a driver at the Indianapolis Motor Speedway, Moore wasted no time cornering onto the throughway. Weaving through what little traffic there was, the subject of our search, and great concern, finally appeared. Off in the distance, with doors flung wide open, sat the taxi, curbside. I hoped I was not eyeing what I had prayed had not occurred. Yet, as we approached the taxi from which the last communiqué from our loyal hounds had been sent, we all knew that it had. The worst possible thing we could have ever imagined had indeed taken place. Holmes put a hand to his brow, confirming for Moore and I that we had lost yet another battle in this brutally escalating war.

CHAPTER IX

Casualties

Fearful of what our eyes would behold the instant we reached the old, severely faded yellow taxi that appeared strewn along the side of the road, like so much rubbish tossed from the window of an inconsiderate passing motorist's vehicle, Moore unconsciously slowed his rented motorized soup can to a virtual crawl. Similarly, the breathing of every occupant in it, including that belonging to the uncommonly fearless master sleuth, was as slow as the proverbial molasses in winter. It was quite an odd sensation to be thrust into a surrealistic state of slow motion by Mr. Fear himself, the very same brute who had set our hearts and minds racing with an acute anxiety only an instant or two earlier. Yet that is how that sadistic villain operates. Like this Engineer chap, he lives for nothing else but to heap layer upon layer of internal conflict upon his victims. It was a skill our earthly opposition had obviously mastered, as we could certainly testify. And though our very cores were plagued with the pounding palpitations of a driving anticipation, it seemed, at our slow pace, a tortoise would reach the taxi a full light-year ahead of us.

Finally, as we cautiously pulled along side the aged and rather dilapidated commercial vehicle, we readied ourselves to view the gruesome scene we were all certain would be waiting for us. Yet, we were stunned to discover our nightmarish expectations wholly incorrect. The taxi was empty. The bloodied and mangled bodies, Holmes, Moore and I were certain we would find sprawled across the seats, were conspicuously absent. In fact, all was exceedingly tidy. Not a single drop of blood, nor even a shaving of broken glass could be seen, hide nor hair, literally. Holmes sprang from the car to examine the scene. Nothing. So clean was the taxi's interior, I was thoroughly convinced that no state-of-the-art forensics team in existence would find more than we had. I looked at Holmes for confirmation of my initial impression. His unwillingness to make any prolonged eye contact told me that this discovery only meant one thing. His American friends had met with an end more grisly than any one of us could ever imagined their deed would have merited, even when taking into account the twisted minds of the Engineer's psychotic ruffians. Punctuating this assessment remained the only trace of Holmes' two faithful soldiers. Lying purposely on the middle of the taxi's rear seat, where Mr. Dudzinski and Mr. Vandenbolt would have certainly been sitting, was our one and only clue, the small cellular telephone the two men had been using to communicate with Holmes.

Without giving the slightest consideration to the preservation of the crime scene, Mr. Moore practically dove for the dwarfish phone as he hurried to collect it. Instinctually, I moved to stop him as he began his lunge, but Holmes held me back. After discovering the pristine state of the setting, Holmes knew it was pointless to concern ourselves with the disposition of the crime scene. The instant he had set those piercing gray eyes on the remnants of the crime, he had determined that any criminal residue or trace of his two chums would not exist. Thus, like a card that arrives with a surprise delivery of a bottle of Chateau Lafite, a box of Belgian chocolates or a dozen long-stemmed roses, the phone was merely a message from the sender, a proud admission of responsibility. However, in this instance, its purpose was to utterly destroy the receiver, not thrill them. And like that usual gift card, it worked to perfection. For Holmes was deeply injured. The message it conveyed had run through him like Lancelot's sword. So great was his agony, he was unable to continue standing and took a seat upon the empty passenger seat where his two friends had last sat, and lost himself in contemplation.

I had not seen him display so much emotion over an individual, or individuals, in all my time with him. And as Moore was about to probe Holmes for our next strategic step I quickly ushered him back to his hired compact, where he and I gave Holmes his time for reflection, regret and mourning. That is until that makeshift greeting card sounded off, playing a highly offensive, sacrilegious even, electronic version of Beethoven's fifth symphony. I looked at Holmes. Nothing. Unbeknownst to me, in the millisecond it took me to check on Holmes, Moore had answered the blasted mobile.

"Hello!" he shouted into the phone, still overly keyed up himself. "Yes!—Who is this?—Yes. What do you want?—What?— Where are they? What have you done with them? Tell me, by God, or I'll have the authorities down on you so fast—."

He fell quiet halfway through his angry warning, then listened intently for what felt like an eternity, though could not have been longer than ten or fifteen seconds.

"WHAT? You must be—Yes!—Yes—Yes, I understand," he finally responded before disconnecting.

He then leaned on the driver side front fender of the abandoned taxi, looking completely devastated and bewildered.

"Well? What did they say?" I demanded.

"It's all one big joke to them, Doctor. A joke!" replied Moore with a repelled resonance in his shaky speech.

"Quickly, man! What did they say?" I implored.

"I am to go to the Gateway Motel on Ninety-fifth street in Oak Lawn. Wherever that is."

"It is a nearby suburb," Holmes quickly interjected, while springing expeditiously to his feet and hurriedly climbing into Moore's hired car. "We've not a moment to lose, gentlemen," he said, sounding like his old, valiant self. "Not a moment to lose!"

"But what have they instructed you to do?" I hastily asked.

"Two things. I am to go to this motel. For what, they would not say."

"And the second thing?" I rather impatiently requested.

"The other directive was to fold, throw down his cards," Holmes excitedly interposed. "In other words, they have assured Mr. Moore that this is a hand he can neither afford, nor win. Thus, my dear friend, they have insisted that our devoted Mr. Moore here drop this entire investigative pursuit."

"How did you—?" Moore cried out in astonishment.

"What else are we to assume they desire, my good man," said Holmes confidently as he buckled himself into the passenger seat. "Now get in!"

And that we filially did, me contorting myself, yet again, in order to fit into the rear seat, a feat I'm sure not even the great Hudini would have considered, and Moore resuming his position at the helm.

"How on earth did you know—," Moore tried to repeat.

"Surely this is a trap, Holmes!" I insisted the instant air was able to return to my lungs after successfully molding my elderly frame to the microscopic rear passenger area of Moore's diminutive transport.

"It is anything but, Watson."

"Oh come now, Holmes. This is so obviously a trap if ever I saw one."

"Yes, Mr. Holmes, I am inclined to agree with Dr. Watson. What else can it be if not a trap?" added Mr. Moore.

"Am I the only one of our small brigade who has not been affected by Chicago's intense June heat?" Holmes prodded. "Take the IL-50 south to the US-20/12," he instructed Moore. "We do not wish to be late."

Moore pounded the accelerator and cranked the wheel hard, violently swinging us around and on our way.

"I must protest, Holmes. Out with it! What is it you undertsand that we do not?" I demanded.

"It is as I said. There is no trap being set. We, or I should say, friend Moore here, is about to be taught an extremely difficult and painful lesson," said Holmes.

"Well forget that!"

"Injuring you, Mr. Moore, is not their intent. From their perspective, it is not in their best interest, at the moment. Or so they believe."

"What the hell does that mean?" our panicked companion shrieked.

"Holmes!" I scolded. "Please come to the point."

"It is like this. Lesters' people have apprehended my devoted American soldiers, whom they obviously assume are now working on behalf of Mr. Moore here. After all, if you will recall, you and I had the misfortune of perishing in a rather nasty accident in the Essex House lift. Thus, the purpose of this errand they have sent Moore on, however hideous I guarantee it shall be, is to educate him on the subject of retribution."

"I thought you said they do not wish to harm me?"

"Physically, no. Emotionally, now that is another story."

"WHAT!" Moore and I shouted in unison.

"Calm yourselves, gentlemen. Calm yourselves. You see, to eliminate Mr. Moore before he has learned the fate of our two entrusted footmen, and has had ample opportunity to relay that information on to the president, would not entirely squelch the chief executive's desire to apprehend this most vile of thieves and recover his country's property. No my friends, bodies alone are not sufficient enticement for abandonment of Mr. Clinton's mission. He must learn, first hand, through his most trusted confidant, the sheer horror and futility of waging war against this all powerful villain."

"Holmes," I said, "are you absolutely certain of this? I should not want to send—,"

"They have unwittingly shown their hand."

"How?"

"During his conversation with these hooligans, Mr. Moore was never once asked his name. Thus, both parties knew to whom they were speaking. Had there been any doubt as to our being out of the picture, that would have most assuredly been question number one. If they had found us out, we would have found what we had expected in that taxi, as well as a bullet or two with our own names on them."

He paused as his spirit appeared to sink again.

"Through my own incompetence, and over eagerness, two very intelligent and particularly caring young men have met with great misfortune at the hands of these extremely brutal Visigoths. I do not intend to make another horrific miscalculation. No gentlemen, we will find no trap waiting for us. What we will find, however, is the price."

"The price of what?" Moore anxiously asked.

"Why the price for challenging this ruthless blackguard, of course."

In no time we had reached the Gateway Motel. How we arrived there I am not clear. A brooding heaviness seemed to have infiltrated the motorcar, stifling all conversation and catapulting my conscious mind into deep reflection and contemplation. Even Moore, in his limited way, fell within himself and was driving by sheer reflex as he followed Holmes' directions. It was only when the vision of the Gateway had penetrated my conscious mind, did I return to the moment. The sight also caused me to realise that Holmes and I had *not* taken the precaution of not arriving with Moore. After all, we were thought to be out of the picture, as it were.

"Holmes!" I said as Moore parked the car and switched off the motor. "We should have—,"

"No, Watson," he said, holding up the back of his hand to me. "There will be no person here we need fear."

He took a large breath, turned and looked at Moore, then back at me.

"We need not bother any longer with concealing our involvement. From here on in we are in Dodge City and we shall walk down the center of Main Street with weapons at the ready."

It was an image I freely admit I did not care for. Pistols holstered at our sides, the Engineer and his menacing men standing a mere hundred yards before us, patiently and confidently waiting, poised for the draw, the moment we were in range.

"Where to, then?" asked an anxious Moore.

"The motel office, I should think, would make an excellent beginning," Holmes answered.

Climbing out of the car, I could not help but keep an uneasy eye out for the slightest sign of attack. And though Holmes walked worry free towards the motel office, Moore and I felt as if we were indeed walking down the middle of an old western town's main street, waiting for that cliché of an ambush and the subsequent shootout to commence.

Once inside the modest office, Holmes asked the middle-aged clerk behind the desk if he had any messages for a Mr. Moore. Indeed he had. Up from his stool he stood and collected the key to room nineteen from a bulletin board of keys mounted on the wall behind him and handed it to Holmes.

"You're friends said to tell you they've gotten started without you, Mr. Moore, and to let yourself in," said the amiable, all too comfortably stuffed man as he strained to look up at Holmes through the top half of his bifocal lenses.

"Why thank you, sir," Holmes returned. "Room nineteen, you say?"

"That's right, Mr. Moore. Room nineteen."

We thanked the pleasant man and hurried off to locate room nineteen. En route, Moore and I were both fighting back a vicious attack of nerves. In fact, in the hundred and fifty watt illumination of the corridor, I got a glimpse of very noticeable hue of green in our American comrade's cheeks. Feeling somewhat peaky myself, I could not feel anything but sympathetic. But all that was overtaken by concern when we finally arrived at the door to number nineteen. Standing before it, we could hear the rapid, teletype-like speech of a sportscaster flowing loudly from the television through the solid eggshell colored door. Quickly, Holmes spread his arms out like the great figure atop Rio's de Janeiro's Corcovado mountain to stop us in our tracks.

"I shall go first. You two wait for my signal" he announced.

"Holmes, I'm a physician, for Heaven's sake. I've seen—," I attempted to protest.

"Not like this. Of that I am certain."

And with that he unlocked the door and cautiously slid inside, closing the door tightly behind him.

Never in my life had I known Holmes to mightily shriek out in utter, overwhelming horror. But that is what came blasting through the solid wooden door.

"Holmes!" I shouted while simultaneously trying the door.

No response. Nor luck with the doorknob, which had automatically locked upon closing.

"Holmes! Are you all right? Holmes!"

Slowly the door began to open. Holmes, though visibly sickened, was careful to pull the door open just enough for him to slide out.

"Holmes?"

Nothing. The great sleuth, the master of all detectives, the man whose rock solid nerves and sinewy constitution, like those of the experienced hardened emergency room physicians I had always envied for their inner strength, had been overtaken by something so hideous, so powerfully shocking that it rendered him utterly speechless. Never, in his long and great career had Holmes ever been dealt a blow from which he could not momentarily recover. Fortunately I always keep a few small medical items on my person, and smelling salts was one I always liked to have at hand.

Moore tried to slip inside the room as Holmes staggered out. But Holmes, even in his extraordinarily distressed state, had managed to close the door behind him, successfully preventing either Mr. Moore or myself from viewing whatever evil he had encountered inside room nineteen. So while I waved my small vessel under Holmes' long, narrow nose, Moore frantically paced the area about us.

"Enough!" insisted Holmes as he shoved my vessel filled hand away from his face.

"You're all right, then?" Moore overeagerly blurted out at Holmes, usurping my own attempt at questioning Holmes. "Here, let me have the key. I'll go in and assess the situation. You and the doctor can wait here."

At light speed I was incensed by this asinine proposal. For not only did it reveal Mr. Moore's unobservant nature, it was disappointingly disrespectful and exposed his narrow minded, stereotypical view of people of advanced years. So outraged was I, I thought it best to refrain, no matter how excruciatingly painful it might be, and ignore this part-time oaf, for his sake, at the very least. Feeling the heat from my boiling rage as I was, I just might have launched into a demonstration of my own formidable left jab and right hook combination. And besides, Moore was on our side. The last thing I wanted was to make the Engineer's defensive campaign easier by igniting a sense of bad blood and, thus, initiating a series of brawls within the rank and file of Holmes' very own troops. Surely there was nothing more lethal to a crusade than that.

Holmes, on the other hand, already having grasped the whole of our companion's psychological and intellectual profiles within the first few minutes of meeting this American civil servant, simply waved Moore off and remained focused upon collecting himself. Then, an instant later, Holmes slowly began to regain his usual poise. He looked Moore squarely in the eye and said.

"It is sometimes best to inquire as to whether the water is deep enough before you blindly dive in, sir."

As expected, Moore slightly befuddled by what appeared to him a statement that had absolutely nothing at all to do with the present situation, reflexively shook his head and with an unabashed mollification replied, "Yes, Mr. Holmes."

Again, it required all of my inner focus, and quite a bit of my reserve, to keep from thrashing him on the spot. Fortunately, Holmes announced he was ready for us, making all such thoughts instantaneously wane from me. And although I had seen the singular state Holmes was in after witnessing whatever was behind that door, I was probably more eager to get to the heart of this business than the hyperactive Mr. Moore. But as Holmes removed the room key from his jacket pocket, he began performing a quick little yogic breathing exercise that transformed my eagerness to pure dread. Immediately, I took care to execute the same relaxation technique and ready my own consciousness for what I was now certain was an otherworld evil. Holmes was glad to see I had followed his lead.

"Gentlemen, brace yourselves," he warned as he turned the lock, then flung open the door.

As was becoming routine, Moore wasted no time and galloped straight into the room without the slightest evidence of caution. Myself, I preferred to tip-toe in behind Holmes.

"AHHHHH! OH, MY GOD!" screamed Moore at the sight before us. He then fell to his knees and wept like a child.

Fortunately, I was rendered speechless, thus spared the agony of making an even greater spectacle of myself than he had. Yet, like Niagara, my eyes sent water streaming forcefully down my face. Soon the rising tide in my line of sight made it impossible to see clearly. It was a godsend. Nevertheless, I managed to examine the vitals of the three revoltingly disfigured bodies found in the room. After a lifetime in medicine, I could easily perform this task in complete darkness.

"They're alive, Holmes!" I announced with astonishment.

"That is most unfortunate," he sadly returned.

As unfeeling as his reply may have initially appeared, Holmes was right. For, regretfully, the victimized, after all they had endured, would have been better off dead.

The furniture and twin beds had been shoved into a distant corner of the room. In their ordinarily reserved space were stationed three pathetically juvenile plastic inflatable Miller-Lite Beer Super Bowl chairs, complete with built-in beer can holders located in each of the arms. A putrid greenish-blue background dotted with stickers, like a bad case of measles, picturing American football team helmets and mementos of Super Bowls past completed the chair's design. Before these horrific armchair athlete thrones sat two televisions, both running at full power. One was broadcasting an insulting and highly nauseating mock news program, which merely spewed out sports statistics and player facts and sports gossip as if the entire process was crucial to the presence of human life on the planet. The other television, with the volume lowered to a faint whisper, ran a rather poorly photographed hardcore group orgy video.

Moore, unable to remain in the room, and too distraught to stand, crawled out on his hands and knees, over the fowl, soggy, sawdust-like mixture of beer, pretzel and potato chip crumbs, which had soaked into the room's carpeting. The stench of which permeated the room so violently that Holmes and I were forced to tie handkerchiefs over our mouths and noses. And like the army surgeons I once knew in India, which we now mimicked, we tended to the battle casualties with a great brotherly conviction. For never in all our born days had we witnessed so vile an assault. Tsung, Hitler nor Stalin had ever been this brutal. Rather than bringing a swift end to the enemy, the Engineer, we now fully understood, preferred his soldiers scar the opposition for life by disfiguring them emotionally, as well as physically. It was simply beyond comprehension. But there they lay, heads back with eyes locked trance-like on the ceiling, in what were hands down the *bowling shoe* of chairs, three completely innocent young men. Two working to earn their country's cultural release from the bite of this parasitical scapegrace, the other trying to earn a mere crust. Yet their gallantry, their uncommon valor, their humility, at the very least, was not respected. Not even the unwritten rule of respecting the soldier, if not the cause, was dishonored. It, like the right of their nation to retain its own uniquely fused multi-ethnical culture, was ignored. Their most basic of basic rights callously violated. It was a sight like no other.

Our two infantrymen and their enlisted driver, in addition to haven obviously been force fed CRAP snacks and beer until their bodies went into severe shock, were stripped naked to the waist. Their heads, faces and chests were cleanly shaven and painted with orange and black diagonal stripes, the colors of the Chicago Bears American football team. Added to the horror were large painted player numbers on each man's torso. Ridiculous, short, plastic mock-Viking, bull-like horns were attached to the sides of their heads. The victims were clad in trousers, so hideously oversized, two men could easily get into one pair. Yet even more egregiously appalling was the manner in which the trousers rode ridiculously low in an effort to, of all things, show off the men's *stars 'n stripes* boxer shorts. It was very nearly more than either Holmes or I could take. But endure it all we did. How could we not? These were our allies.

As quickly as we could, dragging one casualty at a time into the adjoining bathroom's shower, we scrubbed each man down. Luckily, all were so heavily inebriated they slept through the entire process. Bringing them round in that environment, in addition to their physical condition, would have surely accomplished the Engineer's goal of emotionally scaring the men for life. Therefore, as a means of sparing the men as much of the nightmare as possible, Holmes and I viewed their overly intoxicated state as a blessing. And as we laid the last freshly cleansed comrade across the joined twin beds, Holmes called out to Mr. Moore, who had stationed himself in the corridor where he had been vomiting violently and attempting to regroup, while Holmes and I tended to the wounded.

"Mr. Moore," shouted Holmes, "get in touch with your people and instruct them to retrieve the final destination of our Renfield's private plane and relay that information to us. Then order those 'reliable' people of yours to meet that craft upon its arrival at that location. I expect them glued to his every move, his every breath!"

Weak from events, Moore sat on the corridor floor leaning against the wall for support. Although he could not have helped but hear Holmes, it was not initially apparent as to whether Holmes' words had actually penetrated the trembling man's conscious mind.

"Then make arrangements to transport us to that very location immediately!" Holmes loudly and authoritatively added.

Still quivering, Moore was unresponsive.

"NOW!" Holmes commanded, reminding me of a boot camp drill instructor.

It was a bark that must have rocketed the very same image into Moore's mind. For instantly his eyes regained their focus and his thigh muscles their vigor, as he sprang to his feet and very nearly stood at attention before Holmes.

"Get all that Mr. Moore?" Holmes questioned.

As Moore nodded confirmation, he simultaneously yanked out a mobile phone from his jacket pocket and hurriedly began to dial. Holmes quickly grabbed the room's phone and ever so politely, insisted the front desk order a taxi. Then, as our casualties were beginning to regain themselves, Holmes, Moore and I quickly slipped a shirt onto each man, then rushed them down to the pavement to meet the arriving taxi. We felt it crucial to their psychological well being that they not possess the slightest sober visual memory of the terrible setting in which we had found them.

After placing the wounded into the taxi, Holmes retrieved a small notepad from his outer jacket pocket, leaned on the roof of the taxi and quickly scribbled a short, yet heartfelt message.

> *My dearest of friends,*
>
> *I am filled with the greatest of sorrows as a result of this great assault which has been so viciously and callously inflicted upon you. I shall not ask that you forgive my misjudgment of our enemy's intelligence or ruthlessness. Nor shall I ask you to forgive my failure of you. I have erred most grievously and can never amend the injury enacted upon your person. Therefore, I merely thank you copiously for your heroism and say that I shall look in upon you as soon as time permits.*
>
> *Your friend and great admirer,*
> *Sherlock*

As Holmes recited Mr. Dudzinski's address for the driver, he folded his hand written note and placed it halfway into Mr. Vandenbolt's shirt pocket. A second later the cab was off and we three headed somberly back to Moore's car.

"Well?"

"Well?" echoed Moore.

Holmes flashed that famous impatient frown of his at Moore.

"Ah, yes sir, Mr. Holmes, yes," Moore obediently returned, "Las Vegas."

Holmes grimaced.

"Lesters' plane should be landing any minute now. And as per your instruction, my people will be reporting on his actions every half hour, or earlier, if necessary. I assure you, he will not leave our sight."

"Very well, then," said Holmes with a painful reluctance blanketing his face. "If we must, we must."

"Well done, Mr. Moore," I tossed in.

"I have also made arrangements for a plane to be waiting to take us to Las Vegas," Moore added.

"Yes, I concur, Watson," said Holmes before directing himself to Moore. "Well done."

As we were returning to Meigs Field, again by means of Moore's mobile torture chamber, Moore kept mumbling the words, '*the horror*'. Not quite incessantly, mind you. However, in the cramped confines of his car, hearing that phrase every few minutes was rather too much to endure. I was just about to scream, when Holmes, who had been in deep contemplation, finally returned to us and interrupted Moore's all too vocalized suffering.

"You are correct, Mr. Moore. You are quite correct. It was quite horrible indeed. But surely you witness similar such horrors on a daily basis. Would you not say?"

"What?" shrieked Moore. "Never in all my—,"

"Yes, yes. I grant you. It was terribly repulsive back there. But have you not noticed the legions of such casualties spread about the country?"

"Well, I guess so. I mean, after all, I am here because the president and I have been noticing a highly disturbing trend toward the cheap, the disposable and the uncouth."

"Precisely! Do you not see these people as casualties?"

"Well, since you put it that way. I guess I do."

"Then do you not see people who are perpetually pressured by a barrage of clever subliminally influencing advertisement campaigns to purchase, for example, diet soft drinks by the score as casualties?"

"What? Are you serious? Diet soda drinkers as casualties?"

"Considering the facts, how could they not be viewed as casualties?"

"Exactly what facts are you referring to?" I asked.

"The fact that ninety four percent of diet drinks replace sugar with Aspartame, an extremely lethal chemical primarily used as a wood glue."

Struck dumfounded with consternation, Moore looked intently at Holmes. With eyes alit with hope that Holmes' statement was an exaggeration, Moore waited. Yet when, after this silent challenge, Holmes unflinchingly stood steadfast in his position, Moore blasted, "That's appalling!"

"It is quite shocking indeed," returned Holmes.

"Yes," I interjected. "I remember reading a paper published in a fairly recent issue of the British Medical Journal in which it was reported that people who consume these products on a very regular basis developed symptoms extremely similar to Multiple Sclerosis."

"My God!" cried Moore.

"And let's not forget the hordes of people dining at fast food restaurants, despite knowing that these places are nothing more than breeding grounds for the likes of heart disease, diabetes, colitis, high blood pressure and obesity," added Holmes. "All casualties, Mr. Moore. All casualties of an assault being waged upon them by the unfathomably merciless Engineer."

"Yeah, but you'll never be able to rid the country of burger joints and diet drinks!" bellowed Moore.

"Yes, Holmes," I offered, "just imagine what the size an opposing army made up of ranchers, slaughterhouse operators, major food conglomerates and all their employees would look like on the field of battle."

"Rather formidable, I should think. But I fear reintroducing the purloined culture, if we are successful in our endeavor, is none of our concern."

"What? I don't understand. Isn't that why you're here, Mr. Holmes?"

"If you will recall, Mr. Moore, I came to this country in an effort to uncover the identity of this thief and to locate your country's stolen property. That is all. I did not sign on to reintroduce the pilfered cultivation back into this society, once, and if, it is ever recovered."

"Yes, of course. You are right, Mr. Holmes. Forgive me for assuming—,"

"Holmes!" I scolded. "Would it positively strain you to—,"

"I do not intend to be unsympathetic, Watson," he quickly shot back. "But first and foremost, I intend to stick to the facts. The facts, gentlemen! The facts! And, as I have just stated, I am here to attempt to apprehend this fiend. And *that* is what I shall endeavor to do."

He paused to fill his pipe with his private herbal mixture from the small pouch in his inner breast pocket. As he did so, Moore and I quickly seized the opportunity to take a deliberate deep, and calming, breath.

"Gentlemen, I shall repeat," Holmes resumed. "It will no doubt be rather a daunting task to reinstate this country's original culture. However, Watson, that is not on our agenda." He looked at Moore. "You, sir, have my deepest of sympathies." Then, readdressing me, he continued. "With our conversation on the subject of casualties, I strive only to enlighten Mr. Moore as to the actual size of the task ahead of him and to the incomprehensible number of casualties he will need to attend to."

He turned again to Mr. Moore.

"Take, for instance families who know nothing of proper etiquette and find it perfectly acceptable to dine in their underwear."

"AHHHH!" Moore and I harmoniously shrieked.

"And let's not forget those casualties that, as a result of infection, incorrectly believe that music consists only of fifties, sixties and seventies rock and roll radio and compilation CDs available for purchase on infomercials. Or those under the mistaken impression that all you really need know about serious music can be found on CDs like *The Bride's Guide to Classical Music.*"

"OUCH!" I could feel my body screech as Holmes' words pounded it.

"Others," he continued, "are so gravely contaminated by this rancid virus that they actually listen to something referred to as *smooth jazz*, a so-called variation of that musical genre that has absolutely nothing whatsoever, believe it or not, to do with the great Ellington, Monk, Coltrane or Davis. Instead it is rather an eclectic blend of soft rock, love ballads by Luther Vandros and Streisand, overly sugary and extremely schmaltzy instrumental music by the likes of Kenny G, John Tesh, Yanni and George Winston. Then, added to this mishmash, in an attempt to give it a jazz-like substance, is instrumental music that is not jazz, but *fusion*, a rhythmic concoction of R&B and, what is referred to as 'pop', the result, an erroneously assumed notion of jazz. I like to refer to this smooth jazz sham as *Jazzak*. For surely it is nothing more than a 'jazzed-up', if you take my meaning, version of *Muzak*, more commonly known as elevator music."

He puffed on his pipe an instant.

"Imagine the poor misguided fans of this culturally offensive noise sipping glasses of makeshift wines like *Turning Leaf* and white Zinfandel and engaging in a rapturous conversation about the unimaginably sublime, shopping mall art of Thomas Kinkade, the Henry Ford of the art world himself, while Jazzak completes the mood by floating gently throughout the room."

"YUK!" my chorus partner and I agonizingly moaned.

"Grotesque, yes. Yet the examples do not end there. Imagine full grown, even mature, adults carrying on conversations in which the topics being discussed are not actual topics at all but mere gossip. Or, worse yet, pseudo conversations covering nothing but the latest fads, trends and empty, though touted as *"very cool"*, products."

Moore and I badly wanted to grimace at the thought, but Holmes' words were flowing like the mighty Colorado river in full force, allowing us no time to react to any one aspect of his rant.

"Some casualties, I am pained to inform you," Holmes flowed on, "invest themselves in what they actually think are serious discussions. Discussions, believe it or not, which are provoked by the latest sensationalized subjects, and events, delivered by talk shows, tabloid television, CRAP journalism and the latest empty product advertisements. All, mind you, very passionately argued and debated as if such things, like the break up of Roseanne and Tom Arnold, were immensely important and relevant to their own individual lives. Yet all of it, in reality, serving no true purpose, save one."

Taking the bait, I quickly asked, "Which is?"

"*Pseudo*, these rather loathsome conversations I speak of, amongst a myriad of other CRAP-steering ploys, act as a beacon, presenting a strong and very clear signal to the Engineer himself that his *mechanism* is functioning perfectly, achieving its objective, as planned, of 'dumbing down', if you will, the nation's populous."

Poor Mr. Moore, knocked slightly short of breath by the weight of Holmes' dissertation, barely managed to whisper,

"Ah, I think I am beginning to—."

"Yes, but Holmes, do we not have such awfully inept publications and television programming in England?" I challenged.

"Of course. Like periodic ant infestations that besiege our homes, no country is immune to such rubbish filtering in. The difference is here the mundane, the simple and the empty is revered. Here, it goes unquestioned as it amalgamates with the mainstream. Here, the ants are never combated. Domesticated actually. Thus, anything else, anything of greater substance is looked upon as élitist in nature and is actually frowned upon by the great mass as 'pretentious'."

"Surely you exaggerate?" I returned.

"Not at all. Take, for example, the very successful and long running American television sitcom *Cheers*."

"Oh, come on! Don't tell me there's something wrong with that show? I thought it was great," pleaded Moore.

"I much regret I must," countered Holmes. "For it was just the kind of empty product that successfully manages to devolve the viewer while simultaneously satisfying his or her thirst for entertainment."

"Holmes," I said, "perhaps you read too much into such programmes?"

"I sincerely wish I were unable to cite such obviously propagandized fabrics of American life. However, *Cheers* was a programme in which its so-called adult characters approached dating and relationships with the level of maturation and sophistication of a second year high school student. Then, if that were not crime enough, the programme's zenith was reached only by poking fun at anyone possessing even an inkling of an intellect. Anyone holding the slightest appreciation for classical music, art, opera, or science was made to appear an utter goof, one of society's misfits, an oddball. Hence, suggesting to the viewer that no one in their right mind could possibly enjoy an opera or something of a more cultivated nature."

Moore and I looked a one another. His expression, as I have no doubt mine had reciprocated, told me Holmes' contention had made an impact. For surely, when explained in such a detailed manner, Holmes' thesis, though poignant, was, as Holmes is fond of noting, *elementary* after all. Unfortunately, it sent my mind racing with all sorts of memories, most unpleasant memories. Images of CRAP-like things I had the misfortune to catch a glimpse of during previous trips to America. Things that were so horrifically part of the day-to-day of American life that my conscious mind had simply refused to acknowledge them. My defensive shield, I now realise, had, like a mother's instinct to protect her young, automatically flung itself over my brain in an effort to spare me great trauma. *Maniac Mansion, Two Brothers From Outer Space, Hardcopy, Oprah, News at Eleven,* all television programmes which were clearly, and insultingly, targeted toward the simple. *People, US, Entertainment Weekly* and *Sports Illustrated* magazines, sports bars, the Chevrolet *Camaro*, 'dually' pick-up trucks, vehicles with flames painted on them, Elvis, cape donned, giving a Karate demonstration whilst singing the song 'C.C. Rider'. UUUGH! The collage of these past images hustling through my mind nearly forced me into unconsciousness.

"These poor people," I said to myself.

"Yes, Watson," said Holmes, having heard the comment solely intended for my subconscious, "these, although we have scarcely scratched the surface, are the casualties I speak of. People who, as with chicken pox scars, clearly display evidence of Eloisyndrome."

"Ah, I see. The infected ninety-four percentile," realised Moore.

"Correct, Mr. Moore," praised Holmes.

Then, overtaken by a reflection that was all too visible in his eyes, Holmes paused. His voice fell to very nearly a whisper.

"A dear friend of mine, who had moved to the U.S. from Eastern Europe when still in his teen age years, shared with me his experience of that move, which I think, perfectly sums up the situation we are discussing."

We were all ears.

"This dear friend of mine, and his family, had their circumstances unexpectedly change, and moving to the U.S. became their only option," Holmes began. "Since America was without question the world's most prosperous nation, making the choice seemed a positive one. Naturally, knowing the U.S. to be *the* undisputed economic world power, my friend had expected to find a very advanced level of cultivation and intellect. Instead, what he found were teenagers of his own age who could not discuss current affairs, or any issue of social relevance or global importance. They spoke only of jobs at the local *Tastee Freeze*, who had been dating who, and the empty television programmes they had watched the preceding evening. This, he learned to his great dismay, was the extent of their entire universe. Thus, like H.G. Well's time traveler, what my friend found were the Eloi."

We all fell silent for a moment, as if standing over the grave of an old and beloved friend.

'Great minds speak of ideas. Average minds speak of events. Small minds discuss people.'

Eleanor Roosevelt's solemn quote paced back and forth through my mind as we mourned the circumstances.

"Rather a bleak picture, Holmes," I said to break the uncomfortable silence.

"Yes, my dear chap. It would appear so."

"Holy cow!" exclaimed Moore. "What do we do if we do manage to bring this villain to justice and get our culture back? How will we ever manage to reintroduce it?"

"I offer this analogy as a frame of reference. But, friend Moore, think not of just food as I present it."

Holmes' singular ability to captivate his audience was, once again, in full force. Moore and I sat riveted, eager to hear what he had to suggest.

"There is a great famine in this country," he said. "Its pitiful, starving inhabitants have had no substantial nourishment for quite some time. For generations, I dare say. Consequently, as you can now see, like any other famine plagued land, countless casualties abound."

He looked to me as he began to deliver his next statement.

"Now, Watson, being a man of medicine, you would not immediately reintroduce whole food to these victims of starvation? Would you?"

"Why, of course not, Holmes. To introduce whole food would, initially, do them more harm than good. It may even be fatal. I would begin by introducing broth, soups, intravenous saline and vitamin and mineral solutions."

"Exactly! And that is what must take place here, Mr. Moore. Once, and if, the culture has been recovered, it is imperative that the culture be reintegrated in the very same manner in which it was removed. Gradually, bit by ever so minute bit. For if you remember our earlier discussions, thanks to the Engineer's perverse genius, the victims of this outrage have no idea that anything has been stolen."

"How?" wondered Moore. "How on earth do you suggest we begin?"

"Well, let us return to Watson's image of a large, rather menacing army of fast food advocates. Taking the fight directly to them would be absolutely ludicrous. Therefore, in an attempt to rescue fast food casualties, it might be wiser to take the fight to them in an indirect manner. Begin, perhaps, by introducing warning signs and warning labels."

"Warning signs?" asked Moore. "You're joking, aren't you?"

"Not at all. Tobacco and alcohol products have labels on them, do they not? So, why not label fatty, sugary and chemically treated, or enhanced, foods in much the same manner?"

"But we already have very strict labeling guidelines in place, Mr. Holmes."

"You think?" Holmes patronizingly questioned.

"Of course!"

"Yes, well, you may believe so, sir. But I assure you, they are wholly inept."

"Holmes!" I shouted.

"No Watson, pray, allow me to present my argument. Imagine, Mr. Moore, warning signs, a sad necessity, posted in fast food restaurants. Would they not, ever so gently, pass on to the patron of such *cretinistic* establishments a few facts about what he intends to consume? Perhaps point out the extreme risk involved in partaking of such dangerous products as meat byproducts, for example? Would such signs not, at least, imply that he should first determine which end of the swimming pool our Mr. Patron is about to dive into?"

"Are you suggesting we enact laws and regulations which require the posting of signs in fast food restaurants that, like other dangerous vices, might read as:

Warning: Food products in this establishment have been linked to strokes, heart disease and cancer.

"Indeed, I am."

"Oh, come now, Holmes?" I cut in. "No one will ever buy into this."

"Is that not the point?"

"I don't think that's what Dr. Watson meant, sir," assisted Moore.

"I am very much aware of what the good doctor infers. But I ask you. Why is it you can have the Surgeon General's warning on one potentially lethal product and not another? No gentlemen, it will not do! It simply will not do!"

CHAPTER X

Wynnland

As Moore had promised, his people, with soldier like observance, were indeed at Meigs Field ready and willing to carry out whatever directive the celebrated detective should issue upon his arrival. And after a last second request by Holmes to exchange the plane Moore's personnel had readied for us for another, in the off chance that some of the Engineer's miscreants had somehow managed to tamper with it, we were airborne, bound for that mega-gambling-Mecca known as Las Vegas, or as referred to in some casual circles, *Vegas*. However, during all in-flight discussion, Holmes had been using a new and rather unique term in regards to that city. For despite the billions of dollars and expert craftsmanship he poured into the city, hotel mogul Steve Wynn, almost single handedly transformed the city into an appallingly tacky theme park for adults. Subsequently, Holmes felt obligated to contemptuously christen the city, *Wynnland*.

Like Walt Disney's Matahorn and castles, in that collection of *awfully* famous amusement parks of his, *Wynnland* is bursting at the seams with reproductions. A medieval castle, the Eiffel Tower, an eighteenth century pirate ship, Venice, New York, Paris, the Statue of Liberty, the great Pyramid and its very own Sphinx, albeit a rather disrespectful cartoon-like rendering. Added to the ensemble is a clone of the Coney Island Cyclone roller coaster, which proudly watches over the Hotel New York, while another sits superciliously perched high atop the Stratosphere Hotel and casino. If ever there was irrefutable proof that cultural devolution, like a serious case of wood rot, was occurring in the *"good 'ol US of A"*, Las Vegas just might be the *smoking gun*, as they say.

Unfortunately, or fortunately perhaps, I could not offer a judgment in the matter. For in all of my very long life, I had never had occasion, or the slightest desire, to visit Las Vegas. Admittedly, with its plethora of Elvis impersonators, themed wedding chapels and bargain-basement-all-you-can-eat-buffets, that metropolis of nimiety had created a picture in my mind that I found rather repulsive. However, as Holmes himself would attest, without a firsthand examination of the evidence, it would be impossible for one to formulate an accurate assessment. Though, in all honesty, with Monte Carlo lodged in my subconscious as the barometer, I fully expected to view the very physical incarnation of my mind's frightful image upon our arrival in Las Vegas.

RUUURK! THUD, KLANGTHUNK! The aircraft's landing gear announced itself, and our runway approach to Las Vegas' McCarren airport. Swooping in on our target, I caught a glimpse of the fêted city from above. I was struck dumbfound. Had there not been the great desert about that glittering oasis, I would have insisted we had veered off course and were actually about to descend upon either Anaheim, California or Orlando, Florida, the geographical locations of Disneyland and Disney World. I could not help but chuckle at the sight of it. Something about the Statue of Liberty, the great Pyramid, the Tour Eiffel and the Arc de Triomphe residing mere yards away from one another tickled me. I half expected to see an oversized Mickey Mouse walking down the boulevard and stopping to pose for photographs with visiting children. I'm glad I had not.

Lucky for him, Holmes had missed the establishing shot to our caper's Las Vegas chapter. After waking for but a brief moment or two during the flight, his body's need to recover unconditionally demanded a deep, dead to the world sleep. As his friend, I was extremely envious of this good fortune. For adrenalin, I sensed, had appropriated my system's blood and was flowing wildly though my dilated vessels. As his physician, on the other hand, I was very glad to see him replenishing his resolve. He would no doubt need it once we touched down. Round two, I was certain, was about to commence with a tremendous flurry of punches, once we touched down.

THUMP! THUD! THUMP! BUMP! THUD! KURBOOM! BANG!!! Suddenly, in an instant, all was complete chaos. The plane thrust into a violent nosedive. Panicked, Moore popped out of his seat like a jack-in-the-box.

"What the—," he tried to shout before being tossed across the cabin.

Holmes woke, and with a catlike reflex he sprang into action, yanking the cushions from the empty seats about us. Then, just as swiftly, he quickly sat one of the cushions on my lap and pushed the back of my head forward to bury my face in it. He then followed this with a pillow placed over my head.

"Hold that there and breathe," he instructed, which I knew meant make use of my experience with singular focus meditation.

I was about to comply, of course, but like a schoolboy, curiosity got the better of me and I couldn't resist cautiously sneaking a peek at how he was taking charge of the situation.

Holmes took a quick check of Moore, who had been rendered unconscious by the chaos. As he did so, the craft wobbled, bumped, then dropped several feet. Yet Holmes managed to stay erect and lift ally Moore into a seat and strap him in. He then dove into his own seat and assumed the crash-ready position he had rushed me into, when SWOOSH! The aircraft jumped upward. This was followed by a very loud, KURPLUP! Then an elongated EEEEEEK, which was followed by a dull, very heavy sounding KATHUNK-A-FUUUUW! After which, the mechanical bird recovered sufficiently enough to steady out and touch ground with an unexpected, and miraculous, absence of injury to passengers and craft.

The lone steward on the private flight, frozen by shock, was not a flight attendant by trade but was one of Mr. Moore's key people. Both he and Moore, men more than a century younger than Holmes and I, were completely disabled by the ordeal. So, as the small jet rolled its way to a stop, I triaged the two trauma victims, while Holmes charged into the cockpit. Moore was out cold, rendered so by a rather nasty blow to the back of his head. No doubt the result of striking the arm of a seat during the tumult. We would need to get him to hospital *tout-suite*. As for the other young man, my ever-at-the-ready smelling salts had, as the mid-summer Nevada sun would have most assuredly defrosted *Frosty*, that famous American snowman, had he been in the vicinity, quickly thawed the glaciated man out.

"Watson!" hollered Holmes from inside the cockpit. "Quickly!"

Blasting into the cockpit, I was horror-struck to discover Holmes examining the pilot and copilot. Both airmen were slumped lifeless, the pilot in his seat, the copilot on the floor. Vomit, some blood and what looked like coffee was strewn everywhere. The air crewmen's shirts, jackets, the controls, the windscreen, the floor, it was absolutely everywhere. Never in all my days had I encountered such a vast amount of regurgitation. Never!

"What on earth?"

"They've been poisoned, Watson. Help me get them to their feet," Holmes ordered. "We must bring them round before we lose them."

With that we sprang into action. Holmes hoisting the pilot and I the mate. Both men were barely conscious and barely breathing as Holmes and I walked them out, making for the aircraft's main door. Through the plane's porthole-like windows, we could see and hear sirens atop a score of ambulances, fire trucks and airport police cars, screaming towards us. Holmes ordered Moore's man to crank open the craft's door. In an instant it was done, allowing an army of fire and emergency personnel to reach us.

As we handed over our two pilots to paramedics, Holmes dashed back into the cockpit for an instant, returning with a common variety aluminum thermos and handed it as well to our rescuers.

"Gentlemen, you will find that a rather clumsy attempt to poison our pilots has taken place," said Holmes, as he sniffed the silver colored vessel. "A mere dash of vanilla in this coffee is not sufficient to hide that signature almond scent."

"Cyanide?" I cried out in surprise.

"Cyanide?" echoed the large, thick mustached uniformed policeman charging into the plane. "Did you say cyanide?"

"You heard correctly, officer," replied Holmes.

"And who might you be, sir?"

"I am Sherlock Holmes and this is my associate and colleague Dr. Watson."

"You must be joking?"

"Why must that be?"

"C'mon, we're talking over a hundred—"

Holmes has little patience for such ignoramuses, especially those sworn to protect and *stumble*, as he condescendingly prefers to put it.

"Nevertheless," he insisted. Then pointing to Moore, Holmes authoritatively, as was his nature, addressed the medical personnel on the scene, "Our astute colleague here, whom I might add is a counsel to the president of the United States, Mr. Moore, has received a rather nasty blow to the back of his head and I would appreciate it if you and your people would see that he and our supremely skilled flight crew are rushed to hospital and given the very best of attention."

"Now just a cotton pickin' minute!" snarled the sheriff.

Just in the nick of time, Moore's man, who had sufficiently recovered by then, interceded by flashing a credential and whispering a few choice words into our esteemed lawman's egotistical ear, causing the rather unpolished flatfoot's face to immediately go blank and Greenland-like pale with discovery and disbelief.

"It's a great honor to meet you, Mr. Holmes, sir," the officer groveled. "And you, too, Dr. Watson. A real honor! Officer Peele, at your service, gentlemen," he announced in a pathetically wheedling tone. "Now, please, Mr. Holmes, you were saying something about the coffee in the crew's thermos containing cyanide?"

"Again, you are correct. That *is* what I had stated," Holmes contemptuously answered.

Holmes then led the constable and me into the cockpit.

"As you can clearly see, the attack was two pronged in nature. A poison laden thermos of coffee and the obvious sabotage of the craft's landing gear hydraulics—"

"Obvious? Forgive me Mr. Holmes, but the plane's gear is down, sir. And it appeared to function perfectly upon landing, Mr. Holmes," Peele quickly challenged, before popping out of the small cabin for a quick breath.

The cabin reeked of an unusually foul smelling vomit. It took every bit of my concentration to attempt to ignore it while we listened to Holmes. Officer Peele, on the other hand, gave away his inexperience as he immediately began to turn green with nausea, an act any hardened police veteran would surely have been well beyond. I handed him my handkerchief and took hold of his arm to steady him. That display of delicacy, and the inobservance his challenge exposed, stiffened Holmes' face, revealing his immediate bête-noir of the man.

"Pray, allow me to present you with an account as to what has taken place here," pleaded Holmes, with such disdain in his pitch I felt certain officer Peele would lunge for the proudly arrogant sleuth's throat. He did not. He simply gestured, happily, for Holmes to continue, an act that informed me that the vast majority of things had a tendency to sail high over the man's thick head, a realization which caused every microgram of that default tolerance one keeps in reserve for just such people to dissipate completely from me.

"It began, obviously, with the poisoning of the coffee," resumed Holmes. "I am certain that both men had noticed the peculiar aroma emanating from their routine beverage of choice, but paid little attention to it at first, attributing it simply to an imperfect brewing, and kept sipping away throughout the flight. But soon, after each cup delivered dose after dose, the affects of the toxic agent began to tear away at their very fabric. First, a slight headache, one that gradually intensified as the flight progressed. It was soon followed by a mild nausea, which, like the headache, transformed into the most horrific, unimaginable, gut wrenching of pains. Correct so far, Watson?"

"Yes," I eagerly answered. "That is exactly what one would expect of cyanide administered in such a manner."

"Suddenly, the men are on the verge of losing consciousness," continued Holmes. "But our men are clever. One may be ill, but not both, they quite correctly reason. And it is in that very millisecond that they call to mind the slightly odd scent their coffee had to it. Immediately, both pilot and copilot have the presence of mind to ram their fingers down their throats and induce vomiting, something their systems had greatly desired but were unable to accomplish on their own."

"Yes, but what about your claim that the landing gear, had malfunctioned? I see no evidence pointing to its failure, sir?" Peele mumbled through the handkerchief covering his impatient mouth.

"It sounded as if the airplane was coming apart at the very seams," I defensively blurted out, highly annoyed by Peele's boorishly disbelieving tenor.

"Is that so, Mr. Holmes?"

"As I had stated, officer Peele," said Holmes with a firm and obvious condescending inflection which announced itself as more a rebuke for Peele's inept short-term memory function, rather than Holmes' segue into the continuation of his observations. "This, I repeat, was a two pronged attack. The second assault launched upon this craft was aimed upon its landing gear, which our courageous copilot, despite battling cyanide poisoning, fortunately for us, managed to manually lower and lock into position before losing consciousness."

"And how, might I ask, have you put this little melodrama together so—," Peele attempted to ask.

"You forget to whom you are speaking," I lashed out before Holmes waved me off.

"Elementary, Officer Pele. It was quite elementary."

"Excuse me, Mr. Holmes," Moore's man interloped. "I'm going

to ride along to hospital with Mr. Moore and the pilots. Can you and Dr. Watson get to the hotel on your own, sir?"

"What is your name, young man?" asked Holmes.

"Driscoll, agent Aaron Driscoll, sir."

"Well, Mr. Driscoll, we can and will be most happy to take care of our ground transport. Please, give our best to Moore and his exceptional airmen. We are deeply indebted to them."

"Yes, sir. I will. By the way, where—,"

"Do not worry yourself, young man. Watson and I shall ring the hospital later to inform you of our whereabouts."

"Thank you, sir."

After a quick shake of hands, Driscoll shot out of the craft and dove into an ambulance just as it raced off for the local trauma center.

"Now, Officer Peele," Holmes scolded, "I am afraid you have earned a failing mark in this instance. For this little melodrama, as you have so termed it, is actually quite simple to reconstruct. As you can see, the copilot's seatbelt has been neither ripped from its fastening nor cut, thus proving the man in the seat had removed himself from it voluntarily, while the pilot remained fastened, and at the controls. Moreover, as you will observe, the controls to manually operate the landing gear are over here."

He pointed to an area low to the floor where the first mate had been lying.

"Precisely where the second man was found," Holmes confidently announced. "And that, my good man, is why the landing gear appeared, from afar, to function properly. But all this you will discover for yourself, once you and your people conclude your examinations. Now, if you will excuse us, Dr. Watson and I must be off. Our business elsewhere is most urgent."

"Now wait just one—!" the obtuse constable attempted to rage.

"If you wish anything further from us, you may contact us at our hotel. As you might imagine, we are rather spent from our ordeal," Holmes barked back, as he led us off the aircraft.

"And which one would that be?" demanded Peele.

"One what? Ordeal or hotel?" Holmes snidely asked, knowing full well the fumbler was referring to the hotel we were en route to.

"We are booked into the Caesar's Palace," I curtly broke in.

And with that, we were off the small jet and charging our way past a pack of medical personnel that was urging us to allow them to examine our conditions. However, all that occupied our minds at that moment was blasting through the terminal and hailing a taxi. A long, hot bath, I must admit, had also entered my head as we hurtled forth.

Spurred on by the desire to put the latest incident behind us, Holmes and I made short work of the walk to the taxi queue on the street, where we wasted no time in procuring one and instructing the driver to hastily deliver us at the Venetian hotel.

"It is no wonder crime is out of control in this, *the* most advanced of countries on the globe," raved a disgusted Holmes, as the taxi hurried us away. "Dense, myopic peace officers like Peele are a dark, unremovable coffee stain upon law enforcement— Ugh! I cannot verbally express just how infuriating I find such a circumstance."

"This must surely be a first?" I sarcastically quipped, knowing full well Holmes' career-long contempt for inept police personnel.

"Ah, but if you only knew," answered Holmes, with a surprisingly dejected demeanor, "how frequently I have been rendered speechless by the incompetence of my fellow investigators over the last one and one quarter century or so. Their inability to solve the most open and shut of cases from the Ripper Murders to that O.J. Simpson fiasco, has pained me greatly. Particularly disappointing has been the last fifth of the twentieth century. For with all science has recently delivered to investigators, high speed computer processors and colossal advancements in forensics, with DNA capabilities atop the list, officials continue to stumble their way through the most routine of investigations, a criminal act in itself."

Like that belonging to our eavesdropping driver's, my mouth dropped open upon hearing Holmes state, in such a matter-of-fact manner, he viewed some of the most highly profiled and infamous investigations as routine.

"Holmes!" I involuntarily blurted. "Are you saying—"

"I have said too much already."

"In all these years, I have never heard you imply possession of a resolution to such notorious cases."

"It has been a private anguish of mine, I must admit. Considering my efforts to aid such investigations over the course of time," Holmes disconsolately replied.

"Aid those investigations?" I managed to rhetorically ask before my lower jaw fell open from the shock of the news.

I had long known Holmes had been responsible for the vast majority of those so-called *anonymous* tips to police investigators around the world. From simple notes posted from out of the way origins, to internet cafés, to a bit of computer software which redirects and scrambles the sender's identity and location for a genuinely anonymous email message, Holmes was forever offering anonymous contributions to his fellow investigators. But this was the first time he had ever acknowledged having the slightest involvement in the investigations of great legend.

"Why on earth had you not come forward if you had been able to put an end to the anguish and the speculation associated with the Ripper case?" I asked.

"Why do you assume I had not gone forward?"

"What?"

"Whom do you think introduced Chief Inspector Littlechild to Francis Tumblety?"

"Who?"

"Exactly!"

"No. I'm afraid you've lost me somewhat," I returned. "Who, or what, is Tumblety?"

"Dr. Tumblety, as he liked to refer himself."

"Are you saying—"

"Let's just say that, like traveling through New York's Holland tunnel, my contribution found clear passage through the ears of an overly prideful London constabulary."

"Holmes, you never cease to—,"

"Now you understand my frustration."

"Of course!—And that Simpson case, as well?"

"Oh, please! A ridiculously simple case I'd like never to hear of again. But, enough of this for now," he said, steering his eyes in the direction of our all-ears cabby. "We've the present to tackle."

Like the driver's instructions to take us to the Venetian hotel, when Moore had already engaged rooms for us at the Caesar's Palace, this latest revelation was a very curious thing.

"What next?" I silently wondered. But I needn't have bothered. Knowing Holmes' crystal ball-like ability to see straight through a riddle, I should have expected it. I should also have anticipated Holmes's next step. I'd like to think I would have, had I not been so dumbstruck by the news that he has silently held such mind boggling, history-altering information in his head for all this time. It was unfathomable.

"Pay the man, Watson," Holmes commanded as he popped out of our taxi and strode hastily into the hotel Venetian, which I was surprised to learn we had stopped in front of.

It was clear to me that fatigue and the strain of the caper was now getting the better of me. A meal, a bath and a good long sleep, in that order, followed by a deep focus yogic workout was what I was prescribing for myself. Concluding this, I paid the driver and limped out of his transport and ambled into the hotel.

I was awe struck. The great lobby was every bit as grandly palatial as anything I had seen in Venice, or the entire European continent, for that matter. I simply could not believe my eyes and had to literally shake my head to comprehend what was before them. Crystal chandeliers, frescos, renaissance urns, ornate sconces, paintings straight out of the Italian School, Venetian glass and ceramic vases, eighteenth century writing tables and chairs, tapestries and antique settees, chairs and loveseats, all upholstered in fabrics fit for royalty. It was simply breathtaking. I had not, particularly if you consider our mission, expected to stumble upon such cultivated opulence in America. It perplexed me.

"Yes, my friend," spoke a familiar voice from behind me, "it is quite an impressive first glimpse, is it not?"

I could not muster a single syllable, stricken by the sights before me.

"The key word, Watson, is 'glimpse'."

"Pardon?"

"It provides only a glimpse of cultivation. Mind you, only a glimpse."

A passing porter noticed my befuddlement and inquires as to whether we require any assistance.

"His inaugural visit to Las Vegas," Holmes replies, with a nod of his head towards me. "This way, Watson," he announces, steering me through the lush lobby and onto the streets of a faux Venice.

I could feel my mouth drop wide open at the sight before my eyes. Not a single soul could ever challenge the effort put forth in this amazing recreation. Herculean, no doubt. Yet, though I could not quite put my finger on it, it reminded me of something that had immediately made me feel as if I had been shopping at a "five and dime", eaten Christmas dinner at one of the Denny's restaurants that are so abundant in America, or had been reared in a caravan in some lost-to-the-world backwater by powder-blue-polyester-suit-clad-parents whose combined IQs totaled 90.

"Your mind races, no doubt," said Holmes, as he knocked on one of the stone façades, which returned an echo from within its hollow center. "Reminds one of what Disney might have created at that amusement park of his, if you are familiar with it?" observed Holmes.

"That's it!" I cried out, as an analogy suddenly sprang to my now very weary mind. "No, not *Walt Disney*, but Thomas Kinkade! It looks as if this is a Thomas Kinkade version of Venice."

"Ghastly!" said Holmes as he nodded concurrence.

"Ghastly!" I agreed.

"Well, since we are here, what say we make the best of it and dine in Piazza San Marco?" suggested Holmes, with a slight chuckle. "I hear the food is actually quite authentic."

An instant later, under a blue-sky-painted ceiling, we were strolling our way through the great ersatz, complete with Moorish influenced architecture, gondolas, singing gondoliers and canal, albeit a horrid, unrealistically clear, coin-covered-bottom toy of a waterway. Rounding a corner and crossing a *piccolo* bridge, we arrived at Piazza San Marco. Like the original, save for a multitude of pigeons and the famed Basilica di San Marco, the square was filled with a surfeit of sightseers and a gang of highly animated street entertainers. It appeared a huge explosion of mirth. Amongst it all sat a café, safely behind a black wrought iron rail, which surrounded all the eateries in the vicinity. Holmes and I were seated at a table, which had a bird's eye view of the merry entertainment out in the square. The highly skilled singers, dancers and musicians were magnetic and served to revive my much depleted energy and spirit.

"Where are we to spend the night, Holmes? I would dearly love to bathe and lose myself in several hours of some much needed sleep," I asked.

"Do you not think we are here?" Holmes devilishly answered.

"Well, since I know you are fully aware we had been booked into another hotel, yet chose to instruct the taxi driver to make for a different hotel, yet did not register once here, I can only assume that we shall not be lodging at this hotel either. This is merely another exercise in buying time to strategize further," I rejoined.

"Very good, Watson. Very good, indeed."

"Elementary," I quipped.

"Signore," Holmes called to a passing server. "Might we have a bottle of sparkling mineral water?"

With a simple nod of the head, the man promised to quickly return with our desperately needed refreshment.

"But seriously, Holmes," I said, "after that business with the airplane, surely these people must have eyes in all four sides of their heads. Will simply moving from one hotel to another do the trick?"

"We have not much in the way of options, do we?"

"I suppose not."

"Then I suggest we replenish our tanks in this moderately cheerful bistro and continue to do our best to keep these swine on their toes, afterwards."

Thankfully, our liquid revival arrived just then. I dove for it and poured a glass for Holmes and another for myself, while Holmes order an *insalata mista* and a plate of *alio e olio* for each of us. Then to aid in our recovery, a fiddle player launched into a performance of Vivaldi's 'Summer' movement from his most singularly famous, *Le Quattro Stagioni*. Though the piece is somewhat sugary, and well overplayed these days, a masterwork, in the hands of a skillful musician, was a Godsend in that *place de faux*. Yet, while Holmes and I dined on what was a genuinely authentic and exceptional Italian meal, I was slightly bothered by the sight of a very odd character I kept noticing amidst the group of street entertainers. I had not sought him out each time I glanced out at the performers, yet there he was, in my line of sight each and every time, looking out of place by simply pacing about and not giving his all to the performance, as were the other thespians, of which group I deduced he must belong for he carried no instrument. Holmes, with the appetite of a Tour de France cyclist, focused his singular attention on the plate of food before him and paid little mind to anything else.

"Holmes," I started, "could we be in that proverbial fish bowl at present?"

"But of course," he replied.

"Should we not—", I began, but stopped the instant I could no longer find that odd-man-out in the street theater.

"I should think there is not much they would attempt in such a public place. The Engineer is far too clever to risk such—,"

"THAT'S MY TABLE YOU'RE SITTING IN!" charged the gruff, husky voice of that mysterious thespian as he caught Holmes, and myself, off guard with a surprise verbal assault.

He was dark and swarthy and spoke with such an acute anger, it seemed almost contrived, as if it were deliberately induced to complete the character of a villain, another role the actor was merely playing out.

"Would you be addressing me, young man?" Holmes sternly asked.

"Nobody, but nobody sits at my table, and in my seat. Nobody!" he insisted.

"Surely you must be mistaken, sir," replied Holmes.

"I don't mistake anything! Now get the hell out of my spot! NOW!" demanded the bully.

"Forgive me, sir," I rallied, "but this a public café, not a residence. Surely you must—,"

"Must nothing! Now get the hell out of my spot or—,"

"What say we call over the proprietor of this fine establishment," said Holmes as he waved over our server.

I took advantage of the slight diversion to reach for my revolver. To my horror, it wasn't in my jacket pocket. Blast! I had left the blasted thing with my luggage, which was still back on our wounded air transport.

"Doesn't matter what he says, Shakespeare," yelled the brute. "I say get out!" the rough commanded. "Get out!"

Holmes turned to readdress the oaf, but in that split second, the large man had taken a firm hold of the lapels on Holmes' jacket and viciously yanked the heralded sleuth right out of his seat and all the way over the wrought iron rail and out into the piazza.

The café and absolutely every living thing in the square was horrorstruck by the assault upon Holmes' person. Not knowing what else to do, I scooped up the bread knife from our table and poised myself, ready to throw it into the attacker's chest. But just then he delivered a thundering backhand across Holmes' jaw, sending my great friend crashing into the rail and into my line of strike. Myself, and the square's population, held our breath as the elderly gent slowly hoisted himself to his feet with the use of the rail. Then, to our great surprise, Holmes, then on his feet, turned, faced the hooligan, then assumed a boxer's stance.

"You sir, are no gentleman," said Holmes to his foe. "Watson," he said, acknowledging my position behind him, "once again, it would appear, I must deliver a lesson in proper gentlemanly combat."

He then readied himself and readdressed his opponent.

"A gentleman, sir, never strikes with the back of the hand!"

The blackguard howled out a disbelieving guffaw, then snarled at Holmes, much like a World Wrestling Federation brawler might. A second later, he was fuming as that lighting-speed left jab of Holmes' landed on his already disfigured and extremely ugly nose.

"YEAH!" screamed the large witnessing crowd and I, at the sight of the elderly gent's defiance and obvious skill.

"A gentleman, sir, stands erect and leads off with the jab," informed Holmes.

POW, said another jab as it made a quick and surprise forceful landing. POW! POW! Followed two more.

"URRRRRGGG!" growled the now seething oaf. "I'll kill you!" said he, as he swung at Holmes.

A mighty swing for certain, one which would have positively flatten anyone, had it landed. But Holmes, demonstrating a master's ability to bob and weave, ducked as the sweeping strike attempt came his way.

"The jab, my good man, the jab," Holmes continued to lecture. "Never commence with a mighty right, you give away your hand. No, no, no. Measure your opponent with the JAB!" he said, as he delivered the subject of his point. POW, screamed yet another.

Holmes' would be attacker was now beside himself with a raging anger, the worst possible state any warrior could ever fall into. He swung and swung away at Holmes, to no avail, and suffered the consequences each time he lunged forth. For Holmes, with his brilliantly swift footwork, easily dodged every pathetic and increasingly desperate attempt the bigger and much younger man made to thwart the Holmes revolt, and easily countered with either a very stiff jab or a devastating right hand to the body. Soon, it was obvious, the vandal's conscious mind was tapioca.

"And that, I'm afraid," announced Holmes, as his wobbly victim did his best to remain defiantly afoot before the great master, himself, "must be the end of the lesson. However, in closing, I would very much like to reiterate, that a gentleman never uses the back of the hand. And, he always saves his mightiest of right hands for closing out the bout."

SNAP, went the large man's jaw as Holmes demonstrated his final point. BAM! It sent the villain crashing into the same wrought iron rail, where I, ready and waiting with the bread knife, took a firm hold of the ruffian's head and placed the blade firmly upon his throbbing throat.

A thunderous applause drowned out any communication between Holmes and I. It was followed by the arrival of two armed security guards who had struggled to squeeze through the thrilled crowd of spectators. Gladly, I released my stronghold over the oaf to allow the resident authorities to take possession of the fiend. To compensate for the inability to hear over the deafening roar of appreciation, for his part, Holmes whispered a quick word into the ear of one of the constables, who acknowledged him with a very overeager nod, then he and his comrade proudly carted off the perpetrator.

Holmes, mockingly, though that aspect of his action soared high over the heads of his sudden audience, bowed to the crowd, then hoisted himself over the rail, which gave yet another thrill to the already feverish crowd. Then, before retaking his seat at our table, he bowed once again. It induced an A-bomb of appreciation. Ironically, the exuberant crowd had no idea just how deserved their applause actually was. Holmes, a man over one and one half centuries old, had thrashed about a man more than a full centenary younger than himself. For the visiting throng it was simply a superb surprise act the hotel had organized to heighten their holiday experience. After all, this was Wynnland. Reality not required.

CHAPTER XI

The Scent

Returning to our surprisingly authentic Italian meal was an utterly ridiculous notion to entertain. After his encounter with the ruffian, Holmes was besieged by an onslaught of appreciative hotel patrons, who were now queuing up by the score to congratulate him, shake his hand and pose for pictures with him, as if Holmes had been billed the theme park's main attraction, or worse, its mascot.

"Damn, you were great out there," exalted one pleasantly pudgy, forty-five year old man dressed in a pup-tent of a T-shirt, a pair of overly loose and lengthy putty coloured safari styled walking shorts, black socks with matching black running shoes and one of those horrid, ever-at-the-ready pouch gadgets strapped around his waist, who stood at the head of the queue.

"You're far too kind, sir," Holmes disingenuously returned.

"Your getup is so fantastic. I really thought you were some helpless old fart at first."

"How good of you to notice," Holmes sarcastically, yet subtly, retorted.

"Yes, really incredible show!" commented the man's equally stylish and stout wife.

"Thank you. Thank you one and all," Holmes rather insincerely said to his new group of fans in the queue. "But I'm afraid my associate and I have another engagement elsewhere, which forces us to take our leave. So again, I thank you. Hopefully we shall see you another time."

A blasting combination of applause and cheers struck the piazza, as Holmes and I did as he had announced and vacated the café, then forged a path through the runaway glee. Back through the counterfeit city streets, up the bridge and over the disappointingly pale canal, all the while being inundated with congratulatory pats on the back and shoulders, smiles and the obligatory "great show". It was all rather embarrassing, I must say. Yet, just as relief in the form of the hotel foyer revealed itself to us, agent Driscoll popped out from within the heavily populated lobby and ushered us into a small room just past the concierge station. Inside, waited our obliging security men, our semi-conscious hooligan, seated in and handcuffed to a heavy iron chair, and, to our great displeasure, officer Peale.

Considering the grand attempt at opulence the hotel appeared committed to, this room was the epitome of drab. With its flat, magnolia coloured walls, along with the absence of any décor or furnishings, it was a surprisingly stereotypical interrogation room.

"How do, Mr. Holmes?" asked the reliably obtuse Peale. "Hear you managed to survive yet another peculiar mishap, eh?"

Not surprisingly, Holmes was reluctant to reply.

"Thank you, your concern is very much appreciated," I quickly interceded.

Holmes remained silent and let his eye contact with agent Driscoll do his speaking for him.

"Mr. Holmes," he began, "officer Peale and I—,"

"Were wondering if you would be so kind as to explain just what the hell is going on here!" demanded the dense constable, who had rudely interposed Mr. Driscoll in mid-sentence. "Ya got poisoned coffee, tampered with landing gear hydraulics, a government official in the hospital, and now," he said, pointing to the dazed ruffian confined to the lone iron chair in the room, "ya got this idiot tryin' ta take your damn head off? In the Venetian Hotel, of all places? Now, since this boy Driscoll here's been left in the dark and is of no use to me, I'm telling you, I want some answers. And I want them pronto! Government business or not, this is my jurisdiction! And you *will* give me some answers."

"You are right, sir," spoke Holmes. "After all, as you say, this is your jurisdiction."

"Damn, straight! Now, who the hell is this scumbag who tried to clean your clock in the hotel, here?" demanded Peale as he took hold a firm hold of the attacker's ear, much like an angry mother might when her child has behaved unruly.

"My clock, sir?" replied Holmes with a feign naiveté.

"You know, smash your head in."

"I have no idea, sir," replied Holmes.

"You expect me to believe that a man you don't know, never saw before, for some reason or other, wants you dead?"

"I could not have summed it up more accurately myself."

He quickly looked to me.

"Could you have, Watson?" he cheekily added.

"Why no, Holmes," I answered.

"Now look Mr. Holmes, I want a name!" insisted Peale.

"Perhaps you should ask him."

"You know, believe it or not, we did actually think of that on our own," Peale snidely remarked.

"What is your name, sir?" Holmes asked of the brute.

Nothing.

"And he is carrying no I.D.," Peale gruffly added.

"Did you honestly expect him to?"

"Everyone carries a wallet!"

"And if you find no such wallet or identification?"

"Now look here—,"

"Would you carry identification on such a dastardly errand?" Holmes offered, before readdressing the offender. "Now sir, I am certain you would find it an extremely safe haven to remain in this devoted constable's custody. Having failed in your attempt to injure my person, I am confident your employer will not be as hospitable as earlier in your relationship with him. Therefore, I submit to you, provide these officers here with the information they need, or I shall not press charges and see to it that you are released immediately."

"What the—" Peale sounded off.

"I can and I shall!" Holmes curtly retaliated.

"No! No! Okay! I'll tell you what I know," pleaded the hood. "I don't know much. But I'll tell you anything you want to know."

"There you have it, officer Peale," said Holmes.

The official glared at Holmes, then turned his limited attention to the man in custody.

"What's your name, damn it?"

"Hugo Bean, sir."

"What?"

"Hugo Bean."

"I heard, I heard. What the hell kind of name is Hugo Bean?"

"A stage name I should think," offered Holmes. "A rather poor one, but a stage name nonetheless."

That opened the way for Peale, who took to the interrogation process with a swelled chest and an ambush of questions set upon his captive. Holmes stepped back and very quietly spoke into Driscoll's ear. The man nodded and proceeded to follow suit by whispering into Peale's ear.

"What the hell has that got to do with anything?" shouted Peale.

Driscoll repeated his action.

"Well, all right, then," said a reluctant Peale. He then looked his captive squarely in the eye. "What's the name of your theatrical agent?"

"Sid Mellonowski," came the eagerly cooperative answer.

"There, happy now?" a frustrated Peale rhetorically asked of Driscoll and Holmes.

As our American governmental comrade replied with a slight nod, Holmes looked on with an air of indifference to the goings on. Yet, though he was wearing his poker face, Holmes' eyes had that familiar sparkle a hunter gets when he's got the scent of approaching game. Peale, on the other hand, still held the question, and answer, to be irrelevant to the matter at hand. So, like a Great White in the midst of a feeding frenzy, he focused his attention on browbeating his man. As he did so, Holmes gave a subtle hand signal to Driscoll, and while back stepping, pulled me quietly through the door with him.

Returning to the foyer, Holmes wasted no time leading me straight into the vast swarm of fun seekers for camouflage and swiftly through the hotel's grand main entryway. Once outside, I found it rather daunting to actually realise myself standing on Las Vegas Boulevard, that famed concourse of exuberance. But there was not time to marvel, or stand aghast.

"Come Watson," insisted Holmes. "Despite our Mr. Driscoll's aid, even Peale is bound to have noticed our absence by now."

"Where to?" I asked as I matched his stride.

"To our hotel, of course."

"But Holmes, why on earth should you not have wished to question that villain further?"

"I have what I want," answered Holmes.

"WHAT?"

"Yes, my good friend. It would appear our opponent has failed to keep his arm up."

"Pardon?"

"Let us just say I have spied an opening which may afford me the opportunity of landing a solid jab of my own."

"STOP!" I pleaded.

But the wind was clearly behind him. It would be easier to halt a speeding catamaran. Once Holmes was on the scent, all one could attempt to do was to keep pace.

"Fancy a refreshment or a well deserved libation on the way to our hotel, old friend?"

"What is this opening you spoke of?" I asked.

"Just look at this city!" he exclaimed. "Have you ever seen such a spectacle in all your days?"

"No!" I said with a great frustration.

"I should say not."

Then, inexplicably, I froze in my tracks while Holmes strode onward. I tried to move, but I could not. I tried to call out to the swift sleuth, but I was powerless to take control of that function either. Though I was thoroughly exhausted from the events of the day, I felt well. My vitals appeared normal. My pulse, as best I could tell, sustained a regular, moderate rate. Still, I could neither move nor speak. Peculiar it was. For other than with Holmes' usual aloofness, I was not consciously upset or outraged by any one thing in particular. Yet my physical symptoms appeared a textbook state of complete and overwhelming shock. Fortunately, Holmes had quickly noticed my absence and, equally as quickly, had grasped the whole of the situation and hurried to my side.

"I'm so sorry to have had neglected to warn you, my friend, about *Wynnitis*, as I like to refer to it," said he. "I myself had to battle my way through it on my initial visit to this city."

He read the perplexity in my eyes.

"No, no, do not try to speak. It shall pass."

Despite his valiant attempt at a bedside manner, a sense of panic began to power over me, my thoughts running away with themselves, led by the humiliating notion that I, a doctor, was not acquainted with this emotional condition.

"You will find it best to squint so that you may slightly blur your vision," explained Holmes. "Like a soldier who sees a dead body ravaged by war for the very first time, what you are experiencing is the normal cultivated person's reaction to the *images des faux* you see before you."

Though his diagnosis had registered with me, I still could not move a muscle. Try as I might, I was frustratingly incapable of movement.

"Deep breath," Holmes instructed. "Slow, deep breath."

Slowly, as I complied, I could once again feel my life force flowing through me. Stronger and stronger it raged.

"I apologize for forgetting to share my method for a gentle adaptation to this, shall we say, unique, city in advance of our visit, Watson," said Holmes. "Often, on one's initial visit, the subconscious mind simply cannot cope with what it is trying to comprehend. And who should fault it. With a stunted Eiffel Tower, the Arc de Triomphe a mere feet from downtown Venice and the

Sphinx and the Great Pyramid in the background, the mind can lose its perspective all too easily."

Regaining myself completely, I resumed our initial pace, remaining committed to Holmes' prescribed remedy of squinting to blur my vision ever so slightly.

"Where to?" I asked with a renewed determination.

"My plan is this," said Holmes as he rejoined me in our forthright promenade down *'the strip'*, as I understand the city's main street to have been lovingly baptized, "firstly, we shall make ourselves as visible as possible this evening, to placate any concerns both friend and foe may have about our whereabouts. Starting with a bit of a stroll down this most public of thoroughfares."

"Assume the role of goldfish?" I asked. "How will that further our cause if we have no room to operate?"

"Taking our cue from Las Vegas itself, you, my good friend, and I shall make spectacles of ourselves. And, like this *ville de spectacle*, behind the facade shall exist another story."

I was all ears as Holmes laid out the details of his strategy while we continued southward, en route to the Bellagio Hotel and Casino. I was pleased, and most eager, to explore Mr. Wynn's desert palace, for I had been informed it housed a most impressive art gallery. Yet as we approached that grand establishment, I was struck dumbfound, despite my vaccination, by a close look at the nearby Paris hotel.

With its diminutive Tour Eiffel and Arc de Triomphe, standing before me, I could not help but recall Holmes' remark about this city offering only a glimpse of cultivation. For from afar, those two recreated French monuments appeared quite realistic. Yet, from an intimate vantage point, the attention to detail, one could clearly see, was absent, particularly on the Arc. The carved figures and ornamentation on this homage to the genuine article, appeared featureless, plain and shockingly flat, ghost-like. In an attempt to be absolutely certain I had not simply distorted my view by applying Holmes' blurring technique, I decided to temporarily forego my coping remedy. It was a great mistake. For I was further stunned to discover the monument's condition was even worse than I had initially observed. Thus, as you can imagine, I quickly reaffixed my visual shield and joined Holmes in a dart across the grand boulevard to put his clever scheme into action.

Arriving at the strikingly lavish Bellagio's front desk, Holmes announced our change of plan to all concerned by priggishly requesting two of the hotel's best suites. Then, just as sanctimoniously, he instructed the hotel staff to retrieve our luggage from the Caesar's Palace, from where it was to have been initially delivered. This was followed with yet another announcement. We were to take in the hotel's famous art gallery while we waited the arrival of our baggage, dreadful news to me, since fatigue had taken a very firm hold upon nearly all of my *chakras* by then and I had been counting the seconds till I had the opportunity to sleep, meditate and devour a plate of *Tofta*, which is an absolutely splendid, and energizing, blending of rice, tomatoes and herb marinated tofu, the perfect thing for recharging one's center.

Despite this, I knew there was, as always, no other decision to make but to go along with a Holmes strategy. And for the time being, that subterfuge was to make ourselves as visible as possible. Therefore, alongside Holmes, I charged dutifully into the Bellagio's art gallery. Yet the instant I stepped inside the romantically lighted room, I was, again, taken aback. Not by the horror of the sights before me, but by the sheer surprise at spying the genuine and sublime beauty I had always known the great master works to deliver. Suddenly I was refreshed. Not wholly, but enough to carry on, or so I thought.

"Holmes!" I cried. "Pissarro, Cezanne, Monet, Manet, Seurat, Sissley, even Picasso. My God, everyone is in attendance here. This is absolutely breathtaking."

"Indeed," said a rather down in the mouth Holmes.

"Is this not wonderfully impressive?" I asked.

"The works, without question."

"Then why the long face?"

"As you know, you and I have had the great good fortune to have known many of the masters whose works we see before us. And knowing them as we had, it pains me to envision them turning in their graves over the news that their magnificent contributions to humanity are being displayed in this backwater spectacle, much like that mock eighteenth century ship battle, running as scheduled, around the clock, in front of the Treasure Island hotel and casino. No, my friend, these masterpieces are here not for the pleasure of spending time with such wondrous and eternal treasures, but are yet another contrivance designed to steer the great herd to this locale. Yes, Watson, I submit they are nothing more than an essential ingredient in what is an extremely cunning scheme. A scheme which has been constructed to not only lure a great influx of punters to this city, but one which simultaneously, suggests that substance and cultivation can also be found in this greatest of all amusement parks."

Needless to say, after listening to Holmes' brutal critique, my initial euphoria and renewed verve quickly evaporated.

"I even feel a great sympathy for that self-centered, domineering lout Picasso," added Holmes. "Never thought I'd see the day."

The one location within Las Vegas I had actually been rather keen to see suddenly felt like a mortuary.

"When you have had your fill here," said Holmes as he began to make for the exit, "go directly to your room. We've much to do before we depart for Los Angeles."

"Los Angeles?" I shrieked with surprise.

He held his index finger to his mouth as signal that I be careful with mine.

"Of course, Holmes. Of course," I replied, still dazed by the unexpected news.

As he exited the gallery, I elected to remain and savor the awe-inspiring works filling the rooms of the small gallery, despite the picture Holmes' words had painted in my mind. And though I do feel my effort was most valiant, I failed to lose that sense of pity that had come over me since his last harangue. Thus, recognizing that I had joined him in a sudden *down-in-the-mouth* mood, I pushed myself to remain cognizant of the monumental talent and consummate artistry behind each of the great works I shared the room with, even if it did suddenly feel rather like a wake.

After that somber experience, I found myself in the loveliest of suites, where clearly no expense had been spared. However it, like ninety-four percent of the city itself, had that contrived and rather shallow, Thomas Kinkade sense about it. Nevertheless, I took immediately to pampering my thoroughly exhausted self by availing it of the steam sauna chamber built into the bath, which was followed by a leisurely soak in the suite's massive and extraordinarily opulent marble Jacuzzi, accompanied by newspaper and a long overdue glass of Port, taken from the in suite bar. After which, I realised, food would have to give way to sleep, the immediate priority.

A few hours later I was awakened by a determined knock at the door. Slowly staggering my way to answer it, I heard that famous announcement, "Room Service!" After a quick peek through the door's eyehole to verify the presence of a server, I opened the door and allowed the lad to charge through with his large wheeled cart.

"I'm afraid I did not—,"

"No sir, Dr. Watson," spoke the lad quickly, "Mr. Holmes took the liberty of ordering for you, sir."

"Did he?"

"Yes, sir," he answered, lifting the silver lid to the entrée platter. "As requested, *Tofta* joined by a tamari and sesame marinated zucchini and eggplant side. A sparkling mineral water, with a lemon, not lime, twist for the meal, and a pot of Assam tea and a bowl of strawberries and peaches for dessert.—Oh, and this sir."

He retrieved a small silver tray, which bore a single envelope as its payload.

"From Mr. Holmes, sir," he announced as he held the small tray before me.

I quickly lifted the miniature communiqué off its tray and eagerly tore it open.

> *Watson,*
>
> *As you dismiss the server, instruct him to collect his cart later-on. Under the cart's drape, on the under shelf, you shall find parcel and further instructions.*
>
> *H.*

"Everything all right, Dr. Watson?" asked the young man.

"Yes, thank you," I answered. "Oh, and please leave the cart. I must meditate before I dine."

"That won't be necessary, sir. I would be more than happy to set a place at the table," he countered, gesturing to the small, yet luxurious glass and ornamented marble dining table sitting at the other end of the lush sitting room.

"No, no, no! Don't bother with such nonsense," I said rather curtly. "I cannot be bothered with such fanciful fuss."

Indeed, I felt like a brute. But it was all that had come into my head in that instant. It was a painful reminder that, unlike Holmes, I had never been exceptionally quick on my feet.

"That will be all, young man," I said, remaining in character.

"Yes, sir," he responded, looking slightly broken hearted.

As he commenced to take his leave, he paused at the door, took a large breath and turned to readdress me.

"Yes?" I asked in the same false manner.

"Dr. Watson, sir. If it's not too much trouble, I would very much like to have your autograph," said he, as he produced pen and notepad. "When I was very young, before a sudden illness took him, my father often read to me your adventures with Mr. Holmes. They were my favorite, sir, even better than those of Dumas' great trio. And now, here you are before me. It's an honor, sir. A real honor."

"I'd be happy to!" I eagerly offered out of sheer guilt for my earlier crass pretense.

After signing and returning him his pad, a smile was shared between us before he returned to his charge and marched out. Yet the instant he had closed the door behind him, I dove for the cart, lifting its drape and retrieving the expected package Holmes had somehow gotten onto the cart's under shelf. Then, with a borrowed knife from the place setting atop, I sliced the twine that bound the parcel, then slit the brown wrap open.

"What on earth?" I said to myself as I discovered a server's costume, a map of the hotel and the promised instructions.

Dear Friend,

After you have completed your much needed yogic stretching and eaten your meal, please be so kind as to don the guise you find. When ready, make your way, with the room service cart to complete the effect, and exit the hotel as I have indicated on the enclosed map. I shall be waiting on level four of the car park at precisely 11:40pm.

H.

What had Holmes up his sleeve, I pondered? However, after a reflexive glance at the ornate Venetian wall-mounted clock, I would not have to wait long to discover the meaning behind it all, for it was very nearly 11pm. I had scarcely 40 minutes to stretch, consume my meal, dress and deliver myself to level four of the hotel's car park.

RING! RING! RING! bellowed the telephone.

"Hello."

"Dr. Watson?" said the fairly youthful voice on the other end of the line. "Sorry if I've woken you, sir."

"Driscoll?"

"Yes, sir."

"What is it? How is Mr. Moore?"

"Fine, sir. But he'll have to remain hospitalized for a day or two, sir."

"Yes, rather a nasty blow, that."

"Yes it was. But sir, I have tried to reach Mr. Holmes, but was told he's sleeping and is refusing all calls."

"Yes?"

"I'm afraid I have some awfully bad news to deliver."

"What news?" I pressed.

"I'm afraid we've let you down, sir."

"How's that?"

"Lesters appears to have vanished without a trace, somehow managing to fly beneath our radar, so to speak."

"I see."

"What now, sir?"

"I suggest you employ your intelligence dragnet to do its utmost to locate any glimpse of our mouse. Holmes and I have not come all this way only to be knocked out in an early round, if you take my meaning," I answered somewhat sternly, feeling pressed for time.

"Yes, sir."

"In the meantime, I shall break the news to Holmes first chance I get."

"Thank you, sir. By the way, Peale, as you might have suspected, is on the warpath. You and Mr. Holmes should expect a visit in the morning."

"*Oafficer* Peale, as Holmes would refer to him, is the least of ours worries."

"Good night, then."

"Good night."

Frustration, brought on by a mountain of pressing circumstances and time constraints, I sensed, was attempting to commandeer my conscious flow. If only I had not answered the door, nor the telephone, I thought. But alas, thankfully, I was also determined to resist such laments. So, after pausing in my station by the telephone for a few therapeutic deep breaths to commence a regrouping of my continuum of focused thoughts, I elected to put the world on hold and lose myself in a few moments of meditative yogic stretching and controlled breathing exercises. RELIEF! I then dressed in the attire Holmes had delivered, devoured my, by then, cold meal and braced myself for the running of the gauntlet, or so Holmes' next instruction had felt to me.

Cautiously, I cracked open the door to the suite. Nothing. The corridor was perfectly empty. So I thrust the cart and myself into it and dutifully embarked upon this next step of Holmes' scheme. His directions had me take the lift, which fortunately was also void of any other human presence, down to the kitchen level. Once there I abandoned the cart and made for a nearby exit. Proceeding through it, I discovered I had arrived upon a short causeway, which led to the car park. Once there, I hoofed my way up to the fourth level. But again, nothing. Then, suddenly, a pair of headlights awakened and brightly flashed into my eyes. Intense their illumination grew as the car inched casually toward me. Luckily the car park was exceptionally well lit, allowing me the ability to see the whole of the silver Honda saloon as it approached and stopped very nearly upon my toes.

"This is America, Watson. Passengers ride on the right," announced that familiar voice, as the driver window slid down with a fluidity singular to power windows.

"Holmes?" I cried out with great surprise. "What on—,"

"Get in, Watson. Get in!"

I dashed round, taking another dose from the strong headlights and climbed in through the passenger door.

"Dare I ask how you acquired this car?" I cautiously asked.

"Best not."

"Holmes!"

"Right on time, Watson. I take it all went well and according to plan, then?" asked Holmes.

"What plan?" I insisted.

"Los Angeles, old chum. Los Angeles," he answered.

"Now?"

"Most assuredly now!"

"But Holmes, Driscoll rang to say that he and his people have let Lesters slip through their visual grasp."

"I'm surprised they had hold of him for as long as they had. Most remarkable, that," Holmes stated as he stepped upon the accelerator and steered us on our way out of the goliath car park.

"What?"

"It was only a matter of time, Watson. We are not dealing with any run-of-the-mill organization."

"I thought you'd—,"

"On the contrary, Moore and his people performed far beyond my expectations. I never expected to have gained such insight into the workings of this breed of hooligan."

"Insight?"

"Quite right. Perhaps a healthy glimpse then."

"But our luggage?"

"Delivered to my suite while you slept. However, I should think we will survive without it for a day or two. By the way, this promises to be a rather lengthy drive. Would you mind taking the wheel shortly so I may catch a bit of sleep?"

"No, not at all. But first, I would very much like to know why we are en route to Los Angeles, of all places? And why now, at this hour?"

"The answer to your second question, I should think, should be elementary. We've created the impression we are quietly tucked in our beds for the night, which should afford us just the appropriate size window for reaching Los Angeles un-pestered, if you will."

"But why Los—?"

"Sid Mellonowski, of course."

"Who on earth is Sid Mellonowski?"

"Remember Hugo Bean?"

"That villain who accosted you?"

"Exactly! His theatrical representative is none other than Sid Mellonowski."

"And he's in Los Angeles?"

He nodded.

"Why not New York?" I pressed on.

"Come now, Watson. In between substantial roles, an actor of Mr. Bean's very limited capability is far more likely to acquire work as an "extra" in Los Angeles, than in New York. Moreover, and despite his obvious New Jersey accent, I noticed the make up he wore as part of his costume. It was light, not heavy like that of a stage performer. More suited to the cinema, I should think. And, not surprisingly, with Las Vegas a mere three hundred miles to the east, he is probably no stranger to the odd job in that city as well."

"Forgive me Holmes, but have you confirmed that this Sid person actually is in Los Angeles?"

"Would his address appease your apprehension?" he asked, as he took a note out of his breast pocket and handed it to me.

17805 Westwood Blvd.
Suite 106
Los Angeles, CA

"How on earth?" I asked with great surprise.

"With an ever so brief bit of access to one of the hotel's computers, one can easily acquire such information with a quick peek at the Screen Actors Guild website."

"Yes, but Holmes, where does this Mr. Mellonowski fit into all this?"

"He is the conduit through which Mr. Bean provides himself his very meager living."

"And on occasion he portrays an actual thug?"

"Exactly!"

"Yes, but what shall such a revelation deliver to us?"

"Why the Engineer, of course."

CHAPTER XII

Misrepresentation

Amidst the dark wee hour, star-filled sky, and its constant companions silence and stillness, the lengthy and dreadfully monotonous drive along the isolated I15 desert highway, did much to help ease my reaction to all Holmes had announced. Strange that. For I had never much cared for the look and feel of any such wasteland. However, the somewhat soothing and welcomed lull that that stretch of road provided did not entirely dissolve my apprehension to the goings on. The hotel subterfuge, actors transforming into murderous villains, an obtuse constable, shady theatrical representatives, a clandestine car lending of some sort, a midnight escape and all of it leading us, supposedly, directly to the very Devil himself? Had it not been Holmes who laid all this before me, I would have thought it simply a fantastic yarn offered by some long-winded blowhard. For utterly fantastic it all truly was. Yet, on the other hand, I should hardly have been surprised. The circumstances surrounding the whole of this affair were nothing less than extraordinary.

An hour into the drive, I had traded positions with Holmes, who had, seconds later, fallen catatonic with sleep. No problem having to man the left-sided helm, it was the navigation of the task, which had perplexed me. For in the dim, raven night sky, I could scarcely differentiate one cacti, one ragweed, one rock, one dirt road from another? Had the local signage not been in English, I promise you, I would have most assuredly mistaken the area for the vast and extremely remote Gobi itself. Again, I am compelled to reiterate my disdain for the desert. Regretfully, I never could quite understand those who had an appreciation, an affinity even, for the flavor of the desert, particularly the western desert. With its solitary, seemingly endless and narrow, black asphalt road, its abounding desolation, and its brutally hot and relentless sun overhead, it was a visualization that had never failed to turned my stomach. And yet, although I had not ever considered myself to be inflicted with agoraphobia, perhaps my dislike for the desert, *et al* in it, it occurred to me, might have been due to a mild form of that condition. Be that or not, on this occasion, I was indeed thankful to the desert for providing me a momentary reprieve from the breakneck speed of developments in this case.

With the arrival of dawn yanking me back to the moment, I was stricken by the sudden realization that even though I had reached some sort of an attempt at civilization, I had somehow managed to veer off in a incorrect direction. From the map Holmes had laid out across the dashboard, I had expected to deliver us onto what is known as the I10 freeway. Instead, I was reading directional signs, which were proudly announcing, 91 West. How on earth had I gotten us here? I wondered. Where was here? Fighting panic, I decided to exit the rather large artery and ask for directions to Los Angeles at the first petrol station I should come upon. Fortunately, I could see one residing but a quarter mile directly ahead. However, a traffic signal, with its vibrant red light, impeded my progress with its insistence I stop to allow opposing traffic the opportunity to flow freely for a moment or two. By all means, I had my saving grace in my line of sight, which, I might add, brought to me a very welcomed degree of comfort. Unfortunately, it was a sense that would not last. For as I patiently waited for the signal to favor me, I could discern a good portion of that comforting calm rapidly slipping away with each passing oddity that steered its way past. One after another, as if it were some sort of an organized procession plowing straight through the intersection, a series of large and rather peculiar box-like pick-up styled trucks rolled parade-like before me. Most were painted in extremely vibrant colors, particularly yellow, and sporting a kind of color matched firm rubber cover, which lay over the truck's cargo area, which, to me at least, rendered the purpose of owning such a vehicle pointless. Others embellished their presence with odd shaped flames, in a variety of colors, purple, pink, turquoise and magenta for instance, which had no relation to real fire whatsoever, painted on the bonnet and the front-end fenders. Adding to the eccentricity of this spectacle, each garish vehicle, whether it had six tires and a pair of ridiculously extended fenders at the rear or not, rode extraordinarily low, again rendering any notion of the vehicle as workhorse, impossible. Like the horse and the ten-gallon hat, I had fully expected to see the pick-up truck in the west. But surely, these were not those belonging to the contemporary version of the rugged cattle and horseman of the west? My God, I thought to myself in horror, the damage this Engineer chap has inflicted is worse than anyone would have ever imagined.

Pulling, finally, into the petrol station, I noticed a young gent standing about, looking rather bored with his lot in life. Could not blame him really. Shabby, oil and grease stained, pewter colored work clothes, a grimy auto repair garage the center of his professional life. Though I knew such service professionals were of an enormous value to people like myself who know nothing whatsoever about the motorcar, the image saddened me. Yet, despite the gloom I'd fallen into, I pulled Holmes' questionably procured Honda Accord over to where the filthy lad stood, shoved the gear lever into park and popped out.

"Pardon me, sir," I said interrupting his deep, empty stare. "I say, would you happen to know how I might make my way to a thoroughfare known as the 405 freeway?"

He gave me a very queer look.

"What's that?" he answered.

"I say, I'm afraid I've lost my way," I replied.

Another look of astonishment was his only rejoin.

"Looking to make my way to the 405 freeway. Do you know it?" I added.

"You German or something?" he asked.

"No, I am not."

"Where ya from?"

"England," I answered while biting my cheek to keep from reacting to his ignorant initial deduction.

"Oh! Ya speak English?"

"Of course!"

"Ah! Good. I don't know any England, you know?"

"Do you know the way to this 405 freeway or not?" I asked with a little more firmness in my tenor.

"The 405? Oh, heck yeah! That's easy. Where ya tryin' to get ta?"

I retrieved the slip of paper Holmes had written our intended destination on and read it aloud.

"Westwood boulevard in Los Angeles, by way of this 405 freeway, as I understand it."

"Oh, sure, that's easy," said the dullard. "You get back onto the 91 and go west. Now you could take it all the way to the 405, but it turns into a busy street. I think it's better to take the 110 freeway towards the harbor and then catch the 405 north. Got it?"

"Not quite, I'm afraid," I answered, hoping Holmes had managed to overhear the man's directions. No such luck. Like one of those new electric vehicles now infiltrating the market, these days the great elderly sleuth was completely incapacitated whilst recharging. "The harbor, you say?"

"Yeah!" he replied.

I drew a blank.

"Look, it's easy," he continued. "The 110 is the harbor freeway. You take it to the harbor, but get off at the 405 north. Got it? Then take the 405 all the way to Wilshire and take it to Westwood Blvd. Okay?"

"Ah, I see," I said, though I was not fully convinced I had comprehended all the attendant had explained. Nevertheless, I thanked him for his assistance, returned to my seat and drove straight for the 91 West access ramp. Once there, I applied greater pressure upon the accelerator and thrust Holmes and myself back into the westward bound flow of traffic, which was surprisingly formidable for so early in the morning.

Forty minutes on, amidst the considerable congestion, I found myself at a nightmare of a fork in the road. It seemed riding in the fast lane, as we were, was the incorrect procedure for one wishing to remain on the 91 West, which was suddenly veering off to the right, something my good man had forgotten to mention. Hence, being trapped by a swarm of local road drones, I was unable to merge right. Thus, I found myself deposited onto another great thoroughfare known as the 55 freeway and traveling southward.

"Mother of God, will this horror ever end?" I thought out loud.

"Do not fret, my friend," said Holmes, returning to the world, "these little hurdles are but par for the course. Let's have a look at the map."

"I'm awfully sorry, Holmes. I'm afraid I'm rather poor at navigating my way through this network of motorways."

"And which one would we be on?"

"The 55 freeway, I believe."

"My, we have managed to veer off course quite a bit,"

"I don't know how—,"

"No bother, I had a chance to study the map of the whole of the Los Angeles basin prior to our setting off," he announced as he studied the roadmap. "Not to fear, old chum. All is not lost. It would appear we should shortly reach this 405 freeway. Once on it, we shall proceed northward until we reach the Wilshire Blvd. exit."

Prior to reaching the last leg of the superhighway segment of our sojourn, that artery known as the 405, I had prepared in advance by merging all the way right, to avoid any further complication, and made the northbound transition onto it with great ease. What relief. And feeling much better about our position as we entered the Los Angeles basin, I was about to ask Holmes to elaborate as to how this Sid person was going to lead us to the great fiend himself, when I began to notice a very curious thing.

"Holmes," I wondered aloud, "have you been noticing the numerous directional road signs announcing the presence of an array of institutions of higher learning in this vicinity?"

"Yes, I had," he rather aloofly replied.

"Does not their presence challenge your argument on the educational shift in America?"

"Not at all," he confidently answered.

"Orange Coast College, Coastline College, University of Phoenix, National University, Golden West College, Long Beach College, Long Beach State University, California State University, Dominguez Hills, El Camino College. Surely these institutions must possess some merit?"

"Yes, it would appear, the very hotbed of academia, this area," Holmes condescendingly remarked.

"Now Holmes, honestly! That is particularly unfair. Even you must admit the number of institutions in this vicinity is rather impressive."

"Though the number of institutions in this area hopes to imply the region a *think-tank*, that is actually quite misleading. For, as I have previously stated, the vast majority of institutions in this country have become more vocational in nature. Thus, what you see here is an example of misrepresentation, the main ingredient in the very *undertow*, which we are here to stem."

"How can you say that?" I challenged. "Regardless of your opinion, these *are* institutions of higher learning. Are they not?"

"Please, Watson! Let us not toss this issue about again. You may find my observation a bit unfair, however, I would point out, not a single one of the institutions you mention solicits new attendants with promises of developing the individual into the well-rounded, fully educated entity. No! These institutions entice such young hopefuls with promises of degrees, degrees they suggest, which virtually guarantee well paying employment. Which suffices to say, on the whole, excludes the inclusion of the humanities and the sciences for the individual in pursuit of, let us say, a degree in finance. And it is that brutal reality which substantiates my contention."

"But Holmes, do you not think you are out of line when you imply that this, ever so slight as I see it, form of misrepresentation is as corrupt as that belonging to the Engineer's undertow?" I argued.

"There is not one and the other. For they are one and the very same," he quickly returned.

"What!"

"Watson, old friend, there does not exist multiple undertows in this nation. There is but only one, generated solely by the man himself. And, as I have attempted to stress, it is that very current which transports our pestilent enemy throughout this great land, infecting every single aspect of America's cultural life."

"Yes, but education?"

"The main target, I am afraid. For without it, the villain could not have accomplished all that he has."

He paused to allow me to collect myself, then pointed at the small Japanese pick-up truck that was traveling ahead of us.

"Take this vehicle before us. Do you notice the peculiar little decals stuck upon its rear windscreen?"

"Decals?" I confusedly asked. "I fear you have lost me. Are you referring to the stained glass rear windscreen before us?"

"Yes. But what you see before you is not ornamentally stained glass, but small product notices proudly stuck onto the glass."

"Surely you jest!"

"Regretfully not."

"But why? What is the significance of such a display?"

"Misrepresentation, of course."

"What?"

"Yes, my good man, misrepresentation."

"But why?"

"The reasoning behind it is rather convoluted. But I shall try to explain the whole of the matter as simply as I can."

Again he pointed to the pick-up truck ahead of us.

"The virus I now refer to as Eloisyndrome, attacks the key processing functions of the brain, making rational thought a good deal more complex for the victim. As a result, the infected party grows, subconsciously of course, less secure. Thus, in an attempt to regain some measure of self-esteem, the casualties resort to selectively sharing facts about themselves with the society at large in such embarrassingly sad methods as that we have before us. You see, by informing all whom this driver shares this great concourse with that he has the good sense to enhance his vehicle's performance with Toyo Tires, a brand of automobile suspension struts, known by the name Mcpherson, and the ever reliable STP engine lubricant, he hopes to amaze the viewer with what he considers is a rather astute display of his consumer acumen. It is a side effect I refer to as *product pride*. Further windscreen announcements reveal to the world that this particular victim is a devotee of the rock groups, '*Megadeath*', '*Nirvana*', '*Smashing Pumpkins*' and '*The Dead Kennedys*'. All of which, he believes, should single him out as an exceptionally select member of the, and here is that almighty word yet again, *cool* set."

"Is that not a contradiction of impressions?" asked I.

"Well done, Watson. Very well done!" cheered Holmes. "Of course it is. But as I said, this is a rather convoluted state of mind our casualties find themselves thrust into. On the one hand, they very much long to be a popular member of a group, nigh on any group for that matter. Yet on the other hand, they would like nothing better than to be singled out as *the* rarest of all individuals. A person so highly unique they simply defy all conventional categories."

"But Holmes, the nature of this conversation appears more psychological rather than cultural. Have you not gone rather a bit adrift with your observations?" I challenged. "Our goal is—,"

"I'm well aware of our purpose here, but what you fail to note, is that this vicious viral intruder, with its ruthless attack upon the brain's ability to reason, drinks up its victim's self-esteem. A rather brutal byproduct of its free-radical-like nature. Thus, the infected is sadly ashamed of his station, his average-ness, if you will. Hence, the need for this false bravado."

"Ah! I think I am beginning to see it all. Yet surely this driver is anything but average. Would you not agree?"

"And how is it you have concluded this?"

"For the simple reason that his eyesight and peripheral vision must surely be tremendous if he is to manage sight through such a cluttered rear windscreen," I somewhat sarcastically explained.

"Excellent, Watson! Excellent. Now, what else do you observe about our subject here?"

"How do you mean?"

"Well, you now understand the function of the decals is to create the impression that this driver is exceptionally well schooled in what is currently highly fashionable and supremely *hip*, a connoisseur of the *mainstream*, which I might add is simply a gentler way of saying *undertow*. Thus, what you and I, and the rest of the populous, are supposed to see is a completely and utterly together personality. Yet, this is a ruse, a smokescreen created to distract us from observing the truth about our man here."

"And that being?"

"That he is actually highly insecure and desperate for attention."

"But Holmes, might it not be possible that you have rather unjustly judged this driver? Might he simply be an under educated, unenlightened chap? The type who believes that prestige and respect can be purchased as easily as toothpaste?"

"No."

"Honestly, Holmes! How can you be so certain?"

"Because the eyes are unable to deceive."

"What, by Jove, are you on about now?"

"The license plate frame!"

"What?"

"The license plate frame! It is one of those insufferably boastful alumni announcements, which demand we recognize this individual as a true academic. A highly educated member of society which we may feel free to rely upon."

"I too am proud of my educational achievements."

"Of course you are. But you do not view that education a badge of honor. No! You, Watson, correctly understand it rather a personal measure of inner growth and development and would never conceive of advertising your accomplishments in such a vile manner. No, my learned friend, given the vocational current surging through the university system within this nation, it is an offense to intimate scholarship when what we should find more accurate and truthful are license plate frames which state *financier, electrician, optometrist, architect, software developer, dentist.*"

Once again, I found myself at a loss for a rejoin.

"Thus, the misrepresentation," concluded Holmes.

"Perhaps you read too much into the significance of this fad. Might it not simply be an unthinking gesture on his part, an act in which he merely followed suit, assuming it proper procedure for university graduates?" I suggested.

"In other words, *"go with the flow"*, as it is said here?"

"Yes."

"Do you not hear yourself, Watson?"

I drew yet another blank.

"Is not "the flow" the undertow?"

"AH!" I exclaimed as the horror finally sank in and momentarily ripped the breath from me. Simultaneously the realization that a countless number of poor, misguided, and subsequently unenlightened, souls in this plague-ridden country were mistakenly feeling anchored with the use of this reprehensible device known as *misrepresentation*, when in fact, they drifted waywardly about the landscape. It, quite literally, made my heart ache.

Thankfully my eyes locked upon a large green and white sign, which read, WILSHIRE BLVD. Finally something I could easily comprehend. And at last mastering the controls and the congested interstate, I smoothly merged right and exited onto our designated thoroughfare, where destiny was said to be waiting for us. In an instant, Holmes spotted a dark glass tower, situated upon the corner at Wilshire and Westwood Boulevard, which bore the number 17805. Yet how, I wondered, as we drove into the building's adjacent car park, would suite 106 serve as the gateway to our thief? Whilst commanded by a white metal bar to stop and take a time-entry ticket from the automated dispenser, I decided to put it to Holmes. However, after taking the ticket, the bar lifted, ordering me to drive on. I obeyed its insistence, drove through and slipped into the first available parking space I came upon. A great sense of accomplishment and relief washed over me as I shut down the engine. We had arrived. From London to New York, to

Washington, to Chicago, to Las Vegas, to Los Angeles, it had been quite the journey, to say the least.

"Holmes, what exactly is it about this Mr. Melonowski that convinces you that he will deliver the Engineer to us? Does his profession suggest our villain hides behind the guise of a motion picture mogul perhaps?"

"Erroneous as it is, that is the very deduction our thief expects us to form. A clever misdirection."

"How's that?"

"On the surface, it would seem the correct conclusion. However, since it is so obvious an inference, it cannot be the case."

"But how can you be so certain?"

"Firstly, the role of motion picture mogul is too high a profile for our man. Secondly, it restricts his ability to influence and infect other areas of American business and society."

"Then why have an interest in using unemployed actors as miscreant soldier?"

"Because they are readily available in his business."

"I thought you had just dismissed the implication that this Engineer monster is a filmmaker?"

"I have, indeed."

"Confound it, Holmes! Which is it?"

"Think, my friend. Whom else besides movie and theatrical companies might require the services of actors in the normal course of their business dealings?"

"Who? There can be no other."

"Whose business runs the very gamut of industries. Thus, the perfect carrier of a potentially fatal cultural disease?"

After delivering what to me was a very unsatisfactory reply, he exited the car and began to perform a modified variation of his usual morning stretching exercise routine. I immediately followed suit.

"Holmes!" I firmly said as I bent over, locking my knees straight, of course, while slowly lowering my palms flat onto the ground before me. "Enough with this guessing ga—,"

"An ad man, my friend. An advertising man!"

The announcement took the wind completely from me.

"Yes, Watson. Who but a marketer would have use for actors as mere tools to promote his products? Who but a marketer relies simultaneously on the print ad, television and radio commercials? A marketer! The number of products he promotes is vast. Whether rubbish or not, he will not rest until he has swayed the consumer to believe their species has very nearly gone extinct without said product and that it is their good fortune that he has come along to save the day. Thus, he begets the great power needed to steer the market to suit his pockets."

He straightened himself and let loose a short meditative breath.

"By the way, I took the liberty of retrieving your revolver from your bag. I hope you do not mind terribly?" announced Holmes, as he lifted it out of his jacket side pocket and handed it over to me.

As was growing customary on this adventure, I could only return a look of utter surprise as I slipped it into a side pocket of my own.

"It should be a good idea to keep a hand on that," he suggested just as he turned and strode toward the black glass tower.

CHAPTER XIII

The Devil Himself

Approaching the car park exit, which would deliver us onto a walkway that led to the office tower, I was suddenly struck by what I viewed as an aspect of our circumstances which Holmes had somehow overlooked.

"Holmes, our attire!" I exclaimed. "We cannot enter wearing these server's jackets, looking as if—"

"On the contrary, my good man. They are just the guise we need," Holmes swiftly replied. "By visually suggesting that we have been primarily servers, and actors on occasion, our entire professional lives, our cause is furthered."

"Which is?"

"A pair of *two-bit*, as is the American phrase, thespians forever committed to the search of that breakthrough role."

"At our ages? Surely this cannot persuade?"

"Again, I beg to differ. For you see, my intent is to convey to this Mr. Mellonowski that you and I are dreadfully desperate animals. So desperate, in fact, like our good friend Mr. Bean, we are very much willing and able to take on any, absolutely any, assignment he may toss our way. No matter how heinous the employment, we are his men."

"I see—," I began to acknowledge, but was stopped short by the sudden push of Holmes' hand upon my abdomen to stifle my speech and send me back behind one of the car park's support columns.

A second later, as Holmes and I watched from behind a concrete pillar, a lengthy, black limousine rolled to a stop before the very walkway we had been en route to. In the next second, I witnessed the emergence of Lesters from the ostentatious automobile. And while this unexpected arrival had greatly surprised me, Holmes appeared far more thrilled than surprised.

"Holmes!"

"Shhh!"

Silently, we watched and waited as the limousine drove on and Lesters made for the tower entrance. Finally, both were out of sight.

"Holmes! Should we not make haste before we lose sight of him?" I anxiously asked.

Holmes, with the commanding calm of a chess master who spies mate but a single move away, faced me and let out a great sigh of relief, an act I found most unbefitting the moment.

"Lesters is within our grasp! Surely we must follow him before he—,"

"We must do nothing of the kind," replied the rather irksome sleuth.

"What?" I cried with even greater surprise than that which struck at the sight of our Renfield's unexpected arrival.

"Calm yourself, my over eager friend," said Holmes. "He, nor his superior, shall leave this *vitre montagne* until we have set the matter right," proclaimed the supremely confident detective as he checked his wristwatch and leaned patiently back against our concrete hiding place. "Let's give them a minute, shall we?"

"Has your facility completely abandoned you?" I pressed. "The man we are after, our man is in that architecturally void black glass block and you want not to charge in and—,"

"And do what? Apprehend this fiend?"

"Of course!"

"Come now, Watson. How do you propose to do that?"

I stood paralyzed by the surge of reality Holmes' questioned delivered.

"Certainly this ruthless brute must be brought to justice," he continued. "However, you and I are not an army, nor John Wayne. How far do you think we should get pretending to be such?"

"I take your point. Yet surely we must act!"

He sneaked another peak at his timepiece.

"That, we most assuredly shall do."

"When?"

"Now!" he announced as he resumed his dutiful march for the tower's entrance.

In tow, I felt acutely uneasy with Holmes' exceptional confidence towards the outcome of the game. For to me, we appeared to have little in the way of options upon the chessboard. In fact, considering our out numbered position, I determined a stalemate would be a miracle. Nevertheless, Holmes strode unflinchingly through the tower's large black glass doors and into its foyer, where he stopped to study the grand tenant marquee displayed in the center of the vestibule, which, with its contemporary pseudo-cubic designed, brass framed, glass covered name board perched proudly upon a black marble pedestal, resembling more a modern cubist monument than the mere register of occupants it actually was. As to Lesters, not a trace.

"Suite 1101," announced Holmes.

"You mean 106, do you not?" I confusedly asked.

"Indeed, that had initially been my intended destination. However, since the ant has led us to the mound and it is the mound itself that I am particularly interested in, consequently, the ant is no longer of concern to me."

"But why have you focused so singularly upon suite 1101?"

"Do you not see the firm *O.B.&Y.* Advertising listed here?"

"Yes, but—,"

"Does the firm's name not strike a chord with you?"

"*O.B.&Y.* Advertising," I blankly stated. "Should it?"

"Yes, my unobservant friend. For, as with the daring use of the acronym MYND for that corporation's soubriquet, do you not see the insulting boldness this one projects?"

"Boldness? I am afraid I do not."

"Watson, think. Does not the "and" sign resemble the capitalized letter 'e' written in longhand?"

"Perhaps," I replied as my mind raced to transform the acronym before me into the longhand image Holmes suggested.

O. B. & Y.

O B & Y

OB&Y

OBEY

"Therefore," continued Holmes, while I concentrated to construct the visual, "keeping this in mind, could not the acronym then cleverly read as—,"

"Obey advertising!" I nearly shouted.

"The perfect subliminal, wouldn't you agree?"

"Holmes, that's dastardly! Surely it is unintentional?"

"I think not," he strongly answered. "For whom else, other than this audacious adversary of ours, would be clever enough to inform, taunt even, the populous with his sinister intent without the slightest fear of reproach?"

"Yes, but seriously—,"

"I have never been more serious."

"But Holmes, that firm is housed in suite 1004. Not 1101 as you have stated."

"I have not suggested the firm to reside in suite 1101. It is you who have erroneously concluded as such. No, Watson! Look carefully upon this marquee. What do you see?"

I glared at the framed list an instant or two. I saw nothing hugely out of the ordinary, until Holmes interceded by placing his index finger on the fine parenthetically printed announcement just below the *O.B.&Y.* listing.

(A Carpenter Industries company)

Then dragging that same finger over to the listing for *Carpenter Industries*, he was immediately able to explain the relationship without a single word, as the suite number associated with the listed name was none other than 1101.

"Are you suggesting the parent firm, this Carpenter Industries, is the very vortex of the Engineer's machine?"

"*Control room*, I should think, would be more apt a description."

"Are you absolutely certain?" I reflexively asked as my mind struggled to fight off disbelief over this latest development.

"Do you recall a particular media mogul who announced his retirement from the print and television news services by selling off a very substantial portion of his private stock in a number of media companies, an act which sent the markets of the world into a short-lived panic?"

"Yes. I think I do recall such an individual."

"Do you recall his name?"

"Not at the moment—Carpenter!" I shouted into the quick hand of Holmes', which he had speedily cupped over my mouth to silence my reaction to the recollection he knew would race to the forefront of my conscious mind.

"Quite right, old friend. I knew it would not take long for you to put the pieces in this puzzle together. Well done," said Holmes, as he released me from his grasp.

"Malachy Carpenter, the Engineeer?"

"Like Jeckyl and Hyde, one and the same!"

His reply struck me like a desert winter's gust, frightfully cold and dry, not icy. Yet its impact upon my face had still managed to turn it to granite, stiff like one of the four famous faces upon Mt. Rushmore. However, unlike those of the great monument, my petrified expression had been chiseled out of a great shock and its accompanying fear, rather than dynamite and the jackhammer.

"But first," continued Holmes, "we need to become engineers ourselves before we call upon our Mr. Carpenter."

"What?" I cried.

"To the basement," he ordered as he purposefully made for the single black metal door, with sign above it reading '*Exit*', positioned directly across the foyer from us.

"The basement?" I bemusedly asked.

"Where else would one expect to locate this building's maintenance department?" Holmes cavalierly answered.

"Holmes!" I very nearly shouted as frustration began to seize all my senses. "What on earth? I cannot make the slightest sense of anything you say. You bounce from one subject to another."

"Our costumes will no longer serve our needs."

"What?"

"Think, Watson, think! Costume. Basement. Building maintenance."

"Maintenance engineers?"

"Excellent!" commended Holmes as he charged through the small black door and into the empty stairwell. "Excellent!"

I followed him as he raced down the winding, steel gray iron staircase.

"As I have stated, we no longer require the services of Mr. Mellonowski. Thus, our initial stratagem has been made redundant," he mechanically, like the chess master he is, explained. "Therefore, to accommodate our present situation, I have decided posing as maintenance engineers would be the most effective means of gaining unsuspected entrance into the corporate offices of Carpenter Enterprises."

"And how do you propose we instantly become maintenance engineers?"

"I am hoping a quick trip to the maintenance department, of course, will provide us with adequate costume."

"Should we not phone for reinforcements before—,"

"And who might that be?"

I hesitated as I thought to retrieve an answer. Though in all sincerity, I was merely attempting to brace myself, for I knew what was coming.

"No one, not even our allies, has been informed of our presence in this city," reproved Holmes. "And it would benefit us nothing if they had. Moore is in hospital and Driscoll and his comrades are some three hundred miles away. No Watson, there shall be no reinforcements. We ourselves, alone, must put an end to this vile assault."

My nerves a bit frayed, I offered no reply as we hurried down the flight of steps to the tower basement. For despite Holmes' eager, confident and extraordinarily determined demeanor, I must confess, I felt the situation rather desperate. Futile even. Yet strangely enough, though I imagined our efforts were tantamount to placing our heads straight into the mouth of the king of beasts, I dutifully charged along side my great friend and lion-tamer of a sleuth.

The barren basement corridor was alight with annoyingly bright fluorescent tubular lighting, which I found surprisingly antiquated for such a modern building. Worse were the light reflecting, semi-gloss gray walls. And, though all was as meticulously clean and tidy as an operating theater, my mind flooded with images of Alcatraz, imagery which only heaped weight onto my already rapidly sinking sense of confidence. Holmes, to the contrary, charged through the disinfected hallway with a rather maddening buoyancy, the likes of which I had not previously seen him display throughout any of this adventure. It was a mood I did not fully understand. For we were only two, two inordinately aged gents, pitted against a hidden battalion of hooligans, poised and ready somewhere in this eerie black tower. Of this I was convinced.

"Your revolver," commanded Holmes.

I complied. Then, calling upon my experience with Her Majesty's Fifth Northlumberland Fusiliers, I channeled my nervous energy into resolve and readied myself for the impending battle.

"Ah ha!" cried Holmes as we arrived before a door which had the word 'Maintenance' painted in bold white letters upon it.

He paused and turned to me.

"It begins."

Without hesitation, for I knew it would only be detrimental to our cause, I nodded my alliance.

Receiving my response, Holmes swung the door opened and stormed inside what was nothing more than a very large closet of an office. In the center, back against the rear wall, sat a nearly colorless metal desk with a startled, gray-haired, sixty year old man in a uniform that, with its gray color, was certain to make him difficult to discern out in the cold corridor.

"You, sir, would be the Chief Maintenance Engineer for this building?" asked Holmes.

"Excuse me?" returned the startled man.

"My question is quite simple, sir." Holmes stated firmly. "Are you, or are you not, the Chief Maintenance Engineer for this building, sir?"

"And who might you be?" the man indignantly retaliated.

"I am your benefactor, though you cannot know this at present," countered Holmes.

"What the—," cried the man as he rose to his feet.

"Watson!"

With soldier-like obedience, I pointed my revolver at the unsung proletarian, who immediately stiffened, as if he had seen a ghost.

"We are in need of a pair of uniforms," informed Holmes, with a deliberate calm to ease the panic of the, by then, witless man. "Would you, by chance, have any extra on hand?"

"A few new ones are always kept in the file cabinet, second drawer from the bottom," answered our nervous internee.

"Excellent!" remarked Holmes as he opened the said drawer of the putty colored metal file cabinet, which stood directly left of our very cooperative capture, and retrieved two of the garments. Then, taking the roll of duct tape he had observed to be conveniently sitting atop the cabinet, Holmes ordered the custodial chief to retake his seat, whereupon he proceeded to confine the man to his seat by running tape round his entire circumference nearly a dozen times. This was followed with the application of a large single piece of tape placed over the man's mouth.

"My sincerest apologies, old man," said Holmes to our blue-collar detainee upon completion of the task. Then swiftly followed with the toss of a uniform in my direction. "Get into that."

As our victim watched on in great curious confusion, Holmes and I removed our server costumes and clothed ourselves with the drab gray garb we had, rather hoodlum-like, procured. Yet another implement, in the name of the grand noble cause, Holmes had successfully 'borrowed'. Added to the guise were equally dull, baseball-fashioned, matching caps, which Holmes and I, begrudgingly, placed onto our heads. After which, before darting out, Holmes relieved the 'Maintenance Chief' of his key ring and tool chest. Phase one of our assault was now complete. Phase two? Running the gauntlet. However, by then I was ready. Witnessing the efficiency with which Holmes executed his campaigns had an inspiring effect upon me. If need be, I would have happily charged the beach at Omaha. Unfortunately, my orders were to temporarily remain at our makeshift base camp, while Holmes stormed the beach alone.

The ploy was for Holmes to enter suite 1101 and announce he had been sent to resolve 1101's difficulties with its thermostat. Surprising the unsuspecting staff with a non-existing malfunction, Holmes would suggest a call be made to the maintenance supervisor. Once the Chief Maintenance Engineer's phone rang, I would remove the tape over his mouth and instruct him to substantiate the need for Holmes' presence in 1101. Needless to say, the scheme worked flawlessly. Once the maneuver had been completed, I replaced the tape over the supervisor's mouth, unplugged the telephone, picked up a heavy-duty extension cord and strapped on a tool belt, the first workman-like items lying about that my eyes had set upon, before rushing out to assume my role as reinforcement for Holmes.

Reaching 1101, I felt a sudden, unexpected, surge of courage, if not confidence, and strode straight through the black and excessively wide entry doors, into the grand lobby and gazed purposefully at the receptionist sitting behind the all too curvaceously contemporary, laminated desk. To avoid having to adopt the difficult American accent, I signaled to her with a single finger in a direction I chose completely at random. With a matching gesture, the receptionist confirmed my choice of route for locating the other maintenance engineer, whom she correctly assumed I was there to assist. Fortunately, before I should give up the gambit by losing my way, Holmes arrived to steer me in the opposite direction, stating just loudly enough to be overheard by our watchful receptionist, that he had already examined one end of the suite, leaving only the other to be investigated. It was a maneuver which appeared to cause our little eagle-eyed onlooker a great deal of stress. The firm's Chief Executive Officer's chamber was located at the far end of the suite, she had asserted, and by no means, absolutely by no means, were we to consider barging in and disturbing him.

"Wouldn't think of it, ma'am," consoled Holmes. "Wouldn't think of it."

Yet a second later we found ourselves before an office door, which, in small mounted brass letters, subtly announced itself, to me, as the very gateway into the lion's den.

"M. Carpenter,
President and Chief Executive Officer"

Forgive the use of a frightfully overused phrase, but we had reached the point of no return. Few things in life are absolute, yet the realization of our position at that moment appeared one of them. For from that moment on, the course of life for all involved would be altered forever. Whatever the outcome of our intervention, for better or worse, life's *tao*, would undoubtedly veer in another direction. Mr. Clinton, Moore, Holmes and I all new which course we preferred to set. However, despite Holmes' striking confidence at the moment, the setting of that preferred course, unlike that momentous and pivotal moment we had finally reached, was not absolute. The fifteenth and final round of the bout, which would determine our future course, had yet to be contested.

Like any successful assault, surprise was the essential ingredient. And being outnumbered as we were, that component of our stratagem was more crucial to our campaign than any other. We could not allow a nervous receptionist the opportunity to deprive us of that vital element. So, we ignored the 'gateway' for the moment and returned to the counterfeit examination of the vents, air ducts and individual thermostats found in the adjoining offices and corridors. In essence, making nuisances of ourselves with the unsuspecting office population. It was a ploy which successfully placated the nervous pair of eyes that had been, from a distance, monitoring our every movement, our every gesture, our every glance.

Then, once our shadow had relaxed and had happily returned to her duties, it was time to thrust ourselves into the ring, however bloody the brawl promised to be, and derive a conclusion to this affair in one way or another.

Confident surprise had remained on our side, Holmes looked me straight in the eye. His face had a stern seriousness upon it, the likes of which one would have surely seen in the Oval Office during the Cuban Missile Crisis. Like that crucial drama in history, this saga held the very lives of millions within its grasp. One miscalculation, one incorrect decision, and the cultural lives, the dignity and, eventually, the souls of all Americans would be annihilated.

"Three focused breaths, Watson," instructed Holmes.

Joining him in the exercise, I felt a strange mixture of sensations. Hope, doom, the eagerness for a conclusion to this discord, anxiety and fear, yet with an overwhelming soldier-like pride and readiness to charge headstrong before the face of the enemy and run them through, if need be.

"Ready, my friend?" Holmes pensively asked, for we knew there was no going back to the life of old, once we charged forth. We would either meet our demise or succeed and defeat our foe, which meant the promise of a richer, genuine culture for America, which also meant the American landscape and its inhabitants may no longer be the adolescent nation that it has had the misfortune to be perceived as. Unfortunately, it also meant there existed the great possibility that Holmes and I, as Holmes had been after his victory over the late Professor Moriarty, would be forced underground to avoid retribution from Carpenter's, certain-to-be relentless, miscreant militia. Neither outcome hinted at the restoration of calm and tranquility, or the proverbial happy ending. Nevertheless, abhorrent crimes demand swift justice.

"Absolutely!" I determinedly pledged as I took hold of and turned the knob attached to the 'gateway', then calmly swung it open for Holmes and I to stride purposefully inside.

Once inside the contemporarily opulent office, I gently closed the door behind me.

"Can I help you, sir?" asked the man himself.

He was a surprisingly dashing man, of some seventy odd years. Impeccably attired in a lush, navy coloured, silk suit, appearing the virtual clone of the late Cary Grant. Definitely not, the image of the villain I had expected to encounter. And the office, though disagreeably modern and sterile in my eyes, was equally polished. However, even more unexpected for me was the presence of Lesters sitting in a rather silly black, weakly conceptualized futuristic-looking chair before the unbelievably vast acrylic desk which Carpenter sat behind.

"Can I help you, gentlemen?" asked Carpenter, with a markedly firmer tone.

"Yes, you might at that," Holmes answered cockily, as he removed his cap to reveal himself to the opposition.

In a state of sheer supreme surprise, Lesters, the weasel himself, abruptly rose to his feet.

"There is no way this man could have followed me here!" he insisted. Then, quickly looking over to Carpenter, he reiterated his contention. "I assure you, sir, I did not lead this man here, sir."

"That is correct. You, yourself, did not, entirely, lead me to this destination," remarked a ridiculously secure Holmes.

"Melonowski?" Carpenter asked of Holmes.

Holmes nodded.

"My compliments," commended Carpenter. "Well done. Very well done, indeed. And, you are earlier than I had expected, Mr. Holmes. Or should I say, Mr. Meddler?"

"Do not flatter yourself, sir. A Moriarty you are not," rejoined Holmes. "You may be exceptionally cunning, but you are not of the same caliber of mind."

"Ah, you have me there," countered Carpenter, "For my mental function is far superior to that of the late professor."

"You expected them?" asked a nearly panicked Lesters.

"Anything less would have greatly disappointed me," revealed Carpenter.

"I'll call security!" cried Lesters.

"Sit!" Carpenter command, as if he were issuing a directive to his favorite hound.

Lesters, trembling nervously, quickly dropped back into his chair.

"Like Moriarty, you are a master thief and a rather crafty rogue. I give you that," Holmes stated. "However, unlike yours sir, Moriarty's crimes did not strike out against the very fabric of humanity itself. No sir, your actions, I should think are akin to those of the wartime variety."

"Well, Reverend Holmes, might I suggest you and Dr. Watson take a seat, so we may debate the issue in a civilized fashion," proposed Carpenter. "Would you care for a coffee? A pot of tea, perhaps? I have an excellent selection of imported teas."

"Thank you kindly, sir, but no," returned Holmes as he took a seat before the glass-like desk.

"Do join us, Doctor," insisted Carpenter.

"Yes Watson, do take a seat," concurred Holmes. "There is a great deal to discuss."

CHAPTER XIV

The Final Round

The vibrant California summer sun strode proudly through the filtered glass of the black tower and into Carpenter's revoltingly sterile and *minimalistic* office from behind the very man himself. I found it rather an eerie image, grotesque even. For here was a man truly empty of compassion, a man void of even an inkling of humanity within his core. A man so morally corrupt, so psychotic, that neither Hitler nor Stalin could be called his equal. And yet, ironically, the light source from back of him created an offensively holy, aura-like apparition about his figure. Hence, facing him, as we were, I could think of nothing more gratifying than taking a swing at that arrogantly perfect face of his.

"Well, gentlemen, if you don't mind, I think I'd quite enjoy a coffee," announced Carpenter. "Sure I can't tempt you?"

"No thank you!" I quickly, and quite heatedly, answered for Holmes and myself.

"Very well, then."

He looked to Lesters.

"Just one then, if you would?"

Though a billionaire many times over in his own right, the obedient Labrador jumped up and immediately started for the elaborate in-office kitchenette a few feet behind him to fulfill his master's request. Simultaneously, equally as swift as Lesters' reaction, Holmes, seated beside me, tapped my knee with the back of his hand, a gesture I, as swiftly as everything else that had been taking place in that instant, fully understood.

"Allow me," I insisted of Lesters, as I, keeping pace with events, quickly rose to my feet to obstruct his course. "You'll find I am quite the capable server."

"I don't doubt your many talents, Dr. Watson," Carpenter interjected. "However, you are my guest. I cannot allow——,"

"I am afraid I must insist," stated Holmes.

"Insist?" remarked Carpenter.

"Our discussion requires your complete attention. Would you not say?"

"Quite right. You are quite right," returned Carpenter before turning his attention to Lesters. "Take your seat."

And sit the underling reverentially did, whilst I tended to his unholy master's request.

"Well, my dear adversary, it's good to finally have the chance to sit at the chessboard together. Isn't it?" the scoundrel cockily remarked, which conveyed to me that he was equally as profoundly confident as Holmes was. It sent the image of a pair of stags sizing one another up as they prepared to wage battle over America, the prize female, through my mind.

"Quite so," Holmes snidely replied. "And I believe it's your move."

"No, no! I insist, you be white. After all, you're the visiting opposition, if you will."

"I am afraid you have already made the first move. And if you recall, I've already countered."

"Ah, you're right. Lost two pawns in the process, too, didn't you?" toyed a callous, Cheshire-grinning Carpenter, with a remark he knew would sting Holmes like an unexpected uppercut. "Haven't too many pieces left on the board, I should think," added the goading braggart.

"I've quite enough," replied a determinedly defiant Holmes.

Carpenter glowered at Holmes.

"You project a rather surprisingly smug deportment for a pair of lone soldiers behind enemy lines," he suggested.

"What causes you to conclude we are not without reinforcements?" challenged my great friend.

"Come now! This is not the poker table. Let's not waste each other's time with bluffs. Let us be frank with one another, if only out of respect for a worthy opponent."

"There is rather a marked difference between worthy adversary and clever cutthroat," reproached Holmes.

I returned with Carpenter's coffee in time to provide just enough distraction from the rapidly mounting tension that was visible in Carpenter's jaw.

"Very well, then. You may elect to play cat and mouse, if you like. However, I assure you, nothing on the chessboard escapes me. Furthermore, I am fully aware of your circumstances and present position. And neither appear promising," Carpenter sternly stated.

"Promising, is a rather subjective term, would you not agree?" countered Holmes with all the overt condescension he could muster.

"It's no good, you know?"

"The coffee?" Holmes mordantly asked.

"There is nothing, absolutely nothing, you can do, Mr. Holmes. Nothing!"

"Regarding?"

"The virus you're here to inoculate against, and subsequently eradicate. I'm afraid you're too late. Having already been injected, quite some time ago, it's taken on a life of its very own, and there is positively no stopping such runaway trains. And speaking of train wrecks, you do know the kind of damage they can produce?"

Our host looked to Holmes for a response. Save for a cool, defiantly indifferent empty facial expression, none was offered.

"Well, as a result of this one of a kind collision," Carpenter resumed, "I'm proud to say, a unique form of victim has been produced. Initially we viewed them as empty, credulous, zombie-like calves. However, shortly after impact, I observed they were more like ravenous somnambulists, if you will, who craved a CRAP diet—Yes, I've read that obscure little monograph of yours."

"That's beastly!" I uncontrollably shouted.

Holmes, calmly and quickly, waved me back into my seat.

"Pace yourself, my dear friend. We're only in the first mile of this marathon."

"Yes, Doctor," spoke the malicious mastermind. "I mean no insult to Mr. Holmes, nor to you, by my actions. In fact, I am quite grateful to have had such venerable adversaries."

"I promise you, I shall publish a full account of this case. And then we shall—,"

"I sincerely hope you do, sir. I sincerely hope you do," encouraged the blackguard, with a good chuckle in his speech.

"You find that amusing, sir?" I indignantly challenged.

"Though I am certain I will enjoy reading it, I doubt anyone else in this country will, if they bother to read it at all."

I was very nearly at the boiling point, when Holmes, again, raised his hand as signal for calm.

"Scarcely anyone reads in this country," continued the insolent fiend. "I've seen to that with, as Holmes has so observantly labeled, CRAP television and CRAP magazines. For what better conditioning tool is there? You see, CRAP, like all other mind-altering drugs, is extraordinarily addictive. Thus, like any other addict consumed by the drug, the CRAP junky becomes oblivious to all else."

"GET THEM OUT!"

In a sudden and extremely nervous burst of concern that bordered on hysteria, Lesters screeched at Carpenter.

"Get them out of here! No good will come of this, and you know it!"

"Calm yourself!" ordered Carpenter.

"Let's put a bullet in the back of their heads and dump them in a hole somewhere and be done with it!"

"If you can keep your head whilst those about you—," Holmes began to recite.

"Yes, you are quite right, Mr. Holmes," Carpenter concurred. "Quite right!"

He then pointed a stern finger at Lesters, who, overwrought by the stress of our surprise arrival and the blunt verbal jousting, fell, very nearly catatonic, into his seat.

"Get a grip on yourself," commanded Carpenter, before readdressing Holmes. "I beg your forgiveness for this pathetic outburst. I'm afraid my Watson here has seen too many mafia movies."

"You mistakenly understand '*Watson*' to be a synonym for sidekick," Holmes sharply returned. "I assure you, it is not."

"Ah, again, you must forgive me," Carpenter half-heartedly pleaded. "I have a habit of creating such vile little terms, as well as catch phrases like *touch base*, *your guyses* and *irregardless* so that they will embarrassingly take root in this country's vernacular. And, on occasion, as you have just witnessed, one slips out."

"For what purpose?" I disgustedly interjected.

"Why? Because I can, of course!" boasted the brigand. "I cannot accurately express the amount of joy it gives me to ridicule the great horde by introducing one of my gibberish expressions by way of some corporate blowhard."

His back stiffened as he spoke with a heightened sense of excitement.

"By slipping in one of my offensively lowbrow creations during the course of normal conversation with a selected business bane, I can adversely affect, dumb down, if you will, the level of language spoken in this country. You see, when the image-conscious-vehicle I select hears a term with which it is unfamiliar, its face instantly broadcasts a sense of panic and insecurity, brought on by the perpetual fear it lives with, the fear of being unable to keep pace with the *movers and shakers*, that's one of mine, of the world or worse, discovers it is merely an average human being. But since my subject strives, with singular focus, to project itself as the consummate business 'professional', it must unquestioningly accept and adopt the term as one of its own. After all, it was delivered by the epitome of business gurus. Thus, I'm sure, you can imagine the thrill I receive when I overhear these self-professed *professionals*, in what is solely an effort to impress, make use of such CRAP language, if I may again borrow your very astute acronym, as *one-on-one* instead of 'meeting', 'individual' or 'private', or the exceptionally ridiculous *heads-up* in place of 'notify' or 'warn', in the course of conversation."

He paused to let out a condescending spurt of a chuckle.

"I cannot begin to tell you, just how hard I laughed the time I actually heard some want-to-be-metaphoric-and-poetically-impressive-business-guru preach to his telephone sales flock."

Choked by a pesky giggle, he attempted to project a mocking impression of the self-inflated-businessman he had been referring to.

"If you want to fill your basket, you have to get out there and shake the fruit from the trees. And shake them HARD! So, keep your eye on the ball! Establish telephonic connectivity and take no prisoners!'"

The perverse, pitiless brute nearly failed to relate the entire quote, for he was beset with a constant chortle. It was a display that had made me physically ill.

"Can you believe how positively ripe for manipulation these people are?" raved the unfeeling gurgler.

"I assure you, we do not find this the least bit amusing," I chastised.

Again Holmes used a hand to insist upon calm.

"Too bad," Carpenter sneeringly replied. "The results of my interference are beyond amusing, they are simply intoxicating! Why a few years back, I thought I would play around a bit by overusing the word 'community'. Wow, was that a stroke of genius! Now you've got people adding the gentle label of *community* to everything in sight. There's the *plumbing community*. The *construction worker community*, the *secretarial community*, the *airliner community* and the *health care community*. In fact, I once very nearly injured myself laughing at some buffoon of a politician who had the witlessness to refer to troublesome motorcycle gangs as *the biker community*."

He shot out a knifing, uncontrolled, putrid gust of laughter in my direction, which caused me to quickly cup a hand over my mouth and nose.

"It's out of control," he added. "Next, I'll bet you, we'll be hearing *criminal community*."

"Strange you should select that enterprise as further example," I chided.

"Now, now, my good doctor, I have committed no crime, nor any illegal act. Consequently, it is incorrect for you, or anyone, for that matter, to label me a common criminal. Thus, the *law enforcement community*," he said with yet another revolting giggle, "has no business with me whatsoever. Nor, I'm afraid, do you and Mr. Holmes."

"It would not be possible for anyone to regard you as *common*," said Holmes, finally returning to the conversation, after silently surveying all about us.

"Why, thank you, sir," Carpenter superciliously returned. "Coming from you, I take that as the highest of compliments."

"It is merely an observation," Holmes said cheekily. "There are those whose very natures simply defy categorization."

"Deny it if you must, but it is simply the recognition of genius."

"Perhaps. However, perceiving something as genius does not necessarily vindicate its function."

"My word, you've the nerve of two hundred infinitely younger men, of that I am certain. May I say again, it is indeed an honor to have played this game with you, sir. A true honor."

"Regretfully," spoke Holmes in that familiar condescendingly insincere tone, "I did not arrive here to discuss one another."

"Really? Pity," the enemy general satirically countered.

"I'm afraid, sir," said Holmes, with a cold, firm bluntness, "I must insist you return that which you have taken from its rightful owners."

"And what might that be?" Carpenter coolly asked.

"The American culture," stated an equally cool Holmes.

Like every stereotypical evil villain ever penned or portrayed on stage or screen, Carpenter burst out an uncontrollable, maniacal guffaw, which, though actually took scarcely a minute, seemed a lifetime for him to recover from. All the while, Holmes, like a boxer in his neutral corner, waited, allowing his opponent sufficient time to collect himself.

"Oh, Mr. Holmes, you are good. You are really good. Ever think of taking your act out onto the comedy club tour? I'm sure you'd be quite a big hit," jabbed the brute. "You really are too much."

"What causes you to determine I am joking in this regard?" replied Holmes.

"What makes you think I have that which belongs to someone else?"

"Did you not suggest we speak frankly? You are not alone in your ability to sense a bluff of a hand."

"Well then, what say I call and we put all our cards on the table, then."

"Very well."

Carpenter let out a breath and fell, all too relaxed, back into his black, high-back, leather chair.

"Regretfully, gentlemen, I cannot return that which you speak of. For the truth of the matter is there simply never was anything to take."

My blood began to boil and seeing Holmes remain cool, collected and focused only raised the level of flame under me.

"As you are no doubt aware," continued the fiend, "this country, this exceptionally vast country, is a melting pot. And it is that very fact which has all but made the development of a singular culture impossible. Therefore, you cannot possibly point the finger at me," Carpenter insisted.

"Your argument, unfortunately, is flawed," Holmes charged, "for diversity itself is a key ingredient of any society's culture—No sir, instead of allowing the richer aspects of each ethnicity's individual mores to establish root in this country, you have dissuaded that process from taking its natural course by steering it toward the simple, the tasteless, the backward. Furthermore, making full use of your communications and media empire as you have, the vastness of this country, as you errantly suggest as problematic, is of little consequence. Accordingly, what you have calculatingly forced to mutate here is an empty, spiritless society, which spends its time, though without understanding its lack of fulfillment, unceasingly seeking distractions from the mendacity of its existence," admonished Holmes. "No, sir, you cannot refuse blame. For this utterly deplorable state of affairs is your doing and your doing alone!"

The hardhearted brute chuckled at Holmes.

"My, you've quite the imagination, haven't you?"

"We both know that that of which I speak of is not imagined," Holmes steadfastly replied.

"You bestow far too much credit upon me, Mr. Holmes. Surely it is highly improbable that one man alone could garner so much power and control. After all, I am not a God."

"Actually, I was thinking quite a bit farther south than that."

Again the monster chuckled.

"You, sir, are exceptionally quick on your feet. You know that?"

"And you, sir, you agree to put your cards on the table, yet you, rather ungentlemanly, insist upon keeping one up your sleeve," growled Holmes. "Have you no honor whatsoever?"

"You're right. You are absolutely correct," replied the fiend. "Forgive me. It would appear that I am so used to manipulating situations and denying culpability that I have conditioned myself to avoid looking back at the results of my labor with pride. A shameful admission, I must admit. After all, my accomplishments are rather impressive, wouldn't you agree?"

"I would indeed."

Offended by Holmes' congratulatory concurrence, my back stiffened with great agitation. Lesters, on the other hand, appeared even more nervous and panic stricken than earlier, as he began nibbling, hurriedly, away at his fingernails. A weasel of a man, it was difficult to accept he held such high command in Carpenter's army.

"Like the simple, insecure oaf who favors slow-witted women, I much prefer simple consumers," Carpenter proudly shared. "Yes, sir! Keep the product simple and you keep the customer happy. But, more importantly, keep the product simple and you keep the customer simple."

"That's grotesque!" I shouted.

Again Holmes motioned for calm.

"No, Doctor, *that* is the simple truth," Carpenter replied. "Why on earth do you think so many Americans are obese?—I provide them with an over abundance of food that is both exceptionally inexpensive in retail cost, and manufacture."

"You mean preparation!"

"MANUFACTURE!"

Thoroughly appalled, I looked to Holmes. He was unaffected by Carpenter's fulsome admission.

"It is also unimaginably void of any meaningful nutritional value, I might add," provoked Carpenter. "But, what the hell. You can't have everything, right?"

"That is supremely depraved!" I angrily charged.

"Hey, if the FDA is fine with aspartame in soft drinks, despite the extreme health risks, so am I," Carpenter continued to pontificate. "And on another note, Doctor, you and I both know that meat and the human intestinal tract aren't exactly well suited for one another. Right?"

I nodded agreement.

"And yet, possessing this same knowledge, the FDA is all behind the barbaric meat industry. We might also add to this discussion the fact that that organization is also privy to the knowledge that bleached flour products are exceptionally disagreeable to the human colon. Do you know that bleached flour clogs the colon in the very same manner cholesterol narrows the artery?"

"Of course!" I sharply replied.

"Bleached flour products included in the diet, form a cake-like paste, which eventually narrow the colon. Meat, as I am sure you are aware, takes a ridiculously long three days to be digested in the human intestinal tract. During that process, if the organ is overburdened with heavily processed flour, partially digested meat particles become lodged in the paste, where they grow rancid and remain for years, decades even, contributing heavily to the medical conditions *diverticulitus* and colon cancer. All this, under the watchful eye of the good old FDA. And yet you hold me responsible?"

"Come, come, now," Holmes quickly broke in, "do not attempt to shift blame in this instance. It is a waste of our time. We both know full well who has indirect control over the FDA. And while we are examining your culpability, let us not forget to mention those wholly despicable promotional gimmick items you peddle to further lure punters into many a disgusting eatery, which manage to make their way to the landfills of the country in record-breaking time."

"I twist no one's arm to buy."

"It is the mind, not the arm, which you twist," barked an unyielding Holmes.

"That I cannot deny," said the arrogant autocrat. "I guess you could say you have me there."

"I do say."

"Why, did you know that if you associate patriotism with a product, sales of that item simply skyrocket? Even if the product is unbelievably disgusting? Take the hotdog, for example. It is an American icon, yet all we do to make them is add spices and food coloring to the scraps swept off the slaughterhouse floor. Then we tout them as the really American thing to eat, particularly when partaking of America's favorite pastimes. Yes sir, it's insane, but what the hay! What else is one to do when presented with such a golden opportunity?"

"Helpless victim of circumstance, eh?" Holmes insolently asked.

"Well, frankly, yes," the reprobate coldly stated. "Can I help it if most people are nothing more than two-legged sheep? Why, take that exceptionally crass burger slogan I indirectly influenced."

"Which would be?"

"'If it doesn't get all over the place, it doesn't belong in your face.' Disgusting, I grant you. But it's a real winner of a pitch."

Driven by an overwhelming horror I abruptly interrupted the Carpenter and Holmes exchange.

"You honestly mean to suggest an insultingly revolting slogan such as that actually works to draw people in?"

"I'm afraid so, Doctor. You see—,"

"Allow me, if you don't mind?" interjected Holmes.

"By all means," agreed the viper.

"This is a textbook example of the type of horribly magnificent manipulation our masterful Engineer is capable of," Holmes resumed. "For with one very simple, and utterly vile phrase, the dreadfully clever Mr. Carpenter here suggests to a very susceptible citizenry that they ignore the notion that the said hamburger is nutritionally bankrupt, and factually unhealthy. The reality, his reality, is that the said hamburger simply tastes fantastic, though it may actually not. Moreover, to reinforce the scaling down of expectations and sophistication, his slogan also subtly implies it is also good to throw proper decorum and etiquette to the wayside. Forget napkins, plates, cutlery and proper dining utensils. For they, like fine dining, proper table manners and food of quality and sufficient nutrition are simply, I think the phrase is, *totally uncool!*"

"Excellent, Mr. Holmes, excellent! You have it exactly!" Carpenter cheered.

Once again, as if I were the recipient of a lethal body blow dealt by Mike Tyson himself, the conversation knocked the breath completely from me. And, as you might imagine a Tyson opponent would wonder, I wasn't sure I could last the entire round. Worse yet, the thrill of finally having the opportunity to reveal, as Carpenter viewed it, the sheer cunning of his deeds, set the master sociopath off onto yet another depraved admission.

"I tell you, Mr. Holmes, if they'd only reject one single assault of mine, I'd ease up on the poor saps. But no such luck. No matter how revolting a pitch or spectacle I deliver truly is, 93 percent of the populous applauds it."

"94 percent, actually," corrected Holmes.

"You see, even I can't keep up with the success of my scheme," crowed the bandit. "Decades ago I suggested transforming wrestling into a freak show of a spectacle. That was followed by the Ice Capades, which gave way to the notion of actually staging theater on ice. Talk about egregious spectacle! But then, I thought, we've had the *Beauty and the Beast* animated feature film, which then raked in more revenue as a television series, which was followed by the stage version of the film, beast costume and all. And yet, I began to think, people hadn't really experienced the story until they'd seen it 'on ice'."

Once again, he was beset with laughter.

"I tell you, I was flabbergasted by its success. Frankly, my 'ice theater' projects, *Sleeping Beauty*, *The Lion King* and *Phantom of the Opera*, all have been so successful that I've actually been toying with the idea of staging *Madama Butterfly* and *Tosca* 'on-ice'."

"STOP!" I screamed at the top of my lungs. "I can take no more of this sacrilege."

"Easy, Doctor. Easy," goaded Carpenter.

"That was not your best of reactions, my friend," Holmes calmly voiced to me.

"He goes to far, Holmes!" I insisted.

"That is true, but—,"

Just then a pounding at the office door interrupted Holmes. It was accompanied by cries of great concern and panic with regard to events taking place in Carpenter's office, events then brought to everyone's attention by my scream. Events, I am certain, which could only have been unimaginable from the other side of the solid black office door.

"What shall we do?" I quickly asked Holmes.

He hesitated an instant. From Carpenter's face, I could see it was a moment that had given the brigand great pleasure. But it was only a tease, for that momentary pause was all that was necessary for Holmes to conjure upon a diversionary maneuver.

"Over here, quickly!" Holmes commanded Lesters. "Now!"

The minion looked to his chief, but Holmes, stepping between them, blocked that view with his own body.

"Now!" Holmes repeated.

Steering the underling to the telephone on Carpenter's desk, Holmes picked up the receiver and placed it into Lesters' ridiculously nervous hand.

"You will announce yourself and state that all is well. You had screamed upon hearing the devastating news that '*Bette*', the Bette Midler television sitcom, which you were quite fond of, had been canceled and you had mistakenly assumed that Mr. Carpenter here had a hand in its fate."

"What?" protested Lesters.

"Watson," said Holmes.

Recognizing the utterance of my name in that familiar tone to mean *encourage the resister*, I stepped up to Lesters and placed the nose of my revolver upon his right temple.

"Such theatrics, really," Carpenter disapprovingly observed.

As the commotion at the office door intensified, Holmes activated the office public address system via the telephone and pushed Lesters' receiver-holding hand to his mouth. And as directed, with a little encouragement from the cold steel pressed to his head, Lesters stated all Holmes had instructed, with a nearly verbatim delivery.

"Well done," Holmes praised. "Well done, indeed."

"As I said, you are rather quick on your feet," said Carpenter. "However, this little ruse of yours won't buy you very much time, Mr. Holmes. I can assure you of that."

"That is most unfortunate. I was so very much enjoying your dissertation on the art of mass manipulation and the creation of helpless victims of marketing. Truly I was, sir. Truly I was."

"Oh, do come along, Mr. Holmes. You understand all too well. Do not attempt to infer that you are surprised by the reality of that."

"As you misunderstand the purpose of man's existence, you misunderstand my response."

"Human existence? Again, you credit me with far more than I deserve, sir. Although, I must say, I do find it rather flattering."

"No, sir, flattery is not my intent. But this you know full well. My purpose here is to educate and enlighten."

"Educate and enlighten?" Carpenter echoed with a great roaring laughter. "As you know I have read yours, I am certain you have studied my dossier and are aware of my vast educational background."

"Columbia, Stanford and a fellowship at Cambridge. Yes, you are correct, I have reviewed your record. Yet, despite the efforts of those great institutions, you sir, are surprisingly ignorant as to the purpose of humankind's presence on this planet," Holmes replied.

"Purpose? Come now, Reverend. You and I both know there is

absolutely no real purpose to be found for the presence of humans on this sphere. Like every other organism vying for space upon it, humans are merely a mutation of the ameba, nothing more. This exceptionally surreal existence of ours is merely the result of a freak biological and chemical reaction. So spare me the sermon on purpose, if you will.

"I am afraid I cannot," returned Holmes. "For as with all species, particularly homo sapiens, since it has had the audacity to claim itself *the* most advanced of all species, have an obligation to further its collective humanity, or earthly presence, not return itself to its amebic form."

"Amen, brother," offered the insolate hooligan.

"The earth," Holmes went on undeterred, "is an extremely hostile habitat, one which humankind must respect if it is to endure. Earthquakes, floods, fires, hurricanes, to name but a few, give us simply no other option but to adapt. The last thing it needs is a psychopath such as yourself."

"Again, you misjudge me. I've a great deal of respect for the nature of this planet," Carpenter broke in, with a bit of a giggle in his tenor. "Why all of the disasters you mention make for truly fantastic media—people are such rubber-neckers, you know?" he added with a devilishly instigating glow in his cheeks.

"The result of improper nurturing, no doubt," countered Holmes.

"Ah, the old nature versus nurture argument, eh? Well, in my opinion, it's a waste of time to even entertain the notion of nurture as the overriding force behind the development of an individual, or a society. It's simply ludicrous."

"Yet, is not your influence nurturing?"

"Nonsense!" protested Carpenter. "As I have already admitted, I do steer the great herd in directions favorable to my wealth and position. However I am merely taking advantage of its sheep-like nature. No sir, I do not agree with you. I do not nurture. I am simply an opportunist."

"Whose actions have had an extremely adverse affect upon the populous of this nation."

"Again, I disagree. I provide them with an alternative. A choice," insisted Carpenter.

"A choice?" Holmes scoffed.

"A choice!"

"I suppose the devolution of television programming was not the result of your doing, either."

"Ah, now that was strictly a business decision based upon the demands of the viewing public. My hand was forced. The great mass demanded hotdogs, if you will, for the mind. Certainly *Playhouse 90, Studio One, Matinee Theater* and *The Actors Studio* presented outstanding and socially relevant dramas from the late 1940s to the mid 1950s, like *Requiem for a Heavyweight* and *Marty*, for example. But televisions, at the time, were primarily purchased by the East Coast affluent, the people who could actually afford them. That audience, a highly educated audience, I might add, did greatly enjoy such programming. However, Mr. and Mrs. Ordinary, after a day of hard slog, did not enjoy watching such highbrow programming. Thus, in an effort to persuade them to purchase television sets, we needed programming they could relate to. Programming that would provide them an escape from the fierce daily grind. Hence, the arrival of Milton Berle and a host of other clowns, which, of course, did successfully manage to increase sales of television sets rather *dramatically*," stated the infuriatingly cocky lout.

"At the expense of the serious drama vehicles. And yes, I recognize your rather juvenile pun," Holmes returned with a strong dose of disgust mixed into his tone. "Another thing our species does not need, a psychopath who fancies himself a comedian."

"Nor does it need an old, worn out meddler."

"Yet another point we disagree on, I should think."

"Yes, like your expectations of this meeting."

"Why, I assure you, sir, it has been exactly what I had anticipated."

"Its yield, specifically," Carpenter sharply stated.

"Ah, I see," Holmes coolly rejoined. "Actually, I am quite pleased with the harvest. For you, sir, you have been exposed."

"To whom? To you and your shadow, here? Two ancient, though

albeit miraculously well preserved, senior citizens? No, no, no! I'm afraid your ego is a bit too ambitious, Mr. Holmes."

He directed himself to Lesters.

"Wouldn't you agree?"

Though still unable to stifle his nervous twitching, the dutiful rodent broke from the nibbling of his own claw long enough to return a lightening-fast nod of agreement.

"Well, there you have it," said Carpenter. "Now, gentlemen, if you would—,"

The supremely confident posture of Holmes, as he simultaneously dug into his breast shirt pocket, captured Carpenter's attention, interrupting his line of thought. A second later, Holmes produced a miniature micro-cassette recorder and held it up for all to see. And though the sight of it rocketed a shiver through the area where Lesters' spine should have been, yet what did not, it produced but a condescending chuckle from the infamous Engineer.

"You charge in here armed with only that and Dr. Watson's peashooter?" Carpenter mocked, "It would appear, you are fighting a losing battle against senility."

He rose from his chair and began to stroll confidently about the office as he spoke.

"You disappoint me, Mr Holmes. Did you honestly expect me to become panic stricken by the sight of that ridiculous little gismo? Grant you, revealing my identity and agenda to the public would be highly detrimental to my cause. However, that is most unlikely. You two are mere houseflies that have had the great misfortune to haven flown headstrong into the spider's web. Getting free just simply isn't an option."

"Your analogy is a tad over exaggerated. A slug perhaps, a magnificent spider you definitely are not," retorted Holmes.

"Ah, you wish to fight bare-knuckled, eh?"

"At the moment, I can think of nothing that would afford me more pleasure."

"Age certainly hasn't gnawed away at your backbone. I give you that."

"And I will give you just three minutes to relinquish the property we speak of."

"My God! Has this freakish longevity of yours completely blinded you to reality, or what?"

"On the contrary, our longevity, as I am certain you are fully aware, is due to an intellectual awareness as to what and what not to consume, like meat and modern day *junk-foods*, which you have labeled so brazenly truthful," blasted back Holmes. "Watson and I understand the chemistry of such lethal products and simply choose to avoid them. We do not strive to be the exception. We seek to provide example. For in this, the age of information, it is rather a disappointment to notice the absence of, at least, a legion of individuals of our advanced years traipsing the land. Yet, with the likes of *Bovine songiform encephalopathy, Creutzfeld-Jacob* and *Pfiesteria* diseases silently plaguing the land and food supply, it is quite the uphill battle for the uninformed."

Carpenter stopped short.

"You know, you're right. When you're right, you're right. And you are certainly right! Every single thing you assert is completely accurate. I admit it. I care not for what I peddle, so long as it rakes in the cash. And, if by some chance, my good little consumers take ill, no matter, the funds will continue streaming in by way of medical, pharmaceutical and burial costs. Either way, I simply cannot lose."

In that instant, I very nearly put an end to the Visigoth and his vile divulgence with one quick squeeze of the trigger my achingly tense index finger was wrapped round. Had it not been for Holmes' inexplicable confident demeanor, I cannot honestly say I would have found the strength to resist that reptilian-minded urge for satisfaction.

"And, as to your other concern," the madman raved on, "I quite truthfully don't care if an item I sell ends up in the landfill within a month from purchase. My only concerned is its salability, period."

"Yes, I have been acutely aware of this," responded Holmes, coolly.

"But are you also aware that, even if the good doctor here possessed the inhumanity to fire his little weapon at me, there is absolutely nothing you do can about this country's present condition. Like a nuclear powered satellite, the mechanism I have in place now runs of its own volition. I couldn't stop it if I wanted to. Which is just as well, for I've no intention of—"

"One minute!" announced Holmes.

"Did you not hear me?"

"57 seconds."

"No, Mr. Holmes, it is you and Dr. Watson who are running out of time. For, despite involving Lesters in your little charade, my security staff will be charging through that door any second from now."

"50 seconds," said a recklessly calm Holmes.

"You are becoming a rather tiresome meddler. Can you not get it through that thick skull of yours that I direct things, everything, in this country?—Are you familiar with the story of Bull Durham?"

"The Kevin Costner film?" I blurted out.

"Yes! Well, America is like its young baseball pitcher character. Huge potential! Loads of talent! A cannon for an arm! But wild, untamed, no control. I, like the Kevin Costner character, have all the answers. But, unfortunately, unlike that mentor character of Costner's, I am not about to guide these people to success. No, no! I am only interested in my—"

Suddenly, in an uncontrolled panic, Lesters, now thrust thoroughly over the edge, threw all caution and reason to the wind and quickly lunged at me, catching me off guard, successfully knocking me aside and the revolver from my grasp. Then, as awkwardly as a young boy might maneuver during a neighborhood game of war, Lesters rolled, snatched up the weapon, sprang to his feet and began firing wildly at Holmes. BLAM! BLAM! BLAM! However, his target proved quite elusive as it quickly dove and rolled behind the large black leather sofa and out of the line of fire. I attempted to subdue Lesters from behind, as frustration over

Holmes' spectacular mobility drove him even further into madness. Yet, in a split second he was off, in frenzied pursuit of his target and out of my reach.

"Holmes!" I shouted at the top of my lungs, although I needn't have.

The ever-alert sleuth was keenly aware of the lunatic's position and subsequent charge round the sofa and thus, swiftly bolted cross the room, a maneuver which immediately drew another burst of frantic gunfire. BLAM! BLAM! BLAM! Yet, in that split second, Holmes' action revealed itself to be far more than a defense tactic. For though it appeared simple in nature, it proved to be one of *the* most cunning of strategic moves I had *ever* had the opportunity to witness him execute. In one singular act of absolute genius, Holmes would bring our nightmare adventure to an abrupt end and set our host country on a possible course for recovery by directing the course of his own sprint for protective cover past Carpenter himself.

Standing proudly, and glowing like the Baskerville hound from the robust sunlight pounding its way through the window behind him, the abominable Engineer had been highly entertained by the goings on. But in one chaotic half second, one partial blink of the eye, all had changed. Carpenter's proud stance metamorphosed to that which belong more to a fright-stricken child. His delight became shock and horror. Holmes playing the part of rook had glided southward and exposed the opposing king to check. This move, combined with the bullets launched forth by Lesters' ham-handed attack on Holmes, clearly formed mate, as the later half of the combination completely overshot Holmes' galloping and crouching figure and charged their way straight through Carpenter's elegant Italian navy suit and into his formerly pride-swelled chest.

"AHHHHHHHHHHH!" Lesters, I, and particularly Carpenter, screamed, horrorstruck by the sight of bullets piercing into the despicable mastermind, hurling him back, before finally catapulting him thunderously through the tower's thick glass wall and into the waiting rays of the seemingly retribution-minded sunlight, an image that shall stay with me beyond even this incarnation. Then, in the next instant, just as Carpenter had assured us, the office doors burst open to allow a small battalion of armed men to charge inside. However, unlike Carpenters prediction, the men were familiar to me. In fact, to my great surprise, leading the charge was the highly competent young Mr. Driscoll, flanked by friend Moore to one side and a battalion of local, uniformed police on the other. In tow, to my utter amazement and bewilderment appeared the dimwitted Officer Peale.

Suddenly, Lesters, completely over the edge, turned round, pointed his lone, borrowed weapon and prepared to take on his very formidable opposition. But it was not to be, as Holmes quickly jumped into position between the two combatants.

"Hold your fire!" commanded Holmes, as CLICK, my revolver in Lesters' hand announced itself to be empty.

Not having paid attention to the number of rounds fired, I let loose a huge sigh of relief, as Holmes stood with his back to the hysterical gunman.

"I'm afraid he has already had his six, gentlemen," remarked Holmes, as he peeked at his watch. "Forty seconds ahead of schedule, Mr. Driscoll.—Very impressive. Very impressive, indeed."

EPILOGUE

"What on earth has happened here?" asked Driscoll as he and Moore, with bandage round his head, strode into the late Mr. Malachy Carpenter's then less than sterile office behind a swarm of uniformed officers converging upon a hysterically weeping Lesters.

"Our Mr. Lesters here, has rather a poor aim," replied Holmes.

"And this Carpenter fellow?" asked Moore.

"Oh, bad luck. You've missed him. I'm afraid he's just popped out."

Moore, Driscoll and Peale rushed for a glimpse from the shattered window.

"Just what the Sam Hell is going on here?" hollered the painfully familiar voice of Officer Peale. "Who the hell was this Carpenter, anyway? And just who the hell do you think you are stealing my car?"

"Which question would you prefer I answer first?" Holmes cockily asked.

Moore stepped forward.

"Was this Carpenter our man?" he asked.

Holmes nodded.

"But why should Lesters shoot him?"

"As I said, he is rather a dismal shot—Make certain to have insider trading and attempted murder added to the list of charges against him."

"I got a good mind to shoot you myself," blasted Peale. "You stole my damn car!"

Holmes dug the car key out from his trouser pocket and handed it to the irate peacekeeper.

"Actually, according to documentation found inside its glove box, the car is registered to an Emma Peale, whom I suspected was your wife. A wife, I also suspect, who has only recently embarked upon a career at the Bellagio Hotel."

"How the hell?"

"Elementary, Officer Peale, elementary. You see, the fact that the car had an association with you was not my reason for selecting the vehicle, although I viewed that coincidence as the happiest of bonuses, for I took you for a man of extremely quick response," he cheekily added. "Finding the bonnet still a bit warm suggested to me that, since Emma was the wife of such a distinguished officer, she could only be at the hotel at that hour to work the late shift, a shift that was more than likely to be offered to trainees. This reasoning led me to conclude that I had some five to six hours before the absence of the vehicle would be discovered. Yet, essential to my vehicle selection was the presence of a VTS."

"A what?"

"A vehicle tracking system. And, as you see, it was all the signal needed to fetch you, Moore, Driscoll, and very nearly, the kitchen sink. I am deeply indebted to you, sir."

Holmes looked to the rest of the assemblage.

"Indeed, my gratitude is to you all."

"May I have a word in private?" asked Mr. Moore.

Holmes led Moore to an opposite corner of the office, yet not so far as to be out of earshot from me.

"Then it's over?" Moore whispered. "This Mr. Carpenter was this Engineer, our thief?"

"None other," answered Holmes.

"Then it is over then?"

"In a phrase, 'not by a long shot'."

Moore went pale.

"What next?"

"Well, before returning to my bees, I think Watson and I shall take a brief holiday in the Napa and Sonoma valleys. In addition to many a splendid wine, I understand they've some rather exceptional spas in the area."

"No, I meant about our culture?"

"As I said, that is up to you."

Moore was nearly breathless with anxiety.

"The scoundrel is now out of the picture," reassured Holmes. "There is no longer any obstruction. Therefore, you are free to rebuild this great country's culture into something much richer, something much more worthy of the great people inhabiting it. I do not promise it will be an easy task. But it can be done. Look about you. You've much to be proud of here, already. Riches abound!"

"Yes, but where do we begin? What steps should I take to—,"

"Have you ever attempted to free an individual of an addiction to the drugs heroine or crack?"

"Why, yes sir, I have, actually."

"Picture this like that."

Detaching himself from the brief conversation, Holmes stepped back into the room.

"Gentlemen, I leave you to it. And, once again, I thank you for your cooperation and assistance."

He then readdressed Moore, whose body language revealed a man beleaguered by the daunting task ahead of him.

"Please convey my regards to Mr. Clinton. I wish him well in his upcoming retirement."

Moore nodded.

"Much luck to you and yours, as well."

"Thank you, sir."

Then, with a bit of a rather grandiose sweeping, wave-like arm gesture as he made for the office door, a proudly victorious Holmes looked to me.

"Come Watson, let us see if we cannot find a tofu scramble and a pot of Assam someplace."

The End